THE
INN

JAMES PATTERSON is one of the best-known and biggest-selling writers of all time. His books have sold in excess of 385 million copies worldwide. He is the author of some of the most popular series of the past two decades – the Alex Cross, Women's Murder Club, Detective Michael Bennett and Private novels – and he has written many other number one bestsellers including romance novels and stand-alone thrillers.

James is passionate about encouraging children to read. Inspired by his own son who was a reluctant reader, he also writes a range of books for young readers including the Middle School, I Funny, Treasure Hunters, Dog Diaries and Max Einstein series. James has donated millions in grants to independent bookshops and has been the most borrowed author of adult fiction in UK libraries for the past twelve years in a row. He lives in Florida with his wife and son.

CANDICE FOX won back-to-back Ned Kelly awards for her first two novels – *Hades* and *Eden*. She is also the author of the critically acclaimed *Fall*, *Crimson Lake*, *Redemption* and *Gone by Midnight*. Candice's first collaboration with James Patterson, *Never Never*, was a *Sunday Times* and *New York Times* no. 1 bestseller. They have co-authored three further novels featuring Harriet Blue – *Fifty Fifty*, *Liar Liar* and *Hush Hush*.

A list of titles by James Patterson appears at the
back of this book.

JAMES PATTERSON
AND CANDICE FOX

THE
INN

arrow books

7 9 10 8 6

Arrow Books
20 Vauxhall Bridge Road
London SW1V 2SA

Arrow Books is part of the Penguin Random House group of companies whose
addresses can be found at global.penguinrandomhouse.com

First published in Great Britain by Century in 2019
This edition published in paperback by Arrow Books in 2020

www.penguin.co.uk

A CIP catalogue record for this book is available from the British Library

ISBN 9781787462441
ISBN 9781787462458 (export edition)

Printed and bound in Great Britain by Clays Ltd, Elcograf S.p.A.

Penguin Random House is committed to a sustainable
future for our business, our readers and our planet. This
book is made from Forest Stewardship Council® certified
paper.

THE
INN

CHAPTER ONE

SOMETHING VERY BAD was about to go down.

There are things you know as a cop in Boston. You know how the city feels, because its streets are your veins and the voices of its people come through your lips when you talk. You know the smell of the salt in the harbor like the scent of the back of your wife's neck, and it's just as precious, reassuring. The hammering of footsteps out of Back Bay Station for the morning rat race wakes you up, and the wail of sirens in the old Combat Zone at night puts you to sleep. Every Christmas, you gather up some young wide-eyed uniforms to take poor kids from East Boston and Hyde Park into the toy stores, try to show the new cops and the kids that they can get along. You know that in a few years, some of those cops and some of those kids will end up killing each other. But that's how the city works. It's like a living thing. It sheds, and it hurts, and it bleeds.

I could feel what was about to happen in the air. It was an unexpected and dizzying heat, surreal against the snow on the ground outside the car.

When my partner Malone and I got a call to go to the commissioner's office downtown, I knew we were in for it. A Boston cop knows that being called to the commissioner's office is a bad, bad thing.

Malone always made fun of me for thinking I had Boston's pulse, a sense about approaching trouble in the city. On the morning of the marathon bombing, we'd been a mile up Boylston Street doing crowd control and I told Malone I felt hot and weird, like I had a fever. We felt the thump of the first blast under our feet a second or two later.

We were in the back of the cruiser, Malone looking out the window, joggling his knee and picking his teeth.

"Wait. I know what this is," he said suddenly. "This is about that baby. We're getting a medal for the baby last week."

The week before, Malone and I had been walking out at the end of a shift when a woman outside a café two doors from the station started screaming like she was on fire. She was standing in the street pointing at a balcony five floors above, where a toddler was sitting on the concrete ledge, having the time of his life. A crowd gathered, and it was quickly established that the mother was inside but wasn't answering the door or her phone. While some guys went in to try to break down her apartment door, Malone and I watched, pulling out our own hair, while the toddler crawled along the ledge and then, wobbling, stood up.

There was no time to decide who would catch the kid.

Malone and I both went in and snared him in a tangle of arms about two feet off the ground while the people around us hollered and screamed. Turned out the mother had been so damned tired from working two jobs that she fell asleep with the baby on the couch, the balcony doors open and a pot of peas cooking dry on the stove.

It was a good get, the kind of thing that wins you cheers when you walk into the station the next day. Ribbing about how tubby you look in the YouTube footage. Calls from the *Globe*. A medal, maybe. The toddler catch had gotten my wife, Siobhan, on the phone for a week, bragging to all her friends, telling them to watch the news, patting my head and saying she was proud of me like I was some kind of heroic dog.

But today wasn't about the kid. I could feel it in my bones.

"This is bad," I told Malone. "They only send a car for you when they know you'll be too fucked up to drive home afterward. We're in big trouble here. You better start thinking what we've done to piss off the top brass."

Malone, still twitching and joggling his knee, settled back and watched our driver. I gripped the seat belt and let Boston roll by, trying to guess what they were about to tell us.

The car dropped us at the building on Tremont Street. We went in, and as the elevator doors closed on us, I noticed that all Malone's twitching had suddenly stopped.

"I'm sorry," he said. His eyes were fixed on the floor. "I'm real sorry for this, Bill."

"You're sorry for what?"

He didn't answer. I had to hear it from the commissioner.

CHAPTER TWO

BOSTON PD LEGEND says that the visitor's chair in the commissioner's office is an old electric chair. I'd heard whispers around the department that some sadistic jerk occupying the top job had acquired the chair from a prison auction in Ohio and simply cut the straps and headgear off to make it acceptable for the office. Malone and I entered and took two identical chairs, either of which might indeed have been an Old Sparky sourced from the depths of the Midwest. The wood was eerily warm, and there were gouges in the arms that perfectly fit my fingernails.

I wouldn't have liked to be sitting in front of Commissioner Rachel McGinniskin even if the news were congratulatory. The red-haired, narrow-faced woman was a descendant of Barney McGinniskin, the first Irishman ever handed a police baton in Boston. From the moment Barney pulled on his blue coat, his appointment spurred hysterical news-paper reports, violent riots, and Irish bashings nationwide. The anti-immigration, anti-Catholic parties dumped him out of his job after only three years, and years later, Rachel McGinniskin had fought her way up the ladder in the force out of pure spite.

The commissioner opened a laptop and swiveled it on the desk so that the screen was facing us. She pushed a button and a black-and-white video began to play.

Only minutes into the video, I could feel sweat sliding down my ribs beneath my shirt. I looked at Malone, but he wouldn't meet my eyes.

McGinniskin pointed to a guy in the video. "Detective Jeremiah Malone," she said. "Is that you there on the screen?"

Her tone was strangely heavy, like she was the one getting the bad news. Malone didn't say anything. Just nodded, defeated. She let the video play a while longer.

"Detective William Robinson." She pointed at the screen again and looked at me, her eyes blazing. "Is that you?"

"It is," I said. Malone still wouldn't meet my gaze. *Look at me, you prick,* I thought. But the bastard put his face in his hands. McGinniskin turned the laptop back around and slammed it shut.

"You're both out," she said. The muscles in her jaw and temples were so tight, they bulged from beneath the skin. "And I've got to admit, gentlemen, after seeing that tape, it gives me great pleasure to say it. There's no place in my police force for people like you. Your discharge will take effect immediately. If I hear that either of you have inquired about pensions, I'll make sure you can't get a job in this city as a fucking *mall* cop." McGinniskin swept her hair back from her temples, chasing composure. "Give me your badges and your weapons," she said.

It was hard for me to get out of the chair. Gravity seemed to have tripled. I took my gun off, walked what seemed like a hundred miles to her desk, and put my weapon down at the same time Malone did. He finally looked at me as we took our badges off. Then we left. Neither of us spoke until we were outside her office.

"Bill," Malone said. "Buddy, listen. I—"

"I can't believe you did this." I was shaking all over. "I can't believe you did this to us. We're out. That's it. It's over. You lying, backstabbing piece of shit."

My job. My city. The walls of the old stone building were pulsing around me, closing in. Malone had killed us. We were being expelled from the living thing. Shed like dead skin, like waste. I couldn't breathe.

"I'm so sorry, Bill." Malone sounded panicky. "I was trying to—"

I grabbed my partner by the shirt and slammed him into the wall beside McGinniskin's door. It was all I could do not to knock his teeth out right there. I put a finger in his face and eased the words out from between my locked jaw.

"You and me?" I said. "We're *done*."

CHAPTER THREE

Two Years and Five Months Later

THE DEATH TOLL was eight, according to Cline's count.

He knew it was narcissistic, but every day he sat under the big bay windows on the second floor of his house where he could see the ocean beyond the cypress trees and checked the papers for signs of his work. Some days he told himself he was being too proud, and other days he knew it was just good business. Since he had moved to the tiny seaside town of Gloucester, there had been eight over-dose deaths. Two a month. The papers were blaring out words that excited him. *Epidemic. Crisis. Downfall.* Whenever things started to slide, Cline felt happy. Being a criminal meant his concept of the world was upside down. Reversed. A downward slide for others meant an upward rise for him.

That didn't mean it was time to take it easy on anyone. As he sat reading the paper spread flat on the table before him, the way he used to in the can so that he could keep an eye on the movement of other prisoners, his lieutenants started assembling before him. Cline had made sure from the outset that his standards were known and respected. Tailored shirts. Cuff links. Ties for meetings. No speed-stripe buzz cuts, no neck tattoos, none of this gold-chain, bling-bling shit. They were a business, not a gang. The men who entered the room looked like a bunch of lawyers attending a daily meeting, but they came in punching each other and giggling and talking trash, and he silenced them with a glance. They were street thugs and prison bitches and violence-intervention-program dropouts he had recruited from rock bottom, but he'd make them true soldiers before long.

"Where's Newgate?" Cline asked when everyone was settled. "You fuckers know to be on time." There were uncomfortable looks around the crew, and then Newgate appeared with a baby in his arms. No, not a baby, a little girl, though she seemed like a baby in this setting, surrounded by hard men who made their living dealing in death. Cline stood and watched as big, muscle-bound, scar-faced Newgate put the barefoot child on the floor.

"I'm real sorry, boss." Newgate gave a dramatic sigh. "I had a fight with my girl and she dropped the baby on me this morning and ran off. I didn't know what to do."

Cline watched the girl toddling around the room, pulling books off his shelves, slapping her greasy palms on the huge bay windows. He felt a muscle twitching in his neck as he went to the desk and got his gun.

"No problem, Newby. These things happen," Cline said.

"I'm sure she won't cause us any trouble. Let's give her something to play with while we talk. Come here, little princess. Come on."

The lieutenants watched in horror as Cline loaded a full clip into his pistol and flicked the safety off. Newgate's daughter gave a coo of intrigue, tottered over to Cline, and took the gun. Squid, perched on the edge of the couch, didn't dare retreat but he hid beneath his gangly arms like they could protect from the child's aim. The little girl swung the heavy gun around wildly, then lifted the barrel to her eye and looked down into the blackness. Cline's eyes seared into Newgate's, daring him to protest. The little girl walked up to her father and pointed the gun at him.

"Bang-bang!" The girl laughed. Newgate reached for the weapon as his daughter fumbled with the trigger, unable to get her pudgy finger around the steel. Before Newgate could take the gun, Cline reached forward and grabbed it. He pointed it at Newgate, whose face contorted as he realized what was happening.

"Like this, princess," Cline said, smiling.

CHAPTER FOUR

PLANE CRASH, I thought. *That's the only thing that can save me now.*

I'd done everything I could to dissuade the residents of the Inn from holding a memorial service for my wife, Siobhan, on the second anniversary of her death. And yet here I sat at the end of a plastic foldout table in the forest of pines that surrounded the large house, tearing a yellow napkin into tiny pieces, waiting for it to begin, fantasizing about something that could interrupt it. Gas-leak explosion in the kitchen. Ferocious black bear suddenly appearing at the edge of the woods. Airbus A380 plunging into the slate-gray sea just visible through the trees. The truth was, nothing was coming. The people around me were going to talk about Siobhan, and I was going to have to listen.

They'd made a good effort, which was unusual for them,

because it was difficult to get the permanent residents of the Inn to collaborate on anything. They had nothing in common save Siobhan's recruitment of them in the months after I was fired. Siobhan had done everything to set up our new life in the north. She'd found the guesthouse for sale, sourced the furniture, got the licenses and approvals we needed to run a bed-and-breakfast by the sea—her retirement dream realized years earlier than she'd imagined it would be. She'd collected a motley crew of weirdos, down-and-outs, and deeply troubled characters, and she accommodated them all. I'd moped in my sweatpants about my lost job, having no idea that I was about to lose her too.

At the end of the table, Marni stood up. She was the resident wayward teenager, Siobhan's second cousin who'd been sentenced to the house for having constant screaming matches with her mother and running away multiple times. As I sat in my chair watching her prepare to speak, I felt a twinge of guilt. Since I'd lost my wife, Marni had been my responsibility, and like I'd done with everything else, I let her slip. She'd gotten a couple of piercings on her face recently, and there was a little pink heart on her left cheekbone that I wasn't convinced she drew on every day with lip liner despite what she'd told me. She was fifteen. Tattoos, piercings, and the attitude to go with them. She smoothed out a crumpled piece of paper extracted with some difficulty from the pocket of her jeans. A little speech. I rubbed my temples.

"Now, listen," Marni said, wagging a finger with chipped black nail polish at me. "We know you said you didn't want anything like this, Bill. But we've all got something to say about Siobhan, and we think you should hear it. The first year, nobody did anything, you know? It's kind of like we ignored it. And that just makes me totally sad."

"So get on with it, then." I gave a dismissive wave. My best friend in the house, Nick Jones, elbowed me in the ribs. Nick and I pull each other into line whenever we can, but it's not always easy. I like the muscle-bound black man because he's ex-army and has hundreds of horror stories from his time in the Middle East that are so hideous, they pulverize my own trauma like a sledgehammer smashes a walnut.

"Give it a rest, man," Nick said.

"You give it a rest." I took a croissant from the plate in front of me and tossed it at him. He caught it against his chest and started eating it.

"The thing I miss most about Siobhan," Marni told the gathering, "is her terrible taste in music."

Everybody nodded in agreement; some people laughed. I clasped my hands so tight, my knuckles cracked, and I searched the sky for planes.

"Siobhan was a great cook, and she used to play music in the kitchen," Marni said, looking at her paper for guidance. "You couldn't get from the back of the house to the stairs without her grabbing you and making you dance around the kitchen with her. It was so embarrassing. She filled the house with these lame love ballads. Whitney. Bonnie. Celine. Really ancient, weird stuff."

"Ancient?" I scoffed. I leaned in toward Nick. "The prime of Celine Dion's career was the mid-nineties."

"Shut it," he whispered.

"I liked the way Siobhan sang Bonnie Tyler with her arm

out and her face all crumpled up, using her wooden spoon like a microphone," Marni said. "I know all the words to those songs because of Siobhan, and even though they suck, I'll never forget them. I miss her so bad. I've already got a mom, but Siobhan was, like, my better mom."

Everybody looked to me to see what I thought of Marni's tribute. I folded my arms and sighed.

The second person to stand was Sheriff Clayton Spears. He too had a piece of paper with a prepared speech. For a moment, I appreciated the amount of planning that had gone into this breakfast memorial for my wife that I'd been railroaded into attending. The table was cluttered with yellow paper plates and yellow napkins, and someone had filled several glasses with yellow flowers. Her favorite color.

Clay was in uniform, likely because he'd just worked an overnight shift. His enormous belly sagged so low in front, it hid his gun belt.

"You all know, uh, that I came to the house because my marriage broke down." Clay's chin wobbled with emotion. "It's not easy to be a proud man when your wife runs off with someone else. Because of my position as the head of law enforcement in Gloucester, the whole town knows my story."

Sheriff Spears's wife hadn't run off with just anyone. She'd left him for a young male model who had been staying with some friends in the apartment next door to theirs for a single weekend. It had taken him all of two days to convince Mrs. Spears to dump her life with the sheriff, pack a bag, and jump in the car with him and a crew of beautiful nineteen-year-old men. She hadn't been seen since.

"Siobhan stayed up with me many nights, listening to me talk through my breakup," Clay said. "She was the best listener. She was endlessly encouraging. We would sit out here in the garden eating slices of pepperoni pizza and looking at the stars and . . . and she just made me feel like . . . you all know I'm no George Clooney. But Siobhan told me that I deserved love and that I was a great man, and I believed her."

Clay sat down quickly, perhaps attempting to get his butt planted before he burst into tears, and the plastic lawn chair beneath him creaked in a concerning way.

I noticed a car drive up to the house and stop with a spray of gravel.

"My name is Angelica Grace Thomas-Lowell." The third speaker had risen from her chair. Angelica had lived in the house for more than two years, but for some reason she always introduced herself with her full name. "I'm a vegan. Activist. Provocateur. Bestselling author."

The car at the front of the house was a welcome distraction. I leaned to the side in my chair to see around Angelica, but her thin, veiny arms were in the way. The paper she held looked like a full page of typed notes.

"'I'd like to announce firstly my sincere appreciation for Siobhan's constant willingness to act as a confidential sounding board for my ideas,'" Angelica read. "'The creative process isn't always straightforward. It's fluid, magnetic, sometimes chaotic. Though Siobhan's reading history was firmly located in trash novels, I found her somewhat naive critiques of my works in progress—those few I entrusted to her—refreshing.'"

Nick suddenly stood up beside me. I looked over and

saw a woman running from the house toward the gathering. Not a plane crash, gas-leak explosion, or ferocious bear, but *something*. I stood with him.

I recognized the woman from town. Ellie Minnow. She grabbed Nick by his scar-covered arm.

"Nick, Bill, you've gotta help me. It's Winley."

"What is it?" Nick asked. "What's happened?"

"We'll help." I grabbed my phone from the table. "Whatever it is, we'll help."

Marni was already pouting. I brushed her shoulder in consolation as I passed. "Sorry, everyone, duty calls. Feel free to continue on without us."

CHAPTER FIVE

I DROVE, NICK in the seat beside me, Ellie in the back. The gravel road to the Inn became the forest-lined road into town, curving around the marina jam-packed with bright, glossy cruisers and crab boats weeping rust. Nick was giving me the side-eye.

"What?"

"The crew were trying to do a nice thing for you, Cap," he said.

Nick calls me "Cap," short for *Captain*. It's not a habit from his army days but a carefully chosen term that I take seriously. Everybody needs a captain in life—a guiding force, a confidant, a rock, an anchor when tumultuous winds blow in. Siobhan had been my captain. Nick had picked me as his when he first moved in, but I had disappointed him ever since. The expression I saw on his face now hurt me, the way remembering how Siobhan danced and sang and listened and laughed hurt. Like a kick to the chest.

"What do you want me to say?" I asked Nick. "I told them I didn't want a memorial."

"Those people back there, they loved her too, you know," Nick said. "You don't get to be the only person who misses Siobhan."

"Well, they can go miss her in their way, and I'll miss her in mine," I said. "I don't like circle jerks."

"You prefer individual jerks?"

"Something like that."

"You're a lone wolf who's lost his mate." Nick rolled his eyes. "Your heart is broken and it can't be mended, and now you're cursed to wander the earth alone."

"I kind of wish I were alone right now," I said, nodding. I looked in the rearview mirror at Mrs. Minnow and changed the subject like a practiced master. "What's Winley done this time, Mrs. Minnow?"

Gloucester is a small town. When Siobhan and I moved into the area, the story started circulating that I was ex–Boston PD, that I'd been sacked and was bitter about it. I hadn't done anything to quash that rumor, taking up residence at the back of the lobster shack on the waterfront most afternoons, downing JD shots and refusing to answer questions about it. A couple of months after Siobhan got the Inn up and running, people began coming to me with issues they didn't trust Sheriff Spears to handle. They wanted me to talk to the angry neighbor about his aggressive dog. To hustle the scary homeless guy camped out near the pier a little farther down the road. Find the punks who had spray-painted graffiti on an old woman's fence and rattle their skulls a bit.

In truth, being the unofficial town muscle was far more satisfying than running the Inn. Riding around with Nick beside me, I could pretend I was back in the city before my terrible fall. I could imagine sometimes that Nick was Malone, the version of my old friend before he'd betrayed me and morphed before my very eyes into a liar and a schemer. Little jobs like this took me into the past that I never stopped thinking about, a time before I lost everything.

Mrs. Minnow had called me once before about her son Winley, after the boy stole her car and drove it into a ditch off the Yankee Division Highway. She shifted uncomfortably now, perhaps remembering.

"Winnie's much worse this time. He's gone crazy." Ellie was staring out the window, rubbing her wrist. "He's just out of control. I've never seen him this angry. He snaps at me whenever I try to get him out of bed. He just slugs around the house. I got a call from the school saying he hasn't been there in three days. I tried to talk to him about it this morning…"

I turned and looked at her wrist, glimpsed red finger marks. She hid them from me.

"Did the kid hurt you?" I asked.

"No, no." She tucked a curl behind her ear. "He would never—"

"If he's hurt you, I'll kick his ass," I said. "He's not too young to learn what you get if you raise your hand to a woman. Once I've finished kicking his ass, Nick will kick his ass, and then the two of us will hold him down while you kick his ass."

I've got a real issue with men who beat up on women. It's part of a large collection of emotional baggage that would make a team of bellhops throw in their hats.

The Minnow residence was covered in bougainvillea; the mailbox was balanced on the top of a gray concrete post. I turned off the engine and was about to open my door when a coffee table smashed through the front window of the house and landed upside down in a flower bed.

CHAPTER SIX

TIME LOOPS AROUND. One minute you're a washed-up ex-cop with love handles who hasn't shaved in days, and the next minute you're back in time, a rookie with washboard abs who couldn't grow a beard for love or money, adrenaline thrumming in your veins as you wait for the go-ahead to bust into a crack house with your team.

The Minnow residence wasn't a crack house, but it sure seemed as dangerous as one. As I jogged over, I heard Winley Minnow growling and the sounds of glass breaking and something dry, maybe cereal, scattering across the floor. Through the window by the back door, I saw Winley and his father, Derek, a small, round man who was sweating in his polo shirt. Winley held a wooden block of knives under one arm like a football and had one knife in his big fist. Just above Derek's head, beneath a cheerful cuckoo clock with lumberjacks poised to saw tiny logs, a knife handle jutted out of the drywall. I watched as Winley brandished the blade at his father.

"Win, please." Derek put his hands up. "Please, please, son, put the knife down."

"They're not taking me. They're not taking me! I'm not going! They're not taking me!"

I could tell Winley was high as a kite even before I saw his face. He was pacing in a small area, two steps forward and two back. Between the shouts, he muttered something to himself in a singsongy voice.

"No one's coming to take you," Derek said. "You're out of your mind!"

I kicked in the back door just as Nick came in the front. Nick grabbed Derek and yanked him out of the kitchen. Winley turned and hurled the knife at me; it went sailing past my ear and through the open door to the yard. Nick grabbed the boy's hand as he went for another, and I went for the knife block. We wrestled, and the knives scattered on the floor. Nick swept the kid into a headlock that didn't seem to slow him down at all.

Winley had experienced a growth spurt since I'd handled him last, and he'd put on a few pounds. Maybe a hundred of them. The bug-eyed kid picked me up and threw me clean across the room into the kitchen counter, which sent a rack of dishes and glasses to the floor. Nick hung off him like a backpack, but he tightened the headlock until Winley's eyes started rolling up in his head. Winley went to his knees and the two tangled on the floor. I rejoined the fray, and Nick and I shoved the kid into the tiles.

"Winley!" I put my knee in his fleshy back to get his attention. "You're caught, buddy. Give it up!"

The kid growled and howled a bit and then burst into tears. "Don't let them take me!"

"Who's going to take you?"

"The doctors. The scientists."

"This kid is whacked," I told Nick. Typical newbie drug taker shuffling through emotions, grasping at anything. He was crying like a toddler, huffing and sniffing. I sat him up in the glass and cereal and mess on the floor and Nick and I watched as he sobbed into his hands, the ferocious rampaging killer suddenly reduced to a blubbering child.

"Don't tell my mom," he cried. He'd obviously completely forgotten that he'd manhandled her only minutes earlier. "Oh God. I've gotta clean this place up before she gets back!" He tried to get up. I shoved him down.

"Winley, what did you take?"

"Nothing. I didn't—" The sobs racked his big body. "They're coming for me!"

"He's on something," I told Nick. "This doesn't look like the joy and exuberance of glorious youth."

"The what?"

"Never mind."

"Don't call the police!" Winley said.

"He *is* the police, son." Nick grabbed Winley's big shoulder and shook him.

Winley wasn't giving up. He cried and begged us to keep his mother out of it, his dazed state blocking out the reality of what he had done. I stood and walked into the living room, where I saw through the smashed window that neighbors were gathering to console Ellie Minnow on the immaculate lawn. Derek Minnow was in the room, sitting in an armchair by the big kicked-in television set. Winley had knocked pictures off their hooks, punched holes in the drywall.

"I'm so tired of this." Derek looked up at me. A hopeless father.

"This is a regular thing?"

"We knew he'd been smoking weed. But it's never been this bad."

"I've got news for you, Derek," I said. "This ain't weed."

I returned to the kitchen, saw Nick trying to talk Winley out of his mumblings about scientists and doctors. I went to the kid's room and looked in. Curtains drawn, clothes on the floor two feet deep, an unmade bed, and a strange damp feeling to everything. Typical teenage bedroom except for the burn marks on the cluttered desk under the window and the scraps of aluminum foil and cigarette lighters. There were cans of beans lined up on the windowsill and empty ones stacked in the bin by the door.

I lifted some of the trash off the boy's desk and found a small yellow capsule with a smiley face printed on it. I turned the pill in my fingers, shook it, heard powder shift inside.

Nick appeared at the bedroom door and started picking shards of glass out of his palms like they were cactus needles. "What do you think?" he asked. "Crack?"

"PCP, maybe," I said. "If it was crack, he'd be walking around town knocking over fire hydrants. Angel dust makes you burrow. Explains his aversion to going to school. He's been living in his little nest in here where he feels safe."

I showed him the capsule. He took it and looked at it.

"Did he say where he got it?" I asked.

"He says he got it at school," Nick said, giving the capsule back to me. "A kid on a bike gave it to him for free. I don't know how true that is. He thinks some doctors are about to abduct him in a van. Here." He gave me a small piece of paper with a number scrawled on it.

"What's this?"

"Don't know." Nick shrugged. "I asked him where the drugs came from and he told me about the kid on the bike and handed me that. I checked his phone. He dialed this number this morning at about eight."

"Let's chase it down," I said. "I was looking for something to do with my day."

CHAPTER SEVEN

WE DROVE BACK to the house on the edge of the water, both of us silent, thoughtful. Hilly, seaside Gloucester, Massachusetts, sticks out like a thumb into the cold and unforgiving North Atlantic; it's a place of windswept stone beaches and pretty winter trees. The town swells in tourist season, but it doesn't have the pull of Manchester-by-the-Sea, with its glossy storefronts full of work by local artists, or Salem, with its rich, dark history. Roughness comes to Gloucester in hockey season, when Bruins fans pressed too tight into bars built hundreds of years ago get emotional and take the fight from the screen to the beer-soaked boards. It's not a drug-dealer town. It's not a PCP-and-teenage-violence town. Nick and I didn't say it, but we knew that what we'd just seen didn't belong here.

As I pulled up to the house, I winced for the thousandth

time at its condition. The Inn on the edge of the water was old and battered and needed work. Siobhan had been excited about redecorating it, constantly coming home with fabric samples and carpet swatches and those little color cards you get from the paint shop. Even though Siobhan lived here only a few months, she'd left her warm, gentle touch on the place. She'd painted the kitchen a sky blue and filled it with hanging ferns and she'd replaced the backsplash herself, swearing like a sailor and cursing the world, apparently a requirement when she performed any manual labor. When she slipped into the shower with me in the evenings, I'd pick lumps of grout and paint out of her hair, and she'd tell me about her plans for the loft, her major project. That was going to be our place, our sanctuary. She wanted to put a skylight in and open the nailed-shut windows so we could hear the lapping of the waves on the sand as we fell asleep at night.

I hadn't been up to the loft since she died. I lived in the basement and refused almost all maintenance requests from long- and short-term guests who stayed at the house. The plants in the kitchen were overgrown, the plumbing was shot, and the boards on the back porch creaked like an ancient pirate ship.

When we arrived, the house handywoman, Effie Johnson, was crouched by the basement window, sanding and scraping, preparing to paint the house exterior—something I'd forbidden. About twice a week Effie confronted me with a can of paint Siobhan left behind, sunflower yellow, and tapped it sternly with her finger, making a *tok-tok-tok* sound on the lid.

"Nope," I always told her. "Not this week."

I let Effie do some things. She mows the lawns, chops firewood, cleans, repairs broken furniture, and keeps the possums out of the basement in exchange for her rent. She does a good job, but the main reason I like her is that someone tried to kill her once, slashing her throat from ear to ear and making mincemeat of her voice box, so she can't talk at all and thus can't ask me about my grief, how I'm coping, whether I'd like to share my feelings about my dead wife.

When Nick and I approached, Effie looked up at us, then picked up the paint can from beside her, which she must have had waiting in case I came around. She rapped her knuckles on the lid.

"Maybe next week," I said. "You seen Clay?"

She made a sleeping motion with her hands under her cheek. Then she gestured at the cuts and grazes Nick and I had acquired in the tango with Winley Minnow, questioning.

"Just a bit of good old-fashioned kid wrangling." Nick made fighting fists and slow-punched Effie in the ribs until she pushed him off. We told Effie about the situation and she tugged on an earlobe, thinking.

She made a typewriter motion and pointed to the house, and I nodded.

"What is that?" Nick asked. "Piano?"

"Typewriter." I started walking. "She means we should go ask Susan."

"When are you gonna learn proper sign language?" Nick asked Effie. Effie raised her middle finger over her shoulder and went back to work.

I don't know what brought Susan Solie and Effie Johnson to the house or what their history together is. They came not long after Siobhan was killed and asked for cheap permanent rooms, and I knew right away they were not what they seemed. The jagged scar across the beautiful black woman's throat was enough to tell me she had a past, and I'd glimpsed her in her room doing chin-ups on a steel bar she'd erected near the windows; the bed was made impossibly tight, with razor-sharp hospital corners, and the shelves were completely bare of possessions. Susan was ex-FBI and didn't mind admitting it. She explained that she had moved into town after taking early retirement. She'd shrugged when I'd asked about her friend Effie and her mildly psychopathic living habits.

Nick and I trudged into the dining room, where Susan was working on her laptop, writing articles for the local rag. I pushed the laptop closed and Susan gave an exaggerated sigh as Nick sat down beside her.

"We need you," I said.

"What are you two bozos up to now?" she asked, picking up a mug of coffee and sipping it while she looked us over. "I'm on deadline here."

"Deadline?" Nick flipped Susan's blond ponytail. "What happens if you miss the cutoff? The crab wranglers of Gloucester won't have their weather report this week? Oh, wait, you've got a big scoop—yarn-store sale this Saturday, twenty percent off crochet hooks."

Susan gave Nick a withering look. Next to her computer was a sheet of paper she'd been using to design the newspaper's weekly crossword.

"Four across, five letters. The clue is 'intelligent,'" I read. "Susan, that's a bit narcissistic, don't you think?"

"Ah, yes." She wrote the letters of her name in the boxes with a pencil. "I knew I was onto something there. Now state your purpose or leave me be. I'm actually being productive. You might try it some time."

"Clay's sleeping off the night shift and there's a rumor someone's moving in on local high-schoolers with free samples of candy," I said. "You heard anything like that?"

"No." Susan's smile disappeared. "Jesus. Here? In Gloucester?"

"Yeah, here," I said. "Yarn-store central."

We told her about Winley, and I put the capsule I'd found in the kid's bedroom on the dining-room table between us. Susan examined the pill, then took the paper with the phone number from me and turned the laptop away from Nick. As I'd hoped she would, she used whatever mysterious connection she still had with the Bureau to find the number.

"Burner phone," she said. "It's untraceable. Registered to no one."

"Can we find out where it was purchased?" I asked, taking a seat beside her.

"Bill, I'm not your federal connection," Susan said. "I don't work for the Bureau anymore. If you want to go down a rabbit hole, you'll have to do it on your own."

"But you still seem in league with them somehow," Nick said, gesturing to the laptop.

"Just call up your old friends and get them to help us out," I said.

"I can't call up my old friends and ask them for favors any more than you can," she said, looking at me. I felt a chill run up the back of my neck. I wasn't sure if Susan knew what I had done in Boston, what had gotten me severed like a gangrenous limb from the job I loved. Her comment suggested she knew something.

"Look," she said. "A drug dealer using burner phones and giving out free product is probably part of an outfit. Junkies don't have the cash to keep buying devices—they use public phones, and they sure don't give anything away for free. The guy on the end of this number? He's probably just a soldier delivering the goods."

"So what are you saying?" I asked. "This could be a gang or something?"

"What I'm saying is you need to decide whether you want to get involved," Susan said. "You might end up with a whole pack of them on your tail. If you target the wrong guy, you could be in a world of trouble."

CHAPTER EIGHT

THE APPOINTMENT WAS for one Mitchell Antoine Cline, but when Dr. Raymond Locke looked up from his desk, he saw three men entering his small office. From the information in his files, he figured that Cline was the smallest of them, a man with a well-toned body filling out his Hugo Boss shirt and long, narrow feet in patent-leather shoes. He sat in a chair while the two men with him—a thickly built Asian guy with an enormous silver watch and a much bigger black guy with a neat goatee—stood against the wall and looked bored. Locke noted that he hadn't clicked the alert button on the computer screen to tell the front desk to send the next patient in.

"Mr. Cline, is it?" Locke leaned back in his chair. "Uh, this is awkward, but I actually don't take group appointments. I thought you were here to talk about your"—he looked at the computer screen again—"laryngitis. Could your friends perhaps wait outside?"

"My health is fine." Cline smiled. "I'm not here for a medical consultation. I'm here with a business proposal, Dr. Locke. I'm told you're in charge of the pharmacy at this hospital

"I...excuse me?"

"You're a multitalented guy, Doctor." Cline clasped his long hands on his knee. "You juggle many responsibilities. Mondays you're here at the hospital as an internist. Tuesdays to Thursdays, you put in time in the ER. On Fridays, you review the pharmacy inventory and order what's needed, and Saturdays you play squash with two other doctors. Sundays you drive your teenage son, Adam, to acting classes. He dreams of Broadway. Very refreshing in a TV-driven world, you ask me."

The big black man in the corner of the room heard his cue, strode forward, and placed a Polaroid on the desk in front of Locke. It was a profile shot of Locke and Adam walking to the family car in the Fresh Stars parking lot. Locke eased air through his lips.

"I think you're ripe for more responsibility," Cline said. "Our partnership could be very profitable for you."

"This is..." Locke shook his head, tried to find the words. "This is..."

The big guy unfolded a piece of paper and put it next to the photograph of Locke and his son. Locke took it and looked at the items on this list. A part of his brain knew exactly what was happening and what would come next. He'd heard stories like this from friends he'd known in med school, although always second- and thirdhand and always unbelievable. Even as Cline continued speaking, part of Locke's brain could almost say the words along with the stranger in the chair before him. Another part of his brain was experiencing pure panic. Deep, gut-wrenching, red, raw panic, a siren that wailed uselessly as he gripped the paper for dear life. Though he'd always feared this, he'd never made a plan. He tried to tuck himself deeper into his chair.

"You'll have the items on that list shipped here monthly," Cline said. "I'll assign you a liaison, one of my business associates, who will collect the items and adjust the order as necessary. You'll be compensated for your assistance."

"I can't—"

"You're afraid," Cline said. His handsome features were warm, almost kind, and he nodded with compassion. "I understand. You've heard stories about this sort of thing. You think that if you're late or light on a shipment or if you involve the police in our arrangement, my men will come around here with ice picks and baseball bats and teach you a lesson. That's not true, Dr. Locke. Nothing's going to happen to you. We will take our business elsewhere, and you'll go back to your normal, happy life."

Locke felt his legs trembling beneath his desk. Cline took a moment to examine the certificates on Locke's wall almost dreamily before he continued.

"Then one day you'll get a phone call," Cline said. "It might be a couple of months from now, or a year. The caller will be from your son's high school. He'll be wondering where your son is, why you didn't call to say that your son would be out sick. You'll tell them you dropped him at the school gates. He should be there. You'll call 911. There will be an Amber alert. A media appeal. A prayer vigil. People will put flowers and teddy bears and candles on the lawn outside your house."

"Listen. Some of this stuff, I...I can't justify ordering it," Locke stammered. "You...you've got embalming fluid on here. How do I explain that? We're not a funeral parlor. Mescaline I can't get unless I submit for special approval. The Duragesic, the morphine...it's too much!"

"It'll take some time for police to find your son." Cline brushed an invisible piece of lint from the shoulder of his shirt, talking softly, ignoring Locke. "They'll have to access his dental records to confirm his identity. Your wife will want to see him. The medical examiner will advise against it."

"Okay." Locke put his hands up. "Okay. Okay. Please stop. Just stop."

"I'll leave Simbo and Russ here to sort out the details." Cline smoothed the front of his shirt as he stood. "It was such a pleasure doing business with you."

Cline put out his hand. Locke shook it, but he was so numb, he hardly felt the icy contact against his skin.

CHAPTER NINE

I LEFT SUSAN to her work at her laptop and went into the kitchen. Nick followed me. He was jittery, edgy. I'd seen him this way sometimes, bored and searching for conflict, his nerves shot from his time in Iraq and his brain always looking for danger. Just the whiff of trouble could send Nick into a fever. He was like a junkyard dog rehomed to a senior-care facility. Nothing to do. Nothing to guard against.

He stood rubbing his hands together and looking to me as I poured myself a glass of water.

"So what are we gonna do?" he asked.

"Find the loser who gave Winley the junk and cram his head somewhere narrow and dark."

"But Susan said this could be a whole gang. A sophisticated outfit."

"Nothin' gets past you."

"So we've gotta take 'em all out, man. We've got to put a stop to this."

"We," I said, pointing to his chest and then mine, "don't *have* to do anything. We *can* go knock some heads together to ease Mrs. Minnow's mind. But we don't want to get in too deep. If there's a whole posse of these pricks, it's Clay's job to move them on."

"Clay?" Nick scoffed. "Clay couldn't move a throw pillow from one end of a couch to the other without fucking it up somehow and injuring himself in the process."

I shushed him, glancing up to the second floor, where Clay's room was. Nick moved closer to me, lowered his voice.

"Winley Minnow's built like a double-wide and he was *buzzed* this morning," he said. "That shit is strong. What happens if someone like Marni gets ahold of it? She's maybe a hundred pounds dripping wet."

I turned away. Nick was talking like a man who'd already gotten on the train and taken his seat and was beckoning to me through the window as the gears began to grind. I couldn't leave him to wander into a situation by himself, hypervigilant and ready to fight whether there was a battle to be won or not.

Gloucester was not my city, but it had been Siobhan's. My wife had dreamed of running a hotel by the sea since she was a little girl, and she didn't have the time before she was taken to really enjoy what she had built. I knew that at the moment, I was staring into the blood and bone and muscle of a new town with new people to protect. It was a familiar feeling. I was not a cop anymore, but I could throw myself into this mission and become a part of Gloucester, let it take me up into its heart, fight for it. The feeling of having something to love and protect the way I had Boston made the hairs on my arms stand up. No, I decided. Nobody would prey on the kids of this town. Not while I was standing guard.

"It's up to us," Nick said.

"It's up to us," I agreed.

CHAPTER TEN

I WALKED DOWN the hall and saw Marni sitting on the steps, a cigarette clamped between her lips, tuning her violin. Marni had stopped going to school about the time she moved in with Siobhan and me, but she hadn't given up the violin. Music was the only subject she hadn't been failing. I tried to avoid Marni completely, even when Siobhan was alive, having exactly zero experience in the emotional requirements of volatile, vulnerable teen girls. I was aware that, now that Siobhan was gone, Marni was kind of my responsibility. But I'd become a master at ignoring my responsibilities.

I was about to make the girl aware of my presence when she finished tuning the violin, placed it under her chin, and played a few notes I recognized from one of Chopin's nocturnes. I've always wanted to tell Marni that she's a gifted musician. She plays only sad stuff, and sometimes I hear her practicing and just the sound of it tears me to shreds inside. But telling a teenager a thing like that could make her pitch the instrument into the sea and never play again. I stood in the hall and listened, my throat tight and my fists clenched, until she stopped to adjust something else. I crept away and then walked back down the hall loudly and sat on the stairs beside her.

"Here he is," she said, the cigarette moving as she talked. "Mr. Freeze."

"Mr. Freeze?"

"The guy with the cold, dead heart."

"I see." I folded my arms. "You think I didn't appreciate the little thing you organized this morning for Siobhan."

"You sprinted off like someone was shooting at you."

"I had to help a friend," I said. "But I appreciated it. I just grieve differently than you. I'm not a 'Let's all get together and hug it out' kind of griever, Marn."

"Yeah, you're a 'Keep pushing it down until it rises up and explodes' kind of griever," she said. "That's healthy."

"I congratulate you on your career choice of psychologist," I said. "Fifteen might be a bit young to get licensed, but I'm sure your professional colleagues will make an exception in your case."

"Did you come here just to annoy me?" she asked.

"I want to know if you've had anyone approach you with one of these." I took out the capsule with the smiley face and showed it to her. She examined it and then made like she was going to throw it into her mouth. She started laughing when I grabbed it back.

"Jesus Christ," I said.

"You're too easy."

"Have you seen one of these before or not?"

"No, I have not. Why are you asking? Are you the new drug police in Gloucester? And here I was, thinking you'd reached peak lameness. 'Just say no to the drugs, Marni.'" She crossed her eyes and said in a stupid, lisping voice, "Drugs are bad, m'kay?"

"Now who's being annoying?"

"Of course there are drugs around." She looked away. "Gloucester's not the moon. There's weed. The boys in the kitchen at work huff nitrous oxide from the whipped-cream cans we use on desserts sometimes. Whip-its. You ever done a whip-it?"

"No. I like my brain cells too much."

"Well, the boss caught them, so they've mostly stopped now. But I don't blame them. There's nothing to do here. How the hell are we supposed to spend our free time?"

I knew exactly how Marni spent her free time, and it was worrying enough without the drugs. She fit right in with a posse of similarly badly dressed mopey teens who had body parts dripping with piercings or crisscrossed with free tattoos they got from local apprentices practicing in their mothers' garages. From what I could tell, they did the kind of things I did when I was their age. Smashed the windows of abandoned houses. Sat around campfires on the beach talking trash. Threw bottles off the break wall into the water. Kids who, in a couple of years, would either straighten right out or flush their futures gleefully down the toilet.

"I'm not talking weed and whip-its," I told her. "I'm talking about the hard stuff. This here?" I showed her the capsule. "This did about ten thousand bucks' worth of damage to a lady's house this morning and almost got me a kitchen knife in my forehead."

"I don't know anything about it, man." Marni waved me off. "I work at a pizza shop. Everybody there is on something. How do you think they don't go nuts with the sheer mindlessness of it all?" She stuck her chin out, made sleepy eyes. "Thin crust. No anchovies. Double cheese. Thin crust. No anchovies. Double—"

"Not you, though, right?"

"Oh, of course not." She rolled her eyes. I got an itchy, unsettled feeling in my chest. I wanted to come down hard on Marni, tell her all the things Siobhan would have told her if she were alive: that she was too smart to spend the rest of her life wearing a Dough Brothers uniform by day and wasting her time with losers and washouts at night. But I knew too much of that would only push her away. I decided I would keep a closer eye on her, even if I had to do it covertly. Marni was on the edge, and the smallest breath of wind could blow her into a dark place. I had to keep a grip on Siobhan's little cousin.

"Well, then, I suppose if you've never bought any drugs, you don't know how to call up for some," I said, pulling the piece of paper with the phone number out of my pocket. Marni looked at the number with interest, then her big eyes flicked back to me, suspicious.

"I need someone with a young voice," I said. "You ever take a drama class?"

CHAPTER ELEVEN

THE BOY WAS sitting on a wooden ledge outside Dogtown Used and Unusual Books, watching the crowds go by and sucking on a lollipop. A section of Gloucester's main road had been shut down for a street festival, and the curb was lined with carts selling lobster rolls, corn dogs, and ice cream. There were photography stalls selling sunset shots of the boats in the harbor. Nick and I observed the skinny kid in oversize clothes as we stood behind a stand selling nautical antiques, the jumble of polished brass navigation equipment and salt-encrusted buoys providing cover. Marni was casually flipping through tiles painted with colorful starfish on the counter of the stall. She glanced over at the boy when we pointed him out.

"Oh, him?" She laughed. "Can't be him. That's Squid. I went to school with that guy."

"Makes sense," Nick said. "Get a kid to deal to kids. He can walk among them without standing out."

"Why do you say it can't be him?" I asked Marni.

"Because Squid's an idiot. He got expelled for putting a dead squid in the principal's Lexus. The guy left his sunroof open. It was a hot day, too, and he didn't get back out to his car until the afternoon." Marni smirked. "I wonder how much it cost him to get that reek out of his car."

"Where did he get the squid?" Nick asked.

"Science class. It was marine-life week."

"Send him a message," I said, keeping my eyes on the boy. "He's standing where the guy said he'd be. It's got to be him."

Marni took her phone out and texted, and we watched as the kid patted his jeans and then took a phone out of his pocket.

"It's him. All right, get out of here," I told Marni. "I'll see you back at the house."

"No way, man," Marni whispered. "I want to watch."

"I said *move it*." I pointed to the end of the street. Marni sulked off, and Nick and I approached the skinny kid sitting in front of the bookstore. I felt like a bully walking up to the weedy nerd in the schoolyard. The boy looked almost emaciated, he was so thin. Nick could have cracked him over his knee as easily as a broom handle. But I knew that what he had been spreading around was dangerous, lethal stuff. I had to put a stop to it now, before this young man spread his product farther through the neighborhood.

As we got closer, I saw that there was a black backpack over his shoulder, wedged between the kid and the front window of the store.

"Hey, punk," Nick started. I braced myself to take off in case the kid ran, but he just looked at Nick lazily.

"'Sup, bro?"

"What's up is you're peddling toxic shit to schoolkids." I grabbed the boy's backpack and lifted him to his feet with it. "You don't do that in our town."

"*Your* town?" Squid grinned, then shifted the lollipop from one cheek to the other. I could see that most of his teeth were black. "Who the fuck are you? You ain't the police. What, you think you got the local operation around here?"

"No, we're not drug-dealing scum like you." Nick pushed the kid hard enough that he thumped into the glass of the bookstore window. It was an old trick. Never let the perp get his balance. "We want you out of here."

"Oh, man." Squid laughed. "You keep your hands off me, bro. You don't know who you're dealin' with right now."

"Oh, really?" I said.

Squid lifted his white T-shirt and dragged an enormous gun halfway out of the front of his jeans.

"Yeah," the boy said. "Really, bitch."

CHAPTER TWELVE

THE STREET WAS full of people. There were kids gathered around the ice cream stand, families looking in store windows, Marni watching curiously from the other side of the street, only two stalls down from where I'd left her. I saw a trumpet player on the corner, his instrument case open in the sun, heard the clatter of quarters as someone threw change onto the pile. I was suddenly overwhelmed by the noise around me. The gun was comically big in the kid's hand; the tendons of his wrist strained as he flashed the butt at me.

I made a grab for the gun. He shoved at me with his other hand and tried to drag the pistol up above his belt.

"Don't even think about it," I said.

"Fuck you, man," Squid snarled in my face. He raised his voice. "Get your hands off my dick, old man!"

I didn't flinch. "You get your hands off the gun or I'll blast your dick all over the pavement."

Nick stepped in, shielding our struggle from the crowd. All we needed was for someone to spot the gun, start screaming, and cause a mass panic. The kid released the gun and I realized for the first time that every muscle in my body was frozen with terror. I pulled the weapon all the way out of his jeans and tucked it into my coat.

"Where the hell did you get a gun like that?" I eased a breath from my tight lungs. "What are you, fifteen years old? Who are you working for?"

"Doesn't matter where I got the gun." Squid sniffed, trying to act tough after I'd disarmed him. "I'll have another one next time you come knocking. I see you again, I'm not gonna wait, bro. I'll just start poppin' at whoever's around. You got that?"

He gestured with his chin at the crowd, at the children bouncing with excitement in the line for ice cream.

"Now let me go before I start screaming," the boy said. "You ain't the cops. All I gotta do is tell all these nice people here you got a big-ass gun and you're stickin' it in my face."

People had stopped to stare. I backed off, and Squid walked away. Nick and I watched as Squid tried his best to swagger confidently through the crowd, sucking hard on his lollipop.

"I think Susan was right," Nick said. "This is bigger than we thought."

CHAPTER THIRTEEN

I KNEW EXACTLY who killed my wife. In order to get to the bar where Nick and I planned to think through our problem, I had to drive past the house of the woman who'd killed Siobhan. Since the accident, I've felt a tightening in my stomach and a pressure on my brain every time I go by, but there was no way around it now. I gripped the steering wheel as we approached. Nick, his boots up on the dash, looked out the window on the passenger side.

Siobhan had been walking along the strip of grass by the side of the road when she was hit. She was on her way back from the grocery store, a trip she'd made a hundred times, something she enjoyed. She liked the chance to be alone and the little mission of going into town, checking things off her list, talking to people in the supermarket aisles, making connections. It had been a clear, crisp evening, the sun not yet behind the hills, kids riding their bikes in the street, and birds announcing their return home to their nests for the night. The contents of the bags in her hands ended up scattered all over the road, red wine and roast beef for a dinner we would never have.

Some things didn't add up about what had happened to Siobhan. The young woman who had hit her, Monica Rink, had been driving to a party. She'd tested negative for alcohol and drugs after the accident, but in the footwell of the passenger side of the car, there'd been a six-pack of vodka coolers with two missing and one open. The road was isolated but dead straight. Monica had swerved a long way off the asphalt, somehow not seeing Siobhan on the wide strip of grass. The paramedics told me that Monica had been playing with her radio, unable to get the Bluetooth to connect to her phone. She rammed the car into a road barrier after she hit Siobhan and then got out and ran back to assist her. My wife died in a stranger's arms while I was at home on the little porch, watching the purple light settle over the ocean and waiting for her.

I'd never spoken to Nick about my nervous, angry avoidance of Monica Rink's house, but he seemed to get it.

"So I have a confession to make," he said as we got closer to the house.

"Oh yeah?"

"The memorial this morning." He leaned back in the seat. "Marni said Siobhan used to grab her and make her dance with her in the kitchen to her crappy music."

"Mmm?"

"Well." He gave an exaggerated sigh. "Siobhan might have made me do that a few times."

"Really." I looked over. He was smiling to himself.

"Maybe I didn't fight her off so much," Nick said.

"Did you dance close?" I asked.

"Yeah."

"How close?"

"Pretty close." He grinned at me. I found I was grinning too, for some reason.

"One time she made me sing the Kenny Rogers parts of 'Islands in the Stream,'" he said.

I laughed hard. "You're just a man," I said. "What could you do?"

Our smiles faded. When I looked over, Nick's face had darkened. I was steeling myself to pass Monica Rink's house when Nick suddenly put a hand out.

"Pull over," he ordered.

I drove the car onto the shoulder. In the woods, a man with a dark beard and long hair was walking his dog, his eyes on the fallen leaves at his feet. Nick got out of the car and went to the rear tire. I leaned over and watched him in the side mirror as he pretended to examine the tire, then took out his phone and snapped a picture of the man with the dog over his shoulder.

He got back in. "Drive."

"What the hell was that?"

"That dude." Nick was ducking his head to watch the man disappear in mirror as we drove away. "That's the third time this month I've seen him near the house."

"Yeah." I shrugged. "I've seen him around. That's Living the Dream."

"Who?"

"I've spoken to him a couple of times. I just say, 'Hello, how are you?'" I said. "He always says, 'Living the dream.'"

"What does that mean?" Nick said, almost to himself. He was typing something into his phone. I glanced over and saw there was a list of times and dates, pictures of the bearded man. "Living the dream?"

I waited for Nick to tell me he was joking. He didn't.

"Nick, he's just a dude walking his dog."

"Yeah," Nick said. "That's what it's supposed to look like. Just like that mother with her baby."

One of Nick's grisly tales from his time in Iraq was what he referred to as the Mother-Baby Story. His battalion had been traversing the desert from their base camp outside Alqosh to a small town called Jambur, moving supplies. Blistering sunlight, featureless sandy plains so wide you could see the curvature of the Earth. The lead vehicle had stopped when a middle-aged woman in a niqab ran out of a house in the desert waving her arms and crying, calling for assistance. With the soldiers' guns trained on the woman, the unit's interpreter had determined that a baby had stopped breathing inside the little house. The captain gave permission for two armed guys, the interpreter, and a medic to go assess the situation while the rest of the battalion remained where they were in the convoy. The four members of the team hadn't even shut the door behind them when the house exploded, spraying the convoy with dust and debris.

Thinking about Nick's Mother-Baby Story had made me forget completely that I was approaching the house of the woman responsible for Siobhan's death. I realized with relief that the house was now behind us, but the relief was short-lived. Nick's surveillance of Living the Dream and his dog was leading to an episode.

I had seen Nick fall victim to this before, when the mind that was so ravaged by his time in the service inched too far across the sanity line into dark territory and he was suddenly back there on the tour, where people were not who they seemed to be and any moment could be shattered by violent deaths. The bomb of Nick's terrifying hidden memories had been ticking for a while now, and there was no telling when it was going to blow.

CHAPTER FOURTEEN

VIOLENCE WAS ABOUT to break out at the Greenfish Bar.

Nick and I took the short end of the counter and I saw him right away, an old man tearing a cardboard coaster to shreds over a quarter glass of whiskey. His shoulders were up around his ears and his jaw was flexing, and I could see what remained of the muscles in his neck twitching. He was looking away from me and Nick at a group of men celebrating what seemed to be someone's return. A skinny, pockmarked shrimp of a guy at the center of the group kept getting pats on the back and comments on his body, the men busting his balls about his lean arms.

While Nick was in the bathroom, the shrimpy guy walked down the bar and ordered a drink, leaning in a little too close to the elderly whiskey drinker.

"I'm catching those death stares you're throwing my way,

old man," the shrimp said. The old man flinched. "Keep it up. It doesn't bother me. I'm gonna have a few drinks here with my buddies, and then I'm going home to my wife. We're trying to have another baby."

The shrimp pushed the old guy's drink over. It spilled and ran off the edge of the bar. The bartender rolled her eyes and poured the old man another while the shrimp walked away.

I don't make it my business to get involved in bar fights, but I recognized the old guy. He had stood over Siobhan's body in the medical examiner's office the night I lost her. I'd been called in to identify her, and he'd put a hand on my back, warm and heavy. It had felt like the only thing keeping me from floating off and becoming nothing, that hand on my shoulder. The mere sight of Dr. Eric Mayburn now stole my breath away. Siobhan was everywhere. Inescapable.

Nick came back and ordered drinks for us, then slid an elbow out on the bar and surveyed the Greenfish's sticky laminated menu. Lobster rolls and Jack Daniel's–flavored hot wings.

"So here's the plan," Nick said. "We take the gun to Susan. Get her to run the serial number. I'm guessing whoever the jerk is, if he isn't just some poor sap who's had his gun stolen, he's the kingpin and he gave the gun to Squid. We get the address and go around there, threaten him with what we know. He's supplied a deadly weapon to a minor. He won't want his house raided. He'll move on."

"I have a few problems with what you're saying," I said. "First, Susan doesn't want to help us. She avoids anything that has to do with the Bureau."

"I can't work that woman out," Nick said. "What's she doing at the house? Why tell us she used to be Bureau if she's not willing to tell us everything—what she did there, why she left. She's too young to have retired. Maybe she got herself kicked out and she's blacklisted."

I shifted in my seat. Nick was wandering into territory that was dangerously familiar to me.

"Maybe she's undercover, working on something," Nick mused. "But then why tell us she used to be a fed at all? Maybe it's all lies. Maybe she was supposed to marry a guy with Mob ties but left him at the altar."

"You're very creative," I noted. "But whatever it is, I'm sure it's none of our business. In any case, we have to decide what we're going to do with this big-ass gun. Maybe we should take it to Clay."

"What do you need a handgun that size in Gloucester for?" Nick said. "You know, I came to Gloucester to get away from guns, sirens, and crackheads. The fact that these creeps are handing out samples means they're new in town, trying to lock in some long-term clientele. We stomp on them now and we won't have ourselves another Baltimore."

Nick was a Baltimore native, but he'd told me when he moved in here that he had returned to his city to find it worse than some of the war-torn villages he'd rolled through in Iraq. A drug epidemic had ravaged Baltimore, and its overcrowded rehab clinics, overwhelmed cops, and warring gangs had given it a dangerous reputation. Nick left for Gloucester after an elderly woman was beaten to death in the hallway of his apartment building for her handbag. He'd found her lying there stone-cold dead, the other residents too scared to dial 911 for fear of being called on as witnesses.

"Nothing like Baltimore is going to happen," I said. "Not here."

"You're damn right it's not," he said. "So give me your plan."

"My plan for right now is to try to stop this train before it leaves the station," I said, watching Dr. Mayburn. Nick followed my glance. I was surprised he hadn't caught on to the danger already, but once he did, he sat bolt upright. Dr. Mayburn had risen out of his seat and seemed on the edge of making a bad decision about the loud, annoying group at the end of the bar. He took a steak knife from a place setting on the counter and held it by his side, moving the blade up and down.

"I wouldn't do it, friend," Nick said, sipping his drink. Dr. Mayburn was shaking with rage as he turned to us.

"Do what?" he snapped.

"It's not worth it," Nick said. "They're just loud losers. Ignore them."

Mayburn was walking toward them even before Nick finished speaking. Nick and I rounded the bar to intervene just as Dr. Mayburn thrust himself into the group, brandishing the knife at the small, lean man, whose expression was a mixture of surprise and delight.

"I've had enough," Mayburn said, sneering. "I've had enough of you and your filth. You remorseless...cowardly..." His rage was making it impossible for him to find the right words. "Having another baby, are you? You should be ashamed of yourself!"

Nick and I went in to pull Mayburn back but we were stopped by the thick arm of one of the men in the group; it came down in front of us like a tollbooth barrier. Someone shoved Mayburn in the back, almost toppling him, but he got his balance and flailed around with the knife, inches from bewildered faces.

"What you gonna do, you old prick?"

"Go for it, bitch. Let's see what you've got!"

The men had the knife out of Mayburn's withered grip before he even realized it. They started pushing him around like a child. Nick glanced at me, and I could almost feel his body engage, harden, go into fight mode. A switch flipped, and the machine was unleashed.

CHAPTER FIFTEEN

NICK GRABBED THE arm blocking him and yanked it down, then used the momentum to drag the big guy to the floor and sink a knee into his ribs as he went. I heard bones crunch. I thought about the gun in my pocket but grabbed the wrist of the guy with the knife instead and palmed him in the face with my other hand; the shock of the blow caused him to drop the knife. I slid it to the side with my foot, pushed Mayburn out of harm's way, grabbed one of the losers by his flannel shirt, and threw him into the bar, knocking stools over. Nick and I backed the remaining trio into the corner by the men's room.

"He came at us, the asshole!" The shrimpy guy gestured at Mayburn while keeping an eye on Nick, who stepped over the big guy he'd winded like he was a deer shot down in the woods. "We're just trying to have a party here!"

"The party's moving on." I pointed to the doors to the parking lot. "Better catch the bus before it leaves."

The little guy had a chest full of swirly tattoos peeking through his sweat-stained shirt. There were rosy red sores around his throat from a cheap razor. His friends seemed happy to leave, edging toward the door, but it was the shrimp's party and he wasn't giving up without a tantrum. He grabbed a glass from the table behind him and threw it at me.

I wasn't ready for that and I flinched, but Nick caught the glass an inch from my nose and then smashed it on the countertop, leaving a jagged edge to fight with. I imagined myself doing the same thing but ending up with a fistful of useless shards. Nick didn't even have to brandish the weapon. The big guy dragged himself up, and the party of losers walked out. There was a promise in the shrimp's eyes as he glanced back over his shoulder at Mayburn.

The doctor was clutching his chest and gasping as he went to the bar. I helped him onto a stool while Nick went to smooth things over with the bartender before she called the cops.

Mayburn was not a fighting man. His face and neck were flushed, and his hands were shaking. I felt him examining my face.

"Don't I know you?" Mayburn asked.

"Nope," I said.

"You sure?"

"I think I'd remember a crazy old-timer who goes around waving knives at punks in bars," I said. I took the stool beside him, showing him only my profile. "You know that guy, do you?"

"That small one. That's Rick Craft."

"Who's Rick Craft?"

"Google it," he said, too tired to explain.

I took out my phone as Mayburn recovered. The story I read from the *Gloucester Chronicle,* the newspaper Susan worked for, made the hairs on my neck stand up.

"'Two girls, ages three and five, were taken to Lawrence General Hospital in North Andover for suspected poisoning,'" I read. "'They were pronounced dead on arrival.'"

"They weren't poisoned," Mayburn said. "They were Craft's kids. He's a long-term addict. Rick and his wife got high and passed out. Left a bunch of pills on the table. The girls took one each, thinking they were candy."

Nick returned to my side as Mayburn collected himself.

"I'm the medical examiner at Lawrence," Mayburn said, something I knew but Nick didn't. "I was there when the girls were brought in. The pills they took were loaded with fentanyl. It's fifty times more potent than heroin. They never had a chance."

"Jesus," I said.

"That bastard"—Mayburn jerked a thumb at the door through which Craft and his cronies had left—"did just ninety days in prison. Pleaded to child endangerment. *Ninety days*. Can you believe that? I saw the pictures from his house. There were needles all over the floor. He gets child endangerment? It should have been murder."

Mayburn wiped his face with his hand. I now understood his distress at Craft's claims that he and his wife were trying for another child. I felt the rage rising fiery and hard, like a heated steel ball stuck in my throat.

"The drugs even looked like candy," Mayburn said almost to himself, staring into his glass, defeated. "The capsules were bright and colorful with faces printed on them."

CHAPTER SIXTEEN

CLINE COULDN'T UNDERSTAND it. Gloucester was crawling with seafood. Every morning he suited up head to toe in Nike and ran along the empty gray beach, and everywhere there were crab, lobster, and tuna boats returning from predawn runs. He saw the slippery black heads and flippers in the boats' wake, seals that trailed the vessels for scraps and throwbacks. And yet despite that, there was only this one sushi place in town, and it was a dump.

He sat at the windows of the restaurant with his men, gazing at the fading light on the water, his nose wrinkling at the smell from the kitchen. Unchanged industrial fryers, the tang of tartar sauce and lemon. The wine, at least, was passable. He'd certainly been less comfortable than this for much longer in his life.

Attempting to spread the business in the north, Cline had

done all he could to make himself comfortable in seaside Shitsville until he could get boys on every corner, a morgue full of bodies, a police force under his thumb, and a steady population of clients buying his product. As soon as Cline was satisfied, he would be out of here, taking the virus north to cities that better suited his tastes. He had his eye on Portland next. There was great sushi in Portland.

Town by town, higher and higher, Cline planned to spread his business. He was building a franchise. He established control of a town, trained his managers, handed over the reins, and then moved on. Gloucester was a prize Cline had wanted for quite a while. It was untouched territory. *Terra nullius.* A couple of times in Boston, Cline had had to squash local competition and deal with the problems they'd left behind. Resentful cops who were impossible to bend. Burned politicians and judges. Old junkies with high tolerances who couldn't be fed economical, low-percentage product. But Gloucester would be Cline's jewel. His chance to establish things just the way he liked. He'd thought about opening a sushi place here, just to make it tolerable.

Someone shouted something, interrupting a brief by his man Turner that he'd hardly been listening to, and when Cline looked up, he saw a furious late-middle-aged white woman leaving her table and coming over to their booth. One of the locals, he assumed, judging by the stretched neck of her Walmart T-shirt, the bottle dye job, the eighties ice-blue eye shadow. Cline sipped his wine, steeling himself.

"You." The woman pointed across the table at him, ignoring Russ, Turner, and Bones. "I know who you are."

The woman was spitting as she talked. Cline glanced at

the table from whence she'd come and saw the remains of battered-shrimp cocktails, wilted salads. A beer-bellied man cowering in embarrassment and a toddler in a filthy high chair smearing itself and everything within reach with ketchup.

"My daughter goes to your people for oxy," the woman said. "She's twenty-one. Kaylen Druly. Do you know her? I bet you don't know any of their names. Her wrists are like this. Like this!" Cline watched the woman make a circle with her fingers about the circumference of a golf ball. "I haven't seen or heard from my daughter in *two weeks*. I'm raising her son because of you. Did you know that? I'm sixty-three years old!"

Russ and Bones were out of the booth, pushing the woman and swearing, but she struggled with them, knocked Cline's glass of sauvignon blanc into his lap. Cold rushed over his shirt, his thighs; the chilled wine reached into his jock and sent icy fingers around his balls. Cline stood, dabbing at the fabric. He had a huge stain, like he had pissed his pants. A couple of waiters entered the fray. People were leaning out of their booths, pointing, whispering.

"They brought their poison into this town!" the woman howled.

It was a good performance. The crowded restaurant fell silent. Cline knew the story; the girl had probably started with oxycodone prescribed by her doctor for some mild injury. Whiplash from a fender-bender. Muscle spasms from lifting the kid wrong. The girl would be one of the skeletons Cline never saw, the ones who met his boys in beat-up houses on the outskirts of town or in cars in the Dunkin' Donuts parking lot. The oxy would have led to heroin. The heroin would have led to fentanyl—the gray death. Cline smiled. Maybe he'd be on to Portland sooner than he'd thought.

The men returned to their seats as the waiters pushed, prodded, and cajoled the angry woman and her family out. Cline didn't need to say it, but he looked his boys in the eyes anyway as he refilled his glass from the bottle on the table.

"Druly," he said. "Write it down."

CHAPTER SEVENTEEN

THERE ARE DUTIES at the Inn that are mine alone, no matter how desperately I'd like to delegate them, so I headed back to take care of them. I wanted to follow Craft to his house and give him a parenting lesson with my fists, but I knew I needed time to think, to cool down, or I'd get myself arrested and lose whatever leads I had on the smiley-face pills. On my way back, I dropped Nick in town and stopped to watch the waves crashing off Norman's Woe, a rock reef visible from the shore. I'm not the world's most imaginative guy, but now and again, back when I was mourning my lost job and trying to connect with Gloucester, I would go and look at the reef at low tide and think about the ships scuttled there in the night, the sickening grind of the hull, the panic and sorrow of the crew. Gloucester is proud of its shipping history, and for me, looking out at the rocks and imagining the brutal, tenuous lives of the fishermen was a sort of memorial. Sometimes the tourist boat *Adventuress* would come sailing by to add weight to my fantasies, the gaff-rigged schooner slicing through waves toward the harbor as travelers aboard took pictures with their phones.

I got back to the Inn and checked on a few overnight guests—a guy in a suit who seemed to have driven a long way from somewhere and a couple of young lovebirds—all the time thinking about voices calling for help in the stormy night and the reassuring light of shore.

One of my permanent residents, Neddy Ives, lives in a room on the third floor. He actually *lives* there on a permanent basis, seemingly never leaving the room, which is the only one that has an attached en suite bathroom with a shower and toilet. None of the residents, including me, have ever seen Neddy. Siobhan described him as a tall, quiet man in his fifties who wouldn't meet her gaze and who paid his rent into our bank account via a legal firm in Boston called Benkely and Marsh. My theory is that Ned is an ex-inmate most comfortable existing in one room, but I don't know for sure. That afternoon I warmed up the frozen dinner Neddy likes and set it outside his door, then I took away the trash he'd left secured in a little bag on the doorknob. After that I started dinner for the crew, a task that heaped more dread onto the already sizable pile sitting like rocks in my stomach.

I'm the world's worst cook. That's not an exaggeration. There are people who burn stuff, undercook stuff, always turn out watery or misshapen or weird-tasting food. I do all of those things. My fare is burned on the outside, raw on the inside, and the residents of the Inn frequently have to guess what I was trying to make and what the ingredients are. My culinary failures are not for lack of trying. I follow recipes, both the published ones in heavy, sauce-splattered books and the almost indecipherable scrawled ones Siobhan left on the backs of envelopes and receipts.

I decided to make Siobhan's potatoes that afternoon, and as I was peeling them at the sink and looking out the window at the winter trees, Angelica stood chattering to me in the doorway. I give myself too much time to prepare dinner, which never helps, but it also means I'm a captive audience for Angelica, who starts drinking at around three, after she's finished her writing for the day.

Now she held a glass of white wine against her breast and watched with disdain as I reduced the potatoes to twisted slivers in my anxiety to get all the spots out of them.

"You hear some authors, particularly those in the academic sphere, talk about editorial intervention as compromising the author's voice," Angelica said. "No one wanders into a gallery and starts editing a Rembrandt. But the other side of the argument is how a writer evaluates her work without the subjectivity an editor brings to it."

"Mmm-hmm." I rinsed a potato and added it to the pile. I have found that if I keep saying things like "Mmm-hmm" and "How interesting" and "That's a compelling argument," Angelica will eventually wander away, having decided I agree with everything she says.

"For me, there's a dichotomy between the editor as censor and the editor as co-contributor."

Dr. Richard Simeon, who lives on the third floor, wandered into the kitchen and set a brass doorknob on the counter beside the sink.

"Jeez," I said.

"Yes, came off right in my hand."

"I'll give it to Nick." I put the doorknob in my pocket. "He's good with locks and handles and things. Are you able to get in and out of the room?"

"The knob is from the inside of the door, so I'll not shut it unless I want to be trapped inside." He hung his walking stick on his arm. "Not that it would make much difference to anyone if I was, I suppose."

The doctor wandered away again. I thought about his words, how sad they sounded. The old man spent much of his time in his room, which was crowded with books and papers spilling from shelves and the desktop. Angelica kept talking as though the doctor had never come into the room.

"Because ownership of the creative product is such a tenuous thing, you see. It's a highly politicized territory."

"Uh-huh. How so?" I asked, not interested in the answer. A hand reached into the basket of potatoes beside me and plucked one out. Susan Solie gave me a friendly smile.

"Sorry to interrupt." She glanced at Angelica. "Bill, could I speak to you for a moment? I'm having an issue with my room."

Angelica gave the sigh of the unheard and unappreciated artiste and walked off. Susan took a small knife from the drawer and started peeling beside me.

"That creaky shutter still giving you trouble?" I asked.

"No." She laughed. "I just didn't want your ears to fall off."

"Oh, right. Thanks. I only have three pairs left after these."

"Speaking of body parts, is that a doorknob in your pocket or are you just glad to see me?"

I blushed and put the doorknob on the windowsill. I like Susan, but she makes me nervous. I'm well aware that she could use her Bureau contacts to find out what Malone and I did in Boston that got us fired. She'd hinted that morning that she knew, and she seemed like the type to check on those sorts of things, not only for her own peace of mind but to ensure Effie's safety. I didn't know all the details, but I sensed that Susan had brought Effie with her to the house so she could keep an eye on that mysterious, scarred woman. I sometimes saw the two of them in the forest or on the beach, Susan talking about what were apparently grave and troubling things as Effie bent her head and listened. I didn't know if Effie was an undercover operative or a witness in need of protection or what, but I felt like Susan would have vetted me and probably everyone else in the house.

We peeled together in silence for a while.

"So what did you find out on your little mission today?" she asked.

"Oh." I sighed. "I might have a lead on a regular user of the same stuff that Minnow had. I might be able to use him to find the distributor. I think we're dealing with fentanyl."

"I think you are too," she said. She peeled the vegetables like a machine, slipping three perfect potatoes into the bowl for every misshapen one of mine. "I did a little digging around on your behalf," she went on. "The Bureau tried to intercept a big shipment of fentanyl headed for Boston six months ago and got a decoy instead of the real batch. From what the informant says, there might have been up to a hundred pounds of the stuff, and the Bureau thinks it's all heading north. They've had concentrations of fentanyl deaths in Lynn, Manchester, and Beverly."

"This stuff must be pretty bad if the Bureau is interested in it."

"It's serious. Fentanyl is seventy-five times stronger than morphine. One of its analogs is carfentanil. That's a thousand times stronger. They use it to tranquilize elephants."

"I can't remember the last time I tranquilized an elephant myself," I said.

Susan snorted.

"I do remember when the big drug causing everyone panic was cocaine, though."

"Me too." She smiled. "My parents were terrified."

"So people are actually dealing this stuff on the street?" I turned to her. "To *kids*?"

"They're dealing it to whoever will take it," Susan said. "But kids make good customers because they spread information via social media about where to get it and how good it is."

"This is making all the weed I smoked in high school sound pretty tame."

"It was." She gave me another wry smile.

"Why do people need it when there's heroin? Isn't heroin enough?"

"Well, see, that's the problem. After a while, it's not." She shrugged. "If you've been a heroin addict for a decent length of time, it doesn't get you high anymore and you have to hit just to stay well. Fentanyl gives you that high again, and once you build up a tolerance to that, there's carfentanil."

"And what's after that?" I asked, though I already knew the answer.

"A body bag," she said. "And the dealers don't mind. In places where it's really bad, like Baltimore, a few overdose deaths around a particular block just tells the addicts where the good stuff is. The stuff that hasn't been cut up with baby formula or laundry detergent."

"Is this what you did in the Bureau?" I asked. "Drug trafficking?"

"If I told you, I'd have to kill you," she said. Her smile was broad; she was someone who wasn't afraid to enjoy her own humor. Siobhan had been like that. Susan's wet fingers touched mine as we both reached for the same potato, and the collar of my shirt was suddenly hot and tight. "My job wasn't so glamorous. I didn't do anything that would get my picture in the paper."

"All the more intriguing," I said. "International woman of mystery shying from the camera behind aviator sunglasses. Anti-terrorist secret agent."

"Hardly." She rolled her eyes.

"Whatever you were involved in, it must have been hard-core stuff," I said. "Effie's no pencil pusher, and from what I can tell, she's your responsibility. Is she Bureau too or is she just someone you encountered in your job? Maybe she's a spy. Maybe her name's not Effie at all. Maybe those are her initials, *F. E.*"

"Cut it out." She looked mildly alarmed for an instant. "We're not talking about me. We're talking about you and these deadbeat dealers. I want to help you, Bill. I believe in what you're doing. These people don't belong in Gloucester."

I finished peeling the last potato and looked out the window. Marni was wandering on the beach beyond the trees, her cigarette trailing smoke from her fingers into the wind, her eyes on the pale yellow sky wedged between the clouds and the sea.

"They don't belong anywhere," I told her.

CHAPTER EIGHTEEN

SLEEP WAS ALMOST impossible. When I dozed for a few minutes, I dreamed about little girls eating elephant tranquilizers and immediately snapped awake.

I left my basement bedroom and went up to the kitchen, where I found Sheriff Spears in front of the refrigerator, his belly illuminated by the interior light. He turned and smiled at me, a jar of pickles, a package of ham, a loaf of bread, and a bottle of mayonnaise hugged to his chest. I try not to look into the fridge too often. There's a bottle of champagne in there that Siobhan and I had been saving for our anniversary, now a permanent fixture on the bottom shelf.

"Heading out on the night shift?" I asked the big man.

"No, I just got back. Full day of it. Jeez, I'm starved."

I noticed a blue bruise on his fleshy brow as he dumped

the ingredients on the counter and started putting together an enormous sandwich.

"Looks like you brought the fight to crime-fighting today," I said.

"You wouldn't believe it." He slathered a half-inch layer of mayonnaise on the bread. "We've got a bag snatcher in town. I was out all day in an unmarked unit trying to spot the guy. Finally I see him make off with an old lady's handbag outside the barbershop on Burnham Street. I called it in and pursued, lost the guy in the Oak Grove Cemetery."

I sat at the table and listened as Clay pressed the tall sandwich flat with his huge hand, Godzilla squashing a tower of apartments. He took a couple of glasses down from the cupboard, poured a bourbon in one and a shot of pickle juice from the jar in the other.

"So after a while, I find the guy again near Riverside Avenue. But I'm so excited I've finally got him, I accidentally jump the curb with the unit. I go through a fence and a flower bed and knock over a big statue that's standing in this woman's front yard. I get out to chase the snatcher but I'm not in uniform, so the lady thinks I'm just some asshole who crashed on her lawn and is trying to run away. She comes out and smacks me in the face with a dictionary."

"A dictionary?" I pursed my lips so I wouldn't laugh.

"She must have been doing the crossword or something." Clay sighed. "Anyway, another unit caught the guy down on the docks an hour later. The troops let me return the bag to the old lady, you know, which was nice. But when I hand it to her, she says it isn't her bag. The guy must have snatched another bag after I lost him. Get this—the old lady calls me an idiot."

"You're not an idiot, Clay," I said. "You're a fine and dedicated officer of the law."

"Well, I try my best." He sighed again, took a bite of his sandwich. "This afternoon was crazy. I've got a missing person. I mean a real-deal, genuine missing person. I don't think I've had one in . . . well, years."

"Who is it?"

"Guy named D'Aundre Newgate. Moved here from Boston about four months ago. Had a fight with his girlfriend this morning—she dumped their little girl on him and ran off in a huff. She comes back a few hours later, and the child's at home but Newgate is nowhere to be seen."

"Huh," I said.

"I don't even know where to start with something like that." Clay looked stressed. He watched me for a moment, thinking. "Look, Bill. I don't know how to say this, but if you . . . I mean, you're someone who gets around town a bit . . ."

"If I can assist in any way, you'd like me to?" I asked. When I entered the kitchen I'd thought of giving Clay the gun I'd confiscated from the boy named Squid. But his distress and confusion at the missing-person case on his hands made me change my mind. I decided not to share my concerns about drugs in the town.

"I can't *ask* you to assist." Clay struggled to find the words. "Not without officially deputizing you. And I have men of my own, you know. It's just . . . well, in Boston, you got big-city experience. That's why some people around here ask you to do things, I suppose. You know how to handle big-city problems. Sometimes the badge is a blessing, and sometimes it's a hindrance. You'll work faster than me, not having to report on everything, and maybe if someone needs to have his head put in a vise, you'd be able to do that."

The head-in-a-vise comment caught me off guard and I laughed. Clay seemed so gentle on the outside, but I sometimes wondered if a darker, harder man lived beneath the squishy, flabby exterior of the sheriff. A man who wouldn't mind using pain as a tool. I'd watched Clay snarling at the television during a Red Sox game once and I'd been shocked at the malice in his voice and on his face.

"I'll be your eyes and ears, Clay," I said. "Don't worry."

Clay smiled, satisfied. He washed a bite of the sandwich down with the bourbon and pickle-juice chaser, noticing as I grimaced. "You want me to make you a pickle-back?"

"Thanks, no."

"You sure? They're good."

I never like to be the Debbie Downer in a room, so I relented. Clay poured me a pickle-back and I gulped down the salty, sour combination.

"Geesh!" I swallowed hard.

"Good?"

"I don't know if that's the word."

"It's ninety percent amazing," he said proudly. "Ten percent terrible."

"Like most things in life, I guess." I squinted.

"Well, congratulations," he said. "You're a true local now."

"I've been here two and a half years. I was already a local."

"A few more of those pickle-backs and you could run for mayor," Clay said. He fished something out of his jacket pocket. "While you're here, can I give you this? It fell off this morning. I guess I don't know my own strength."

He put a brass doorknob on the table between us.

"Just what I need," I said. "Thank you."

The boards beneath us shuddered as someone hopped up the back stairs of the house and then burst through the door. Effie. She stopped at the sight of us, pointed at my face, and made a sign I recognized: her hand above her head, indicating a tall person.

Nick.

She put her index finger out, thumb extended, her eyes wide with alarm. I recognized that sign too.

Gun.

CHAPTER NINETEEN

I LEFT CLAY to guard the house and followed Effie into the night. The sea beyond the trees was illuminated by a nearly full moon, but she led me into the forest where she must have seen Nick disappear, the pine needles silencing our footsteps. In the blackness, we stood together, holding our breath, listening. Somewhere, an owl moaned and took flight, startled by our presence.

I took Effie's bony wrist and led her to a slice of light between the trees.

"What did you see?" I asked. "Is he hurt?"

She put both hands up, fingers out like pistols aligned. A rifle. She ducked her head and I made out her features becoming pinched, the eyes narrowed and mouth hard.

Nick was stalking someone out here with a gun.

I felt the air leave my lungs in a heavy rush. A collection

of horrible possibilities flashed before me: Nick hunting down and shooting someone out here, Effie or a stranger or himself. My thoughts tumbled into one another. Nick coming to himself, realizing what he had done, what the trauma of his past had bred in him. A distressed, tormented beast pushed down too long. I had to find my friend. I called his name, and my voice seemed closed in by the dark, hardly reaching.

Nick was suddenly upon us, a hot, heavy presence. I could feel he had been running; his sweat-slick hand brushed mine. I grabbed him, tried to draw him to me, but his body was hard, tensed with energy.

"Nick!" I said. "What the hell is going on? Are you okay?"

"I'm glad you're here, Cap." He dragged me into a crouch, seeming to miss Effie's presence altogether. "I tracked the target from the northeast. We've got him pinned in a dead end between the cliffs."

He pointed. There was, of course, no dead end to speak of, no cliffs anywhere near where Nick was pointing. Beyond where his finger stabbed into the dark, there was more pine forest, the distant road, the curve of uninhabited beach. The rifle was slung over his shoulder, the barrel pointing up toward the sky. My heart ached as I realized he was not with me. His eyes were blind to the trees around us, to the night.

"Nick," I said. "It's me. It's Bill. We're home. There's no one out here—"

Effie's approach to Nick's fantasy wasn't as calm and collected as mine. She grabbed the rifle, underestimating his whip-fast reflexes in his heightened state of fear. Nick reached out and shoved Effie away like she was a child, sending her sprawling on her back.

"Nick, buddy," I said, grabbing at his sweat-soaked shirt. "Look at me. Listen—"

He held up the gun, aimed into the distance. I braced for a shot, my hands against my ears, my stomach dropping as I imagined who he might be targeting out there in the wild. Instead of firing, though, he shouldered the gun and ran off. Effie, who'd struck her head on the back of a rock, touched her scalp and checked her hand for blood in the light. We ran after Nick, now only a shadow among thousands of shadows, dissolving in the dark ahead of us. Branches whipped at my arms and face. All my senses were waiting for that terrible sound—the gunshot in the night.

Please, please, please, I prayed to whoever might be listening. *Bring my friend back safely.*

In my search for Nick, I lost Effie briefly. I saw her silhouette against the sea and followed.

We stopped short on the smooth gray stones before the sand. Nick was waist-deep in the water, standing rigid, his hands on the gun and his back to us. I approached, not completely certain it was him, his unnatural stillness making him seem like a man-shaped tree standing sentinel in the glassy water.

"Nick?" I called. He didn't move. I sighed, exasperated, and walked into the water.

Cold needles pierced my calves, thighs, buttocks, crotch. The icy water crawled into my boots and around my feet. I could feel the edges of my bones grinding together in the painful cold as I waded out. I huffed and tried to steel myself against the freezing water, but my upper half was shaking furiously by the time I reached him. Nick wasn't shivering. His eyes were fixed on the black hump of Milk Island on the horizon. I could see what fueled his delusion that he was in the desert. The featureless surface of the ocean interrupted only by the island could easily have been a desert cast in eerie blue light.

"I lost him," he whispered.

"Nick, please." I stuffed my hands helplessly into my armpits. "We're going to get hypothermia if we stand here too long. Look at me. It's me. It's Bill. You're home in Gloucester."

"Living the Dream." He looked at me. "Devil Nightmare."

"What?"

"Devil Nightmare. That's the name of their unit. The six. Living the Dream was a code. An anagram. A warning. They're at the back of the convoy. They positioned them-selves back there so they could block us in. We pursued and cornered one of them. Now he's out there." Nick gestured to the horizon. "In the desert."

"Nick—"

"He'll come back," he said. "He warned us because he wants to come in. Cross over. Give us intel on the traitors." He hefted the enormous weapon in his hands, scanned the horizon with the scope. I watched his wide eyes in the moonlight. His skin was covered in goose bumps while his body struggled against the chill. I had to get him out of the water. I saw Effie at the edge of the sand. She snapped her fingers to get my attention, then saluted, clicking the heels of her boots together. I didn't get what she meant. She pointed at me and did the gesture again. I understood.

I turned to Nick. "You've done a good job, soldier." I hesitated, trying to see if I was getting through. "You've, um, identified the target and now we'll pass it on to command. I'm ordering you to terminate this operation for the night. Give me, uh . . . surrender your weapon and return to camp."

"Cap." Nick nodded, lowering the weapon. He slammed the slide open, ejected the round from the chamber, and popped the magazine. He handed the gun to me and walked back toward the shore.

CHAPTER TWENTY

WE FOLLOWED NICK toward the house. I could see that the light in Marni's room was on. Clay was waiting for us in the doorway, his face creased with concern, his big eyes under his heavy brows trying to analyze Nick.

"You all right, soldier boy?" he asked as Nick approached. I knew from past experience Nick would be exhausted after his little dance along the edge of reality. The last time this sort of thing happened, Nick had convinced himself that he could hear gunshots in the distance and tried to mark down their frequency in a notebook with a series of strokes and dashes. He'd kept up his surveillance of the distant gunshots for an hour, sweating and recording furiously, then he crashed and slept for fourteen hours. I'd never tried to get Nick out of his delusions before by pretending to be a part of them. I grabbed Nick in the back doorway and wrapped my arms around him. It was like hugging a sleepwalker. Though he was barely with me, I needed to know he was safe, to slap his hard shoulders.

"Buddy," I said. "Jesus. You can't go scaring us like that. You really can't."

"Hmm?" Nick patted my back halfheartedly. "What did you say? What time is it?"

"It's bedtime," I said.

"Right. Yeah. I knew that."

Clay, Effie, and I watched as Nick walked away, leaving wet footprints in his wake and muttering to himself.

"Got room in your gun safe?" I asked Clay. Effie handed him the rifle. He took the big black weapon by the barrel with reverence, hefted the stock in his hand to check out the sight.

"Jesus. What's the guy hunting?" Clay asked. "Moose?"

"Shadows," I said. "He was off on one of his trips into the past again."

"You know, I think you should talk to Doc about him."

It was a good idea. I knew Dr. Simeon kept odd hours. I changed in my basement bedroom and headed up there, but when I got to his room there was no light under the door. On the way back downstairs I passed Marni's room and heard her clattering away at her laptop. I rapped on the door and walked in to find her in the lotus position on her fluffy pink desk chair, her fingers racing over the keys.

"What do you want, Freezy? I've got five conversations going on here," she said.

"Oh, don't mind me," I said. "I'm just here to practice my scales." I picked up her violin, put it under my chin, scraped the bow across the strings, and made a sound like a rusty belt sander running across concrete. She sighed and shut the laptop, took the instrument from me. I lay on her bed.

"What'll it be tonight, sir?"

"'Flight of the Bumblebee.'"

She laughed in that open-mouthed kid-like way she rarely did, a beautiful habit she was losing as she grew up. It made me smile. She played "Orange Blossom Special" because she knew I liked it. When she finished, I watched her fiddling with the strings, my head propped up on my elbow.

"Hey," I said.

"Hey what?"

"I think I was a real dick about the memorial thing."

"Is this an apology? Oh my God. I love apologies," she said.

"It is an apology," I said. "You're right when you say I should stop pushing my feelings about Siobhan down. I should talk about her more and let you talk about her more. I'm not trying to build some kind of cone of silence here."

Marni came and lay on the bed beside me. We looked at the plastic glow-in-the-dark stars she had stuck to the ceiling, impossible constellations of unicorns and butterflies. Marni's fingernails were freshly painted purple, but she'd already started picking the polish off. We heard a thump in the next room. We both looked instinctively at the wall beside us.

"We gotta talk about a room change," she said. "Neddy Ives gives me the creeps."

"He's all right. In fact, as a houseguest he's great. He doesn't complain. Doesn't make a mess."

"What kind of person lives in one room all the time?" Marni frowned at me. "He must be crazy. And then there's the ghost on the stairs."

"There's a ghost on the stairs?" I asked. "This is news to me."

"Someone runs up and down in the middle of the night," Marni said. "I heard it a few nights ago, waited until I heard whoever it was coming up to the second floor, and threw open the door. Guess what? No one there."

"Well, that's done it," I said. "I'm never sleeping again."

"Me either," she said. "At least the weirdo next door is only creepy during the daylight hours."

"Siobhan thought he belonged here." I shrugged. "If he was good enough for her, he's good enough for us."

"Siobhan would have taken in Charles Manson," Marni said. "Everybody was good enough for her."

We watched the stars in silence for a while.

"I feel lost without Siobhan," Marni said. "She was so smart. She always knew exactly what to do. She always had a plan. Didn't matter what problem I had, I'd come to her with it and she'd say, 'Let's make a plan,' and by the time we were done talking, everything was fine."

"What do you feel lost about?" I said. "Maybe I can help. I *should* help. You shouldn't have to feel like you're in this on your own. I can't replace Siobhan, but I can maybe be...I don't know. A better version of myself. Someone you can bring your problems to."

Marni said nothing for a long time, tracing the stars with her eyes.

"There's nobody around who I want to be like," she said

eventually. "There's no blueprint for what I'm supposed to be doing. No map. Siobhan was pretty cool, so I thought, *I'll just try to be like her*. But she's gone, so now it's like, who do I follow? Who am I supposed to be?"

I knew Marni didn't mean it, but her words hurt me. The kid in my care didn't respect me enough to use me as a guide, a role model. But why should she? I'd spent the last two years hiding from my problems, running from grief, failing to make plans or see anything through. Well, all that was going to change. I didn't tell her this, but I decided she was going to see a whole different side of me from then on. It was time to man up and show the kid she could rely on me.

CHAPTER TWENTY-ONE

A CRISP, COLD morning. Frost on the windows and on the lawn at the back of the house. I leaned against the door frame of the shower in the third-floor bathroom, Angelica behind me. Effie was looking down the shower drain with a flashlight, her nose inches from the tiles.

"It's the men," Angelica announced, her arms folded defiantly. "They're very hairy, and it's coarse hair. I'm the only woman who uses this shower and my hair is fine and light. Almost silken. I'll bet you get to the bottom of the blockage in that drain and find it's men's hair. That or soap slivers. They're notorious for beginning a new soap too early and letting the sliver slither down the drain."

"Sliver slither," I said. "Very alliterative of you, Ange."

"I try," she said without irony, shrugging.

"You know, I'm happy to do the gross stuff," I told Effie.

She waved me off without looking up and began poking experimentally down the hole with the end of a plunger. The women in the Inn didn't mind attacking the less-than-desirable jobs, but it made me feel bad to let them do it. Maybe that was sexist. When Siobhan arrived at the house, she'd tackled the stained and rust-marked toilets first, not allowing me to take the job from her. I'd suggested we replace the toilets on every floor, but it was her mission to get them stark white with what she had. She'd gone at the second-floor toilet with every available cleanser, scrubbing with wire brushes and industrial sponges. Finally she decided that she needed to block the toilet and make a chemical soak. She sloshed all the ingredients into the bowl and walked away, but she had accidentally created some kind of spectacular reaction that caused the chemicals to expand, bubble, and flow out of the bowl and across the room. The toilet tiles on the second floor were white as snow, and there was a large white patch on the red carpet. The toilet itself still had rust stains.

Effie started plunging the shower drain, her whole body jerking up and down, two hands on the stick.

"There's something metaphorically wonderful about a blocked drain," Angelica said.

"Oh?" I said, trying to prepare my mind for what was to come.

Angelica, her finger on her chin, mused, "We cleanse our physical selves and the waste goes into a hole at our feet. A portal to a destination we don't know or care about. It's a penetrative act. Our waste goes into the earth. And then at some point, the earth decides it can take no more and it rejects us, and we must reflect on ourselves, on consent, on the fact that bodily secrets cannot simply be washed away. It's almost spiritual. A daily baptism ritual interrupted by the protest of the raped earth."

Effie stopped plunging and looked up and over her shoulder at Angelica. Then she widened her eyes at me and returned to her task.

"Perhaps I'll recount this experience in my current work in progress. The chapter could be called 'The Shower Drain: Baptism, Penetration, Earthly Desire.'" Angelica looked at me for my opinion. I nodded and tried to look impressed.

Effie examined the shower drain again with the flashlight. She made a small noise, like a raspy laugh, and plunged her gloved hand down into the hole up to her elbow. Angelica and I watched, fascinated.

Effie brought up a brown, wet, slippery lump and set it on the tiles beside her.

The lump unfurled, shook itself off, and began cleaning its ears with its tiny pink hands. Angelica took one look at the rat in the shower, gave a strangled scream, shoved past me, and ran out the door.

"How does a rat fit into the shower-baptism-penetration metaphor?" I asked Effie. She picked up the rat by the nape of its neck; the creature hung from her fingers, its pink belly dripping with shower water. She looked at the rat, then at me, then she rolled her eyes.

CHAPTER TWENTY-TWO

THE STRESS HIT me like a hangover, stripping all the joy from the morning-shower-rat experience. I stood at the edge of the boatyard smoking my first cigarette in more than a decade, my eyes aching and my stomach rolling. Nick, as usual after an episode, had little recollection of his adventures the previous evening. He'd been cheerful and upbeat when he'd dragged me out of bed before dawn and shown me an address for Rick Craft that Susan had reluctantly tracked down. I knew that Susan was regularly up before sunrise. On my way to the bathroom one morning, I'd seen her setting out for a run along the beach, wearing some black skintight ensemble with gloves to guard against the biting wind. I'd imagined her back when she was a routine-crazy FBI recruit getting sweaty on the tracks around Quantico before class.

Nick did a quick lap of the graveyard of vessels beyond the wire and then appeared from between a disemboweled crab boat lying on its side and a stack of rotting wooden dinghies marked with the wet footprints of enormous gray gulls.

"I've got them." Nick pointed. "They're toward the back."

"Why is Craft's mail coming here? Don't tell me he owns this boatyard," I said.

"No, but whoever does seems like a gifted entrepreneur. You'll see what I mean. Come on."

I followed. Amid the dead and dying repossessed boats lying in the gravel and mud or propped up on wooden frames, signs of life were present. A bag of garbage lay outside the carcass of a partially burned houseboat. A T-shirt hung from the porthole of a tugboat to dry in the morning sunshine. People were living in the carcasses of the old vessels, probably paying someone cash for the privilege. It wasn't a bad business model—the boats were useless scraps left over from a tourist and fishing trade on the downward slope. The residents here were most likely junkies and criminals who cut the landlord in on whatever mischief they cooked up to survive.

I stepped over electrical cables running between Craft's boat and two others, all of them sharing power leached from God knows where. We climbed a wooden ladder to the deck of the old dry-docked crab boat, startling a seagull that had been wandering among the rusted cages picking at sun-dried pieces of bait.

The wheelhouse was full of bags of rotting garbage and discarded clothes; pigeons nested on the sprawling control board before the windows. We were drawn forward by the sound of rhythmic moaning. I followed Nick down the narrow stairs into a small room that smelled of the sleeping bodies there. Two men I recognized from the Greenfish were lying on their sides on narrow couches. Beer bottles were everywhere; my boot crunched a syringe on the rough carpet. The moaning was coming from a television screen bolted to the ceiling with wires hanging down to a DVD player balanced on a pile of old magazines. A porn film had been playing and was now stuck on the menu, the moaning a looped clip of a woman using a candle in a manner contrary to its intended purpose.

A woman was lying on her side under a small table. Rick Craft, apparently asleep, was sitting on the floor with his back against a wall, a blanket around his shoulders like a big, stained coat.

"The children," I whispered to Nick. "The ones who died. They weren't living *here,* were they?" He shrugged. I looked at the woman on the floor. Her greasy hair fell across her brow, and as I bent to get a better look, I noticed white foam at the corner of her mouth. I put two fingers on the side of her neck. Her pulse was faint.

"Hey, asshole." Nick put a boot into Craft's side. "Rise and shine."

Craft opened his eyes and looked at Nick, then scratched at the sores on his badly shaved neck. Nick dragged the waking man to his feet and then slammed him against a wall as if he were banging an old television set to get the picture to clear.

"What — what the fuck do you want?" Rick seized Nick's

arms, his eyes wide now. "I ain't seen the guy! He was never here!"

"You don't even know who I'm looking for," Nick snapped. I went to the table by the sleeping men and found exactly what I'd expected—two colored capsules. One was the yellow smiley identical to the one I had confiscated from Winley Minnow; the other was bright red, the face frowning.

"Where are these coming from?" I showed Craft the capsules. He took a moment to focus, then tried to pry Nick's hands off him.

"You're those fucks who were at the bar with Mayburn," Craft snarled.

"We weren't with Mayburn," I said. "We just find you as repulsive as he does."

"The man asked you a question." Nick gave Craft a shake so hard that his oversize head jiggled on his scrawny neck. "You the one who's been handing those pills out to schoolkids?"

"Fuck off!" Craft yelled. I glanced at the men on the couches, but they were down for the count. "You're not cops. I'm not giving you shit. Get out of my house! Get your hands off me! Get—"

I took Craft from Nick and pushed him down the narrow hall out of the sailors' mess. I knew what I was looking for, having sensed its presence by the faint reek in the room. The toilet was at the head of the boat, beyond the upper freezer hold. I marched Craft through reeking water to the toilet cubicle and kicked open the door. Exactly as I'd expected— the junkies had no plumbing, so they'd simply pretended that they had. Craft saw what I planned to do and braced himself in the tiny doorway before I could force his head into the bowl heaped inches high with human waste.

"Oh God, no." He twisted in my hands. "No, no, no."

"You and your pals need a cleanup crew to come through here," I said. "A man's home is supposed to be his castle, isn't it?" I realized I was biting into Craft's flesh with my fingers.

"Let me go!"

I tried to force Craft into the cubicle, putting all my weight behind him, my hand on the back of his neck. I got him bent above the pile of feces. The smell was eye-watering.

"Tell me where those pills came from."

"No!"

"Tell me where they came from or you'll be picking shit out of your nostrils for the next year and a half."

"His name's Cline!" Craft howled, sinking to his knees. The arms that slipped through my grip were reed thin and covered in scabbed sores. Craft was sobbing on the wet rubber floor. "Mitchell Cline. He lives in town. Don't tell him I gave him up, man."

"You mix with violent people, you get violence," I said. "If Cline wants to hurt you for snitching on him, I'm not going to intervene. You signed that deal yourself."

"I don't care if he hurts me." Craft sniffled, rubbing his nose on his arm. "I just don't want him to cut me off his list. He can ban whoever he wants. I need the gear, man, and Cline's got all the dealers wrapped up around here." Craft looked up at me, his red eyes full of tears. "Please," he said. "I need him."

I left Craft sniveling and feeling sorry for himself in the wet, reeking hall outside the head and walked back up to Nick. He had lifted the woman from the floor and was holding her in his arms like a baby, her head against his shoulder.

"You get a name?" he said when he saw me.

"Yeah."

"Good, because we gotta get out of here." He turned toward the door. "This woman ain't right."

CHAPTER TWENTY-THREE

NICK SAT IN the back of the car with the woman from the boatyard, her head in his lap, and monitored her pulse, his fingers on her carotid. We exchanged worried glances in the rearview mirror all the way to Addison Gilbert.

The nurse behind the ER triage desk, an African-American woman whose name tag said BESS, took one look at Nick and the woman in his arms and pulled a microphone sticking up from the counter toward her mouth. Her fingers sported bright yellow nails that were two inches long and pointed like claws.

"Code Orange in the ER, please, Code Orange," Bess announced. She spotted me and ran her eyes up and down my form.

"Can I have the patient's name, please?" Bess said.

"We don't know," I said. "We found her like this. I believe she's probably had—"

"Fentanyl," Bess said. "It's the flavor of the month." She dragged the microphone to her lips again. "I said Code Orange in the ER, please. Code Orange."

Whatever the term *Code Orange* was supposed to initiate, it didn't seem to work. I looked around the waiting room. There was a young couple on gray plastic chairs watching the television in the corner, ice packs and a paper towel on the man's wrist. Bess sighed and walked through a side door, then reappeared through double swinging doors to our right pushing a gurney. The emergency room behind her was filled with life. Nurses in pale blue scrubs jogged across the crowded space; family members stood in corners looking worried.

"It's a bit hectic today." Bess walked up to Nick, took the woman from his arms like she weighed nothing, and laid her on the gurney. She pulled on a pair of surgical gloves. "We've had two other dreamers like this young thing already this morning. One's got brain damage, and the other didn't make it."

I stood by Nick, feeling oddly self-conscious as Bess checked the woman's vitals.

"You seem shocked, honey," Bess said to me. "You okay?"

"I'm fine," I lied. Bess's total lack of panic about the unconscious patient rattled me. She made a note on the nameless victim's chart with a pen she took from her breast pocket, pink with a fluffy poof swinging from a chain.

"You need somewhere to sit down, you let me know. I'll find you a nice warm spot." She winked at me. Nick pursed his lips. Bess wheeled the woman into the emergency room and returned to her desk a couple of minutes later.

"I don't suppose you've seen these floating around the emergency room lately," I said, showing her the pills I'd confiscated from Rick Craft's boat. Bess reached over and took my hand.

"Let me get a closer look." She examined the capsules but kept holding my hand, stroking my thumb with hers. "Oh yeah, sure, honey. We sucked a couple of these yellow ones out of a girl's stomach yesterday."

"What's the difference between the yellow ones and the red ones?" Nick asked.

"The red ones are the angry ones." Bess held the pill up, still holding my hand in hers. "They'll straight-up snuff you if you're not a long-term serious addict with a tolerance. They're not for a party. You want a party, it's the yellow smileys, the purple dopeys, or the green winky faces. Just different combinations of uppers and downers, cerebral and bodily effects."

She let my hand go and took a folder from behind the desk. Nick was barely keeping it together over Bess's obvious affection for me. I kicked him in the ankle as Bess opened a page to photographs of colorful pills. "We started seeing them about four months ago, but we already knew they were on their way. Lots of deaths down in Boston. You two local cops or something? How come I've never seen you in here before?"

"He used to be a cop." Nick nudged me. Bess perked up.

"My brother is a lawman," she said. "You're good people. Me, I wasn't so interested in locking folks up. I'd rather care for them. I can spot someone who needs a bit of tender loving care from fifteen miles out. You running an investigation?"

"We're just concerned citizens trying to protect our town." I gave Nick a warning look. "Renegades, I guess you could call us."

"Outlaws dealing justice." Nick nodded.

"That's pretty sexy," Bess said.

"Undeniably," I agreed. "It's a sexy job, but someone's got to do it."

Bess shrugged. "Well, you two want to protect something, you ought to just stand out there." She pointed between us at the glass doors of the entrance. "Last week we had a guy in here fell off a ladder and broke his clavicle. We gave him two weeks' worth of oxy to get him through. He got attacked in the parking lot. Didn't even make it to his car."

"Jesus, they're robbing people for their meds?"

"Sometimes they rob them, sometimes they beg them or threaten them. That's the addicts who do that. The dealers, they don't need to use violence. They pay the doctors to write the scripts."

A man in a white coat came out of the emergency room, walked to a cabinet behind Bess, and extracted a chart from a drawer. He was young and sharply dressed, fiddling with the ID badge that was clipped to his lavender shirt. One look told me he'd been listening to Bess from behind the door. He glanced at us quickly, taking in our faces. I wanted to warn Bess, but she hadn't seen the man walk in behind her.

"We had an old lady come in our pharmacy trying to get her methadone prescription from over on Amble Street filled," Bess said. "Enough methadone to kill a horse, you ask me. She obviously hadn't been taking the prescribed dose because she wasn't stone-cold dead, so she must have been giving the pills to somebody. The pharmacy sent her to us."

"Excuse me." The lavender-shirted doctor came over with his hand up like he was ready to start pushing people around. "It's not our policy to chitchat over the triage desk about our patients. Who are you?"

"Bill Robinson. I own the Inn on the water."

"I've seen that place," Bess said, apparently unfazed by her superior's tone. "Looks real nice. Maybe I ought to drive out there one time, take a weekend off, rejuvenate myself. You one of those live-in owners, Bill? Place got a hot tub?"

"We were just talking about the increasing overdose numbers," I told the doctor. When he stopped fiddling with his ID badge, I could see his name: Raymond Locke. "You must be concerned, the way things are going. Are doctors in this hospital being investigated for writing false prescriptions?"

"If you have no other business here today, Mr. Robinson, I suggest you move on," Locke said. "This is an emergency department, not a coffee shop."

"I'll need your number, Mr. Inn Owner, before you go." Bess smiled. "You know, just in case."

CHAPTER TWENTY-FOUR

SUSAN WAS ALREADY at her laptop when I called from the hospital parking lot and asked for Cline's address. I could hear birds in the background and the clunk of her coffee mug on the dining-room table.

"I know you don't want to use your Bureau connections," I said.

"It's okay," she said. "I'm trying to do it discreetly. Hopefully I won't get any menacing calls from my old colleagues. It's not the kind of job you can keep one foot in and one foot out of. Once you're out, you're out."

I gripped the phone hard, remembering McGinniskin's words. *You're both out.* Shame flooded me, made my face burn.

"You keep it up, and I'll have to start charging a fee," Susan said. I heard her tapping the keys.

"They say if you're good at something, you should never do it for free," I said. "Can I pay my debt in terrible dinners? What about questionable life advice?"

"You could let Effie paint the house. Local kids are going to start thinking a witch lives here."

"Don't talk about Angelica like that—she's just eccentric."

"Oh Jesus." She sighed, then read me an address. "I've also got the rap sheet here. This is not a nice guy we're dealing with, Bill. Assault. Assault. Public nuisance. Possession with intent to sell. Assault. Quite a bit of arson in his younger years. You know what arsonists are like."

"Not really."

"There have been a few studies on the link between pyromania and psychopathy," she said. "Think about it. You carry a lighter around in your hand, you hold the key to big, glorious, spectacular destruction. Fires consume, dominate, kill indiscriminately. Cline set a lot of fires as a kid. He wasn't charged in any of them, though—this is all from a psych report I've dug up."

"It's a bit like pills," I mused.

"How so?"

"The key to indiscriminate destruction in your very own pocket," I said. "You dole out drugs, you spread addiction like a disease. People like Cline go from town to town distributing a product that consumes, ravages, destroys."

We were both quiet, silenced by the weight of our thoughts.

"Hey," she said suddenly. "Dough Brothers called here looking for Marni. Said she didn't turn up for her shift. Have you seen her? She's not answering her cell and she's not in her room."

"I haven't seen her. I'll keep an eye out. Thanks, Susan."

I hung up and started the car. Nick had his boots on the dash again. As we rolled toward town, we passed Living the Dream getting into his car on Washington Street. Nick's eyes flickered over him but his expression didn't change.

"Can we talk about last night?" I asked.

"What do you want to know?" Nick stretched and yawned.

"I want to know where you got that big-ass rifle, for one thing," I said.

"I've got a couple of guns left over from the service. I keep them under the bed, but I'll keep them in Clay's safe if you're worried."

"I am worried." I looked at him.

"Well, don't be. Sometimes I get a bit turned around, that's all."

"Nick, you were standing in freezing water talking about secret agents and anagrams," I said. "I had to spend the rest of the night chiseling my balls out of solid blocks of ice."

"I like anagrams," he said. "Did you know *William Robinson* is an anagram for *Rainbow Millions*?"

"You're doing that thing you always do, trying to combat criticism by pretending it's no big deal. I'm serious, Nick. I think you have an unhealthy obsession with Living the Dream."

"Living the Dream?"

"The dog-walking guy," I said.

"Oh, him. I don't even know him."

"That's the point," I said. "It's him this time. What'll it be next time? Cryptic messages coming through the floorboards? A midnight raid?"

Nick let his seat back, put his hands behind his head. "I ever tell you about the time we found an arm?"

I sighed.

"There was just this arm in the middle of the desert," Nick said. "A bunch of little kids from this village were all gathered together looking at something and we thought we'd go investigate. What do you know? A dude's arm. No sign of the dude, not in the whole village, not in the surrounding area. The arm had a watch on it and everything. Every time I put my watch on in the morning, I think about that guy's arm and wonder what the hell happened."

"I think you need to see someone," I said.

"I'll see someone when you see someone." Nick laughed. "Maybe we could see each other? Save the money."

"I don't need to see anyone."

"Really?" Nick shifted in his seat. "Is there some reason you prefer living in the basement with the rats and the paint cans and the boxes of Siobhan's stuff rather than in the loft, as she intended? See? Don't go poking around in my brain and I won't go poking around in yours."

"The veterans hospital will help you find a guy," I said. "And if there is an up-front fee, you can take it out of your rent."

"No, thanks," Nick said.

"Nick—"

"No, thanks," he snapped.

I drove us toward town in silence.

CHAPTER TWENTY-FIVE

I DON'T KNOW what I was expecting of Mitchell Cline's house. I suppose I thought that anyone who dealt the life-destroying products Cline did would have some stain on his home. But his house was not the filthy, smelly, half-burned bedroom of Winley Minnow or the reeking-of-excrement, forgotten seaside hole of Rick Craft.

Cline's Queen Anne–style mansion dominated the end of Stuart Street, a curved cul-de-sac on the water. I could see why he'd chosen the spot. There was one way in and one way out by road, and an acre of forest had been cleared behind the house, making a surprise raid by the police difficult. The other houses on the block seemed almost to shy away from Cline's; his property was bordered by towering cypresses and hedges that two gardeners, a man and a squat, sweating woman, were trimming as we pulled up. I parked at the bottom of the driveway. Two black Escalades loomed at the top of it, watched over by men who I assumed were their drivers along with some others. I counted five people near the cars and three on the porch just hanging out, texting or moving to music coming from inside the house.

Noise. It hit us as soon as we popped the doors of my car. The whir of the gardener's trimmer and the thumping music, a pair of girls sitting on a wicker couch, laughing. It was clear who belonged to the house and who didn't. Cline's employees wore glimmering cuff links and tailored trousers, a jarring contrast with their scarred, tattooed knuckles and the muscles bulging against the fabric. The crowd stopped and watched us approach.

"Cline here?" I asked a big lug leaning on the front of one of the Escalades. He was missing the top of his left ear, and he sniffed the air like a hound as he looked us over.

"Who?" he said.

"We want to talk about these." Nick, looking impossibly small next to the brute in a suit, held up the red pill we'd taken from Craft.

"You chumps are on private property." The goon pointed to our car. "Move the shitbox before it leaks oil on the driveway and someone has to clean it up with your face."

"Yeah. Fuck off, po-po!" one of the girls yelled, barely getting the insult out before she and her friend descended into giggles. It was clear to me that Cline and his people would require a convincing display rather than an eloquent proposal. I calmly plucked up a bucket-size potted plant from a collection by the mailbox.

"Special delivery," I announced.

Nick watched, his arms folded, as I hurled the pot into the windshield of the Escalade.

The crunch of glass shattering, then the blaring alarm. Three of Cline's guys rushed forward like dogs who'd been let off their leashes; two went for Nick, while the biggest one grabbed me by the shirt, put his face inches from mine. I barely maintained my calm, but as I'd expected, the noise of the crash summoned their leader.

"Boys" was all he had to say. I was let go. The two goons who had backed Nick against the car stepped away.

Cline, at the top of the stairs, cut the music with a tap on his mobile phone, which he then slipped into the back pocket of his gray slacks. He waved a hand at one of the goons on the porch, and he took out the keys and silenced the car alarm. The gardeners ran off around the side of the house, aware, it seemed, when they needed to make themselves scarce.

Cline did not act like a drug lord being harangued by a pair of local desperadoes. He seemed more like a mildly curious homeowner inspecting the work of gophers on his lawn. Cline walked down the steps, a slight frown on his otherwise perfect brow, taking in the sight of us as he tucked a hardcover book under his arm.

"I hope that's a guide to New Hampshire," Nick said, pointing at the book. "You're going to need it."

The silence Cline had seemingly willed into existence was eerie. He gave a gentle sigh, looking at the pot in the car windshield.

"Anyone get a name for these punks?" he asked.

"Bill Robinson," I said. "Nick Jones." I nodded at Nick. "We're returning something you lost."

I took the pill from Nick and tossed it at Cline's chest. He didn't try to catch it. Didn't flinch. It bounced off his chest and landed on the pavement.

"I have witnesses who can connect you to the distribution of at least two of those pills," I said. "One of which caused an overdose and another that destroyed a family home. After I ride around for a couple more days surveying the shitstorm you've brought down on this town, I'll be able to connect you to some fatalities."

"Listen to this guy." Cline smiled. Perfect teeth. He still hadn't addressed me directly yet, like he was a rock star and I was a hopeless fan yelling up at him from the crowd at a concert. He would choose who he wanted to shine his light on.

"There are plenty of prosecutors in Boston who will run a murder charge on a dealer who supplies a fatal dose of an illegal narcotic," Nick said. "Especially if someone connects the dots for them."

"Gentlemen," Cline said. "You've made a very interesting choice of how to spend your afternoon, coming all the way out here to give me a legal lecture. It's very kind of you. I haven't actually had anyone volunteer to give me a talk on the local laws in the four months I've been here. Not one police officer has darkened my doorstep with such outrageous accusations."

I looked at Nick, knowing he was thinking of Sheriff Spears. If he hadn't been here already, that meant that his employees could be on Cline's payroll. Clay was advised of the region's serious crime leads by his sergeants, and their failure to even come sniffing around Cline was worrying.

"We're telling you to pack this shit up," I said. "Crawl back under whatever rock you came out from. We're not threatening legal action here, Cline. We're promising it."

"You own the Inn on the north side, don't you?" he asked me as though he hadn't heard a word I'd just said. I felt prickles of pain spread out from the center of my chest.

"I do."

"Lovely property. I haven't been out, but I looked at it online just now."

Dr. Raymond Locke. He'd heard me talking to Bess at Addison Gilbert and called ahead. And then there was Craft. He'd probably called to let Cline know someone was roughing up his clients and wanted an appointment with the top brass. Before them, there was Squid, who I spied now sitting on the arm of the wicker couch with the two young girls on it. He watched me closely from behind his leader.

"I've been keeping an eye on properties near the woods there," Cline said. "I like to hunt when I get the chance, and it's so quiet. I'm sure the gunshots wouldn't bother anyone. Maybe I'll come out. Take a look around. Make you an offer."

"You come anywhere near my property or the people who live there and I'll feed you into a meat grinder," I snarled. The loss of control had been sudden, shocking; I'd been blindsided by thoughts of Siobhan, her house, her people, her dream. My reaction was exactly what Cline wanted. I stepped off the curb, turned away for a moment, rubbed my brow. Nick was by me, his shoulder like a brick wall, reassuring.

That reassurance was short-lived. One of the girls pointed up the street and started laughing. "Someone called the *real* boys in blue on your asses."

I turned and saw a familiar vehicle heading our way. Sheriff Spears's friendly beep of the patrol-car siren was made more cheerful by his wave through the windshield as he approached.

CHAPTER TWENTY-SIX

CLINE SMILED THE thin-lipped, dead-eyed smile of a snake as he watched Sheriff Spears ease his bulk from the squad car. I noticed Marni in the back of the vehicle, leaning over to look up at the turret at the front of Cline's house.

"Someone else call in Cline's crew?" I asked Clay. "You got backup on the way?"

"Ah, no." He looked puzzled, then glanced at Cline and his cronies. "I'm actually here about you. Some quack at Addison Gilbert called in a disturbance in the parking lot, gave us your license plate."

"Tell me this fool ain't the local sheriff." The big goon with the knuckle tats eyed Clay. "I knew cops liked chillin' in doughnut shops, but this guy looks like he owns the chain."

The punks around us snickered. Clay smoothed the front of his shirt and swallowed hard as he took in the sight of the crushed Escalade windshield. "Is there some kind of trouble here? Can I offer assistance?"

"You cool, you cool," one of the girls said. "We ain't got no leftovers to get rid of."

The whole crew laughed, but not Cline, who wasn't paying much attention to Clay at all. His eyes followed me as I walked Clay back to his car. The sheriff was blushing at the collar of his shirt, sweat spotting his sides.

"Ignore those idiots," I told him. "What's Marn doing in the back of your car? Is she in trouble?"

"No, no." Clay wiped his brow. "I got a call about a kid walking the train tracks. She told me she was just taking a shortcut home."

I asked Nick to take my car back to the Inn, said I'd ride in the squad car with Marni. Cline watched us roll out, one corner of his mouth turned down regretfully, like he'd been enjoying the banter and wanted to toy with us a little more. I hoped he got what I tried to communicate as I climbed into the back of Clay's car: I was not done with him yet.

Marni watched the people at the house through the back window as we turned for home.

"Squid again," she said. "Does he live there? Wow. He's done pretty good for a kid who couldn't turn up to school on time even once in his whole life."

"He's not done well at all, if you ask me," I said. "And I'd like it if you didn't go anywhere near the people at that house, Marn."

"Whatever." She folded her arms.

"I know, I know." I put my hands up. "You don't want lectures. But this is serious. They're bad news. Your friend

Squid is tied up with some very dangerous people and I don't want you doing the same."

Marni chewed her nails, shrugged.

"Why didn't you go to work today?" I asked.

"I don't know," she said. "I'm just bored with that place."

"I'm not surprised." I imitated her lazy face from the day before. "'Thin crust. No anchovies. Double cheese.'" She grinned.

"You're better than that and you know it," I said. "But if you're going to quit, you should quit right. Line something better up first. Give them notice."

"I guess." She looked out the window, watched the world go by. "I'm supposed to have a shift tonight too."

"Call them when you get home and tell them you're sick," I said. "Take the night off. We'll have a nice dinner and then you and me will sit and make a plan for what you're going to do."

"I wouldn't know what else to do." Marni sighed. "Wherever I go, it'll be the same sort of thing. Make pizzas at Dough Brothers. Sell stamps at the post office. Gut fish on the docks. What's the difference?"

"Marni, that is not your future," I said. "I'm telling you. You're smart, funny, and tough. Better things are waiting for you. You can't see them, but I can."

"Things like what?"

"Like music," I said. "You've got talent, Marn. Go ahead. Roll your eyes. But you've got something there, something special. You tell great stories, and you kick ass on the violin. You know what that sounds like to me? That sounds like a born musician. Someone who plays and writes music for adoring crowds. Who tells interviewers that she dropped out of high school and worked in a crappy pizza joint before she made it big."

She looked at me, and I knew she was wondering if I could be right. I tried to look as confident as I could. But she knew, and I knew, that I hadn't done well predicting my own future over the past couple of years. Siobhan was the plan maker, not me. But even as I sat doubting myself, a smile grew on Marni's face, and I felt for a moment that I had done my job.

CHAPTER TWENTY-SEVEN

WHEN WE ARRIVED home, Clay followed me to the front of the house, his head down and his shoulders high, as if he expected to be hit.

"I've got a problem," he said. We stopped by the corner of the porch. "I actually know those guys back there."

"Cline and his crew?" I said.

"Yeah." Clay kept smoothing his shirt over his belly like he might be able to flatten his gut with his hands. "The missing guy? Newgate? He was one of them. I've got a witness says she saw two of Cline's guys, Russell Hamdy and Christopher 'Simbo' Jackson, dropping Newgate's kid at his house on the morning he went missing. Newgate leaves with the kid, then later the kid's dropped home, no one sees Newgate again. A cleaner found his phone and wallet in a garbage can near the beach."

"He's dead," I said. "Must have pissed off the boss somehow. These guys go through soldiers like tissues."

"It gets worse."

"How?"

Clay took a deep breath. "They found a head."

"A what? A head? Newgate's head?"

"Nope." Clay massaged his brow. "Local woman named Mary Ann Druly. Her daughter's an addict. Couch-hopping around Boston, so I heard. Mary Ann Druly confronted Cline in a restaurant last night. Made a big scene. I get a call at five this morning at the station from a couple of hysterical tourists down from Maine. They found a head in front of the memorial."

The memorial to fishermen lost at sea was a bronze statue of a man at the helm of a ship positioned right on the waterfront in town. It was a symbol of all that was Gloucester, its pride in its history as America's oldest fishing port, its tenacity in times of crisis.

"I've never seen a head before. Just a head on its own like that." Clay looked queasy. "The crime-scene tech picked it up by both ears like it was a soup pot."

"Did they find the rest of her?"

"Mary Ann's husband followed her cell phone signal out to Dogtown and located the body in the woods. Got there before we could." Clay looked helplessly at the sky. "I'm out of my depth here, Bill."

"You're not out of your depth," I said. "You just need to take this one step at a time. Bring in the witnesses from the restaurant. The ones from outside Newgate's house. Get the security-camera footage from the waterfront."

"That's the thing," Clay said. "The witnesses—the ones in the Newgate case and the Druly case—they talked to me on the phone and told me everything they saw. Then I sent my guys out to get it on the record, and suddenly no one knows anything. All the witnesses have clammed up. The cameras on the waterfront seemed to have been working last night but no one can find the tape. It almost makes me think... but no. It's not possible."

I waited. Clay lowered his voice to a whisper. "It makes me think they might be on Cline's books. *My* guys. That's ridiculous, right?"

"Clay." I put my hand on his shoulder. "Just do what you can. Keep working on it from your end. Don't accuse anyone of anything."

"I gotta stay calm." He took a deep breath. "But if you get anything, bring it straight to me, okay? I don't know who I can trust right now."

CHAPTER TWENTY-EIGHT

VINNY ROBETTI WAS just where I expected him to be, on the corner of the porch, soaking up the last remnants of fading sun. Siobhan's first resident, he'd spent three days alone in the house with my wife before I arrived from Boston, where I'd been packing up the last of our belongings.

We were both startled by the sight of each other. I knew Vinny Robetti by his birth name, Leonardo Roberri. In his prime, he'd been one of the deadliest gangsters in Boston history. I'd conducted raids on Roberri's properties a bunch of times as a patrolman and I'd guarded him on his trips in and out of court for murder charges and RICO violations, none of which ever stuck. I'd responded to the scene when some stupid-ass *cugine* tried to make his bones with a rival family by shooting Roberri; he'd hit him in the back, paralyzing him from the waist down.

I might have objected to the old wiseguy's presence in my house if Siobhan hadn't loved him so much. The two had been like spaghetti and meatballs by the time I arrived. Vinny and I silently decided to leave our prior affiliation unmentioned.

As I neared the old man on the porch, I saw a bucket by his feet and a glimmering knife in his fingers.

"What's all this?"

Vinny gave that classic Mob-guy shrug. "I'm doing arts and crafts. So what?"

In his big, knobby hands he held a small piece of wood on its way to becoming some kind of four-legged thing, a pig or a bear on all fours. I took the wicker chair next to Vinny and he handed me the item for examination.

"Look at this! This is great," I said.

"Eh, I do all right." He took the animal back and started carving it again, catching the little blond shavings in the bucket. "I went to see the doc about my hands. This one's been broken five times since I was a kid. This one six." He held up his right hand. "Last guy that got me was Bobby Russo. You know that guy? Smashed both my hands with a club hammer. This thumb nearly came off completely. Guy heard I was stepping out with his *gumad*."

I opened my mouth to respond but Vinny kept on. The man liked to talk.

"Maybe I was. Who knows? Long time ago; I can't remember. Anyway, the doc says I need to do something to strengthen my hands. Suggested I start knitting. What does he think, I'm gonna sit here making little doilies and frilly fucking tablecloths?"

"I think that's crocheting."

"Whatever the fuck."

"You're pretty good at this," I noted.

"I know my way around a blade." He tossed the knife up; it spun three times in the air and landed with a *chunk* in the arm of his wheelchair. He pulled the knife out and kept whittling like it was no big deal.

"The kid's supposed to be at work." He nodded toward the side of the house where Clay and Marni had just disappeared. It was probably Vinny who told Susan that Dough Brothers had called looking for Marni. When I wasn't around, Vinny was in charge of answering the phone, because he never strayed far from the house.

"Yeah, she didn't go. I'm worried about her."

"You and me both," Vinny said. "Kid told me some fucked-up story yesterday."

"What was it?"

"Get this." He scratched at the white streak at his temple with the knife. "It was a story about this farm. Barnyard. Man and his wife, they sell these animals, have them taken away in trucks. Only sometimes one of the animals doesn't go because it's fucked up or whatever, like a chicken with only one wing or a cow with a broken leg or a pig with some weird skin disease. So it's like a reject. The farmer guy plans to whack the animal, but the wife always sneaks up and lets it go, and it runs into the forest behind the farm."

Vinny shook his head. I waited for more, but he was concentrating on his work.

"So what happens?" I asked.

"Nothin'." He shrugged again. "The fucked-up animals all

live in the forest and they have adventures and shit. They're all sad about how they never got to go on the trucks but they're kinda happy that they're together."

"I assume the trucks were taking them off to be slaughtered?" I asked.

"Maybe. I guess so. Probably supposed to be irony that they don't know about it. I don't know. I'm not a poet. What do you want from me? She was just telling me because she said that's us."

"What's us?"

"The fucked-up animals." He jerked a thumb toward the house. "You, me, Marn, the sheriff. Everybody who lives here. We're them. The reject animals who don't know how lucky they are."

I thought for a moment, watching the trees.

"Kid's cuckoo, you ask me." He tapped his forehead with the tip of the knife.

"While you're doling out advice," I said, "can I get some on a different subject?"

"Shoot."

"What do you do when you've got a dangerous new guy on your turf, and you're not willing to stand by and let him destroy your neighborhood?" I asked. "You probably had stuff like that happen when you were in the . . ."

"The waste-management business?"

"Sure."

"Well, way I always saw it, you got three options," he said. "And those options get steadily less friendly. First, you can divide up the turf. Make sure he stays on his patch and you stay on yours. Charge him something for the privilege."

"Right."

"That doesn't work, you convince him to go somewhere else. Send a guy in talking about how sweet the pussy down in Florida is or something. Grab his *gumad* and give her a squeeze and tell her if she don't get her guy to go down there, they're gonna have problems."

"What's the last option?" I asked.

"The last option?" He pointed the knife at me. I watched his lips form the very same snake-like grin I'd seen on Cline. "You blast him and his crew full of holes."

CHAPTER TWENTY-NINE

IT WAS FAST work, but if you had the funds, Cline knew, you could get the job done. The previous night's fun and games with the Druly woman had filled him with a violent energy, and he'd used that energy all afternoon making phone calls, reading out credit card numbers, watching Squid, Turner, and Bones making their own calls. As the sun set, they started arriving. The caterer came first and took over the bottom floor with six waitstaff. Then there was the DJ, the sound guy, the lighting guy, a team of college kids setting up portable heaters on the patio and cabanas around the heated pool, the firepits. Cline felt like Jay Gatsby watching the lights across the water for Daisy. He kept Squid close at hand. Didn't want the young idiot to mess this up.

"Is she coming?" Cline asked at six.

"Of course she's comin'." Squid held up his phone.

She arrived in the initial rush, a youthful face among a hundred other youthful faces, the desperate and bored of Gloucester, Rockport, Hamilton, all pouring through his doors and flooding into his yard. The big house rattled with bass; the body heat of already too-drunk guests made condensation bead on the windows. Beer pong in the kitchen. Strippers in the pool area. Morons doing backflips off the second-floor balcony into the pool to screams and cheers. Cline watched her picking her way through the crowd, narrow shoulders slicing between big bodies, her tongue nervously worrying that piercing in her lip. The girl called Marni had talked to Squid first, a quick, awkward conversation by one of the bars. And then she was off into the safety of a crew of girls she must have known from high school.

Cline watched her, waited for her to come into his orbit. She was strangely beautiful in a haphazard kind of way, like she had been assembled from pristine but mismatched parts. Her lips were a little too red for her white skin, her arms slightly too long for her body, the eyes a little upturned at the corners. Dark mutant girl transforming, only now realizing that she was different from those around her, powerful. The things he could do to her with a little time. Show her how to dress, how to walk. Take the stupid piercings out, fix the crooked nose, dazzle her with big money, big cars, big guns. She had no idea, this little coastal urchin from nowhere, just how far she could go. She could have men with their balls in a twist at the sight of her. Empires at her feet. Cline leaned on the rail and watched her and swam in his fantasies.

CHAPTER THIRTY

ANGELICA STOPPED ME as I tried to make my way into the house, putting a hand out like a traffic guard.

"We have a problem."

"You don't know the half of it," I said, sighing.

"Come with me," she said. We walked through the house to the porch, where Effie, her back to me, was sitting cross-legged on the edge. Angelica and I came around in front of Effie, and I saw she was eating a large chocolate chip cookie. On her left knee, a plump brown rat sat on its haunches, a small shard of cookie in its hands. It was turning the cookie crumb around and around, nibbling the edges as it went.

"*This* is happening." Angelica pointed sharply at the rat on Effie's knee. The little animal didn't flinch, and neither did Effie.

"Effie is eating a cookie with a friend," I noted.

"That *thing* is not a *friend!*" Angelica threw her hands in the air. "It's a parasite-riddled, flea-bitten rodent!"

Effie and I looked at the rat. It sniffed the air between nibbles of the cookie shard, its tiny pink nose twitching.

"To be fair," I told Effie, "this is a pet-free household."

Effie froze at my words, shocked. She put down her cookie and gestured to the rat, then she pointed to herself and shrugged dramatically. After that she spread her hands to indicate the porch, the house, the forest.

"He's not your pet, you're saying," I surmised. "He goes where he wants."

Effie picked up her cookie again.

"This is ridiculous," Angelica said. "The house has always had rats. I understand. We live in the woods. It's bound to be a problem. But Effie, it's your job as the groundskeeper to keep them *outside* the house."

Effie stared at Angelica, munching her cookie, totally unrattled by her tirade. The rat finished its treat and started cleaning its ears.

"If it bites one of us, it could give us rabies!" Angelica cried.

"Perhaps we could have the rat seen by a veterinarian?" I suggested. "Given a little flea bath, maybe?"

"You can't be serious. This is beyond belief!" Angelica cried. "Rats are not pets! They're vermin!"

"Is it likely to bite anyone?" I asked Effie. "I mean, it's something to consider. Why is it so tame?"

Effie shrugged again. She made a chopping motion at her neck, which was quite startling, given the huge scar running across her throat. She used her thumb and forefinger to indicate a small amount, an inch, and then tapped her forehead.

"Die...almost...when you almost die, you...go crazy?"

Effie nodded. Pointed to her chest, tapped her forehead, tapped the rat's head.

"You're crazy. The rat's crazy," I translated.

Effie nodded, winked at me. Angelica gave a growl of frustration and stormed away. I sat beside Effie and looked at the rat. I reached slowly toward it with my index finger, and the creature took my finger in its small pink hands, gave my fingernail a gentle, experimental nibble, then turned back to cleaning its ears, apparently having decided that I was inedible. I gave the little rat a stroke on the head. Effie was watching me, smiling.

"I guess we can make one exception to the no-pets rule," I said.

CHAPTER THIRTY-ONE

SUSAN FOUND ME in the kitchen picking dried sauce off one of Siobhan's old recipe cards. She must have sensed my desperation, because she came and put a hand on my shoulder, then took the card from my hand.

"You look stressed," she said.

"Siobhan used to make this lasagna," I said. "It was Marn's favorite. I'm going to make it tonight, try to cheer the kid up a bit."

"I thought I saw Marni leaving just before." Susan pointed to the back door.

"Oh. She might have gone for a walk. She'll definitely be here for dinner. We're going to have a talk. Decide some things about her future." I took the card and frowned at it. "I'm trying to get my head out of the sand and take some responsibility for that kid. She needs guidance." I found my phone and sent Marni a quick text asking where she was.

"Well, this recipe's not much to go on." Susan laughed. "It just lists ingredients. There are no amounts."

"Siobhan was a bit of a creative chef." I sighed.

"Let me help." Susan took a big chef's knife from the block on the counter. "I may be old-school Bureau but that doesn't mean I'm not creative."

She took an onion from the basket on the counter and started peeling it. I hesitated by her side, paralyzed with guilt.

"You know," she said, "you can ask for help around here. I know you've got Effie doing the chores, but I've been feeling like there's stuff I could be doing. Things I'm good at." She was turning the onion into tiny, impossibly perfect squares with the speed and precision of a machine.

"Well, it's not your responsibility." I looked away. "I mean, you're just a resident."

"Just a resident." She rolled her eyes. "If you think we're all just residents here, you've lost your mind."

I poured us a couple of glasses of wine and turned the radio on. The sun had set, leaving a stripe of purple light on the ocean. I caught my reflection in the window above the sink and I realized that even with the horror of what Clay had told me that evening and despite the way my skin burned over Cline's words and my heart sank with thoughts of Siobhan and how Marni needed her, I was smiling. Smiling with an unfamiliar but welcome sense of hope.

"Oh, I almost forgot," Susan said suddenly. She put the knife down, reached into her pocket, and brought out a brass doorknob. I took it and sighed.

"You too? Why are they all giving up at once?"

"I don't know." She laughed. "Maybe the ghost on the stairs is doing it."

"You've heard the ghost on the stairs as well, huh?"

"Yeah." She went back to her work. "You probably can't hear it down in your scary basement. Seriously, Bill, you ought to move up to the loft. That room is so pretty. I can't understand why you keep it locked up."

"I can't understand why you won't tell me what's going on with you and Effie," I said. "What the hell happened to her? Who tried to kill her? Is she here under your protection?"

"Whoa!" Susan put down the knife, held her hands up. "That was a swift right-angle in the conversation."

She was right. I'd leaped at her, pushing about things I knew she didn't want to talk about in response to her hitting on something I didn't want to talk about. The loft had been Siobhan's dream place. Sometimes I'd catch her looking out the cracked window at the sea, her shadow stretched on the floor. Our bedroom. Our safe place.

"I was just thinking about Effie." I cleared my throat. "She's got a little pet now."

"The rat. I saw." Susan nodded. "Look, Effie and I met through the Bureau, yes. Something terrible happened to her, yes. We're both here, and we'd like to keep that discreet, yes. But that's as far as I'll go on that, Bill."

I took up my knife.

"Siobhan wanted us to take the loft," I said. "And I'm not ready to be up there without her. That's as far as I'll go on that."

There was tension in the kitchen. We both worked on our separate chopping blocks, waiting for it to melt away.

CHAPTER THIRTY-TWO

HE WAITED UNTIL she was in that golden haze, tipsy but not taken, swaying to the music and smiling at boys who wouldn't know what to do with her even if they got her in their grasp. And yes, it was only boys who surrounded her, some of them frat douchebags who couldn't carry on a conversation with her without looking down her top or letting their eyes rove over other girls, others local dropouts hunting for easy prey they could take to the woods behind the house. Cline, resting his arms on the second-floor banister, watched her come up the stairs, a confident smile on his face.

Self-assurance. She'd probably never seen it before. She was drawn to his stylish clothes, his superior gaze, the expensive wine in his hand. He could see her recognizing him from that afternoon, when he'd been surrounded by men he owned and commanded. She probably wondered if this guy was the king of the castle. Of course he was.

"Nice place," she said, trying to be casual. "What's the party for?"

He shrugged and walked over to her. "When a man's successful, he ought to celebrate it every now and then."

He could tell that his words tickled something inside her, stroked her in that exact right spot, piqued her interest. Success wasn't something that rolled around here in waves. She was looking for it, the key to the door that led out of her small-town world, the path to the kinds of things she saw in movies. Big houses, lavish parties, trips to New York, yachts. Dreamland on the horizon. Cline had her pegged. She was probably washing dishes in a café around here somewhere, scraping fried food off plates for minimum wage. Cleaning toilets. Daddy was absent—one of the crab wranglers who left and returned in the dark—and she'd promised herself a long time ago she wouldn't end up with someone like him. Cline watched the pink lights dancing in her eyes.

"You want a little tour?" he asked, sliding his hand down her arm and curling his fingers around hers. He saw goose bumps rise on her neck.

"Sure."

"We'll start with the VIP room." He smiled.

CHAPTER THIRTY-THREE

THE SMELL OF the food and the sound of the music brought people into the kitchen. Nothing I'd ever cooked before had smelled this good, but Susan had helped, and she had the chef's wisdom. She knew the onion went into the pot before the carrots and the meat needed to be browned before the wine was added.

Nick came into the kitchen and lifted pot lids and smelled and stirred things and raised his eyebrows at the sight of me drinking wine and cooking and bopping around the little space with a woman who was not my wife. I ignored him.

Soon Effie was there tapping her wrist, demanding to know when this glorious-looking feast would be ready, and I shooed the two of them, which left room for Doc Simeon to come wandering in. He was carrying his ivory-handled walking stick and had a book under his arm that was so thick, it threatened to capsize the guy like a small, fat tug-boat. I tilted my head to look at the title. *The Science of Flight in Apoidea*, whatever that was.

"I've been meaning to come up and talk to you," I told him as he watched Susan spreading garlic butter on thick slices of bread.

"Yes, I see you've hired a professional chef." He went to the pot of meat sauce and scooped out a taste for himself. "Will this mean a rent increase?"

"It's just lasagna." Susan rolled her eyes. "Everybody's acting like Nigella Lawson is in the house."

"Have you tasted this guy's oatmeal?" Doc pointed his walking stick at me. "How on earth does one miscalculate the preparation of oatmeal?"

"My culinary miscalculations aside," I said, "I want to send Nick your way."

"Ah, yes." The doctor nodded. "I've heard about his night-time adventures. Bill, I spent fifty years as a general practitioner. That's half a century, you know. The temptation was always there to branch out, to follow my proclivities into other, more prestigious rooms. The operating room. The psychiatrist's consultation room. But you know, I was never happier than when I had a small office and it was just the patient, his sore throat, and me."

"I think you might be underselling yourself, Doc," I said.

The doctor turned to go and then turned back. He beckoned me to the small alcove off the kitchen and stood there, apparently debating with himself about something. In the closeness of the space I realized, not for the first time, how small he was.

"Look." He hung his walking cane over his arm and fiddled with the book. "I know what's going on with you and this... this local drug-lord character. I think you should consider backing off."

"Backing off?" I stood straighter.

"I've dealt with addicts in my time," he said. "I remember when heroin hit. People walked around looking like skeletons, like zombies, their teeth and hair falling out. You'd think that when a person woke up in the morning and saw a living corpse reflected in the bathroom mirror, that would be enough to make him stop. But these people can't stop. There's no rationality to it. The body starts to need it to function."

"I've seen that sort of thing too." I shrugged. "I was a street cop for nearly twenty years. I've seen my fair share of junkies."

"What I'm trying to tell you is that if you get rid of Cline, you'll leave maybe hundreds of people lost in very dark, turbulent seas," he said. "We're lucky. We have a rehabilitation center in Gloucester, which is more than I can say for much of New England. But they'll get overloaded. People will be turned away. They'll get desperate. They'll rob the local pharmacies, try to cook the stuff themselves, start hunting one another for what little supply is left."

"It sounds like you're trying to tell me not to go after this guy at all," I said.

The doctor sighed, took the heavy book from under his arm, and held it in his hands.

"This is not like you," I told him. "I've been in your room, Doc. I've seen all those certificates on your wall. Last Christmas, every second letter through the slot was a card for you from some old patient. You're not the guy who says 'Live and let live' for scumbags like Cline."

"I just want you to consider the fact that there are thousands of guys like Cline out there," Doc said. "It won't make any difference if you bring this guy down."

"It'll make a difference to me," I said.

The doc shrugged and wandered off, still holding the enormous book in his hands. I checked my watch, wondering where Marni was. She hadn't answered my last text, so I sent another. Susan had taken the sauce off the heat and was laying sheets of lasagna in a baking tray. I went to her and dared, in the warmth of the wine and the strange new calm the doctor's words had brought down on me, to reach out and touch her arm.

"Thanks for this," I said. "Marni's going to love it, wherever the hell she is."

"I'm sure she's on the way." Susan put her hand on mine. "She'll be back before you set the table. You'll see."

I picked up a handful of cutlery and a stack of napkins.

The gunshots started just as I opened the dining-room door.

CHAPTER THIRTY-FOUR

THE BULLETS TORE through the room, punching holes in the weatherboard exterior, ripping and splintering the walls and shattering the windows. I dropped to the floor with no idea where the shots were coming from. A cabinet beside me seemed to explode, peppering the table with shards of glass. In the chaos, I saw Angelica at the end of the dining-room table holding a thick pile of papers that disappeared in a cloud of white from under her hands.

The drive-by shooting took only seconds; the house was blasted with noise and destruction for less than a minute before the car outside skidded on the gravel and sped away. But it felt like much longer as I cowered on the floor, my face in the carpet, listening to the screams of my friends.

Their voices rose at once, a confused wailing.

"Oh my God! Oh my God! Help!"

"What happened?"

"Is everyone all right?"

Susan burst through the door beside me and ran through the room to the front of the house. I followed. The car was gone. We grabbed at each other; her nails bit into my arms and shoulders.

"Are you—"

"Are you okay? I'm okay!"

"I'm okay." Susan ran her hands over herself, gripped her hair. "Jesus!"

Nick and Effie were bent over Angelica on the floor. The author was clutching her upper arm as blood ran between her fingers. Pieces of her exploded manuscript marked with slashes of a red pen were in her hair. Susan dashed to the medicine cabinet. Doc Simeon hadn't decided the coast was clear yet and remained under the table, his eyes huge and his mouth downturned.

"How bad is it?" I went to Angelica.

"I've been shot," she said, her voice more wonder than surprise. "Can anyone believe it? Someone shot me. Someone shot me! In my own home!"

I heard a groaning on the porch and ran out there to find Vinny slumped sideways in his wheelchair. A bullet had shattered the hub of the left wheel, collapsing the wheelchair to one side. I grabbed the ancient gangster under the arms and lifted him onto the bench on the porch.

"Motherfuckers!" he howled, shoving me off as I set him on the bench. "You know, I came here hoping I'd been shot at from a moving vehicle for the last fucking time, Robinson."

"I'm sorry," I said for some reason.

"All those guys inside okay?"

"Angelica got hit in the arm." I couldn't catch my breath. I saw the blood on him, fell to my knees, and lifted his thin, useless leg. "Looks like you got one too."

Vinny pulled his tattered trouser leg tight, revealing two bullet holes. "Fuck!"

The fury was descending on me fast, falling on me like a red-hot cloak, tightening around my neck. I found myself grinding my teeth and staring helplessly at the road between the trees, daring them to return. "You see anything, Vinny? You see the car?"

"Black Escalade," Vinny and I said at the same time.

CHAPTER THIRTY-FIVE

SUSAN AND I put Angelica and Vinny in the car to take them to the hospital, and Nick decided he wanted to come along too, so I was relegated to the back seat to make room for his long legs. Then, before I could close the car door, Effie slipped onto my lap, leaving only Doc and Neddy Ives to guard the house. I tried to protest over the sound of Angelica's wailing, but it seemed the journey would be a family affair.

Dark thoughts swirled as I watched the trees roll by. Effie turned and looked at me, seemed to sense my trepidation, and hugged my head to her chest briefly. It was an unusual gesture for her, and I should have felt comforted. But I took it to mean she knew that I blamed myself for all this. As we pulled into the hospital, I worked my phone out of my pocket and texted Marni.

Call me immediately.

We waited in the emergency room for two hours, no one speaking, the television playing a documentary about sharks. I watched the big, beautiful animals gliding through the depthless blue and felt a hunger for Cline's blood shimmering through me. By midnight I had resorted to reading pamphlets about Zika virus to distract myself from violent thoughts.

I turned when Sheriff Spears walked through the automatic doors. He was stunned by the sight of us all. I hardly noticed the gurney behind him, the bundle of white sheets that three paramedics took straight into the emergency room.

"Clay." I went to him, Nick at my side. "You heard about the house? Did Doc Simeon call you?"

A strange stiffness had come into Clay's face. It was an expression I had seen plenty of times in my career, emotion barely held in check, a jaw locked, trapping fury or sadness inside. He glanced at the others, then took my arm and led Nick and me outside into the freezing night.

We huddled under the blazing red emergency sign.

He didn't beat around the bush. Cops never do.

"I'm sorry, Bill." Clay eased the words out carefully. "Marni's dead."

CHAPTER THIRTY-SIX

I COULDN'T LOOK at Clay, at the truth of it burning in his eyes. I turned and put my hands on the wall, pressed my forehead against the cold bricks. Some deep, dark corner of my mind knew that this was exactly where I had been standing when they told me Siobhan hadn't made it. I'd been drenched in sweat, having driven like a madman to the hospital after receiving the call. My legs were shaking now as I tried to focus on the mist of my breath in the light of the illuminated sign.

It was Nick who asked the questions I couldn't bear to.

"Mitchell Cline had a big party at his place tonight," Clay said quietly. "Hundreds of people there. Marni was last seen alive hanging around the pool area. The party spilled out into the street and the beach and the woods behind the house. They found Marni in the woods about a half an hour ago, unresponsive. The paramedics are calling it an overdose."

"Where's Cline? Have you arrested him?" Nick asked.

"We have no—"

"Tell me you've arrested him!" Nick barked.

"There's no reason to." Clay sighed. "We have no cause. There were hundreds of people at that party, and anyone could have given Marni whatever it is she took. It could have happened on or off Cline's property, we can't confirm anything at this stage. If we—"

Nick punched the neon sign beside my head, shattering the fiberglass and splintering the light inside, darkening the first *E* in *Emergency*. I didn't intervene when he grabbed the steel casing of the letter and ripped it off the wall, taking the *M* with it, and smashed the letters into the pavement. I could barely breathe but I managed to get out some words as Nick stormed off toward the end of the lot, pushing over anything that wasn't bolted down.

"Didn't they try?" I asked.

"They tried," Clay said. "But she was cold when the party-goers found her. Someone started CPR then and the medics carried it on."

Clay put a hand on my shoulder. It was like he wasn't touching me at all. The weight and warmth of it had no effect. I stood in the cold and tried not to scream.

"Bill," Clay said. "We're going to find out what happened. I'll chase down everyone at that party and get all their photos. My team and I will talk to witnesses. I'm going to do everything I can do to make this right."

"Yeah," I said, frightened by the sudden evil intent in my own voice. "So am I."

CHAPTER THIRTY-SEVEN

THE MIND SHUTS down in these situations and the body does what it can to maintain calm. I followed impulses that came from nowhere, getting a cab home from the hospital, walking into the house without talking to anyone, climbing the stairs to Marni's room. The cluttered space smelled like her, the way everything seemed to smell of Siobhan after she'd been lost to me. I lay down on the floor on the fluffy pink rug and let the hateful thoughts rage.

I had done this.

The circle had closed. I had stood in the very same spot at the very same hospital where a man had told me that another woman in my care had died in the woods.

Between the internal blows I threw at myself, I had visions of Cline, his throat in my hands. I listened to the house fill with people, all talking and crying. The air was full of questions that had no answers. How had this happened? Why had she gone to the party when she'd said she'd be home? When had she been invited? Who invited her?

As the pale light of approaching morning lit the window above the bed, the house fell into sudden silence, everyone exhausted and numb with grief. I realized I was succumbing to sleep when the sound of a door opening nearby snapped me awake. As I sat up on the floor, the door to Marni's room opened. A man I didn't recognize stood there looking at me. Neddy Ives was as Siobhan had described him, tall and long-faced, a kind of grayness to his skin from his days inside that gave him the air of a figure in a faded photograph. He glanced down the hall as though to make sure we were alone and then took Marni's violin from the stand and weighed it in his big hands.

"Did she suffer?" he asked.

I climbed onto the bed and sat on the edge, my body like lead. I supposed Ned had learned of Marni's end from the house itself, the voices downstairs climbing through the walls, the vents. I wiped my face, which was hot and damp with tears.

"I don't know," I said. "I don't know what happened. I...Clay's told me some stuff, but I don't think I can believe it right now."

Neddy put the violin down and patted the top as though to tell the instrument to stay in place. He nodded and turned to leave.

"Don't bring any more music makers into the house, please," he said, pausing in the doorway. "I don't want to forget what she sounded like."

CHAPTER THIRTY-EIGHT

A DAY CAME and went. I lay on Marni's bed, facing the wall, unable to move. People tried to talk to me. At some point Susan and Angelica sat down next to me and cried together. I handled things from the pillow, my head too heavy to lift, the phone ringing sometimes with questions I couldn't answer.

When Marni's mother called, we talked in low voices, both our throats husky with grief. It seemed a friend of Marni's from her high-school days had invited her to the party. Francis Whitman, known about town as Squid. There were no signs of sexual assault on Marni's body, but her lipstick was smeared, and she'd been found without the tights she'd been wearing under her skirt in photographs sourced from the party. The cause of death was thought to be respiratory failure consistent with an overdose, but there would need to be a toxicology screen, an autopsy. Marni's mother didn't want me to go and see her. She had, and she said Marni looked small and cold and tired.

At midnight, hearing Clay's lumbering footsteps on the porch, I got up and walked downstairs. Everyone was gathered in the living room. I sat on the arm of a couch near Nick, whose face was ashen with anger. As I settled in, I heard floorboards creaking outside the door of the living room. Neddy Ives must have been listening in.

Clay eased himself down into an armchair, put his hat on his lap, and ran his hands through his greasy hair. I wondered how long it had been since he'd sat down.

"It's as you'd expect," he said. "No one admitted to giving Marni anything or seeing her take anything. She was seen in the company of Mitchell Cline, the owner of the house, but she conversed and associated with a great number of people. I'm going to do another round of interviews in the morning. But so far I haven't dug up anything we can use to press charges."

"Was she high? Do we know for sure she took something?" Susan asked.

"There will be a full autopsy, but according to the tox screen, she had narcotics in her system. A lot of them."

Nick got up and left the room. Everyone watched him go.

"Marni wouldn't have done this." Angelica wiped her eyes with a handkerchief. "She was a good kid. Our little baby of the house. We all looked out for her, and nobody's seen her do anything really bad, right?" She looked around. No one met her gaze. "Yes, she got up to some mischief. But nothing like this."

"My mother thought I was only getting up to mischief when I was a kid," Vinny said. He seemed to fall into his memories, his eyes darkening; he turned away. His words seemed to break something in Angelica.

"What are we going to do for Christmas?" Angelica cried. "Marni loves Christmas."

She hid her face and sobbed. It seemed to me that she felt silly for making the comment, but she shouldn't have. We were all going to have to face the things that Marni loved but without Marni around in the coming months and years. Effie, in the darkest corner of the room, rubbed her nose on the back of her hand and shielded her eyes.

"Surely you can bring Cline in for questioning," Susan said. "He owns two Escalades. One was spotted at the house during the drive-by."

"He had an alibi." Clay sighed. "All I can do is ask him to come sit for an interview and submit his vehicles for forensic testing voluntarily. Until I have more, my hands are tied."

Silence passed over us. I cleared my throat.

"New house rules," I said. Everyone turned to me. "No one stays here alone. I want the curtains drawn morning and night and all the cars parked at the back. We don't want to make it obvious who's here and who isn't. Until this is over, we've got to take care of each other."

I stood, trying to think of something to tell my people about the loss of Marni that would help them in their hour of pain and confusion. But all I could see around me were the memories that tied them to our lost girl. I remembered Vinny sitting in the morning sun telling Marni about champion boxers from New York in the fifties. Marni and

Clay watching Red Sox games together, eyes locked on the screen, munching cheese balls and swearing under their breath. Marni shaking the ladder jokingly as Effie climbed up to clear leaves from the roof gutters.

"I can't bring her back," I told them all. "All we can do right now is try to weather the storm. This is our house. We need to be ready if he comes at us again."

There was a ripple of something in the room, fear or sadness, maybe. I heard the truth in my own voice, and I think they did too. I beckoned Effie from the dark corner, planning to take her to Nick so we could strategize.

In the hallway, Clay stopped me. "I need to talk to you," he said. Effie left us together, and the big man turned his hat in his hands. "I know what you're going to do."

CHAPTER THIRTY-NINE

I PUSHED THE door to the living room closed behind me. Clay looked exhausted in the light from the stairwell. In the tight space I could smell him; he'd spent forty-eight hours pounding the pavement, running down useless leads.

"I don't know what you think my plan is," I said, "because I haven't fully formed it yet."

"That's why I want you to listen to me now." Clay pointed a finger at my chest. "I know what kind of man you are, Bill. After what happened in Boston—"

"What do you mean, you know what kind of *man I am*?" I squared my shoulders and looked at my friend. Clay sighed. He had probably heard a version of what had happened to me in Boston from other cops. That version probably had all the major details correct, and I knew, even before he went on, what he was going to say.

"You're a man who wants justice whether it's inside or outside the law," Clay said. He filled his chest with air and immediately seemed inches taller. "Well, I love the law. It's why I do my job. I think it's . . . it's beautiful. And yes, sometimes it actually prevents people from getting what you think they probably deserve. But that's the system. It's all part of something bigger. And it's my job to protect it. I don't care if I have to find somewhere else to live. I'll make you uphold the law if I have to."

"You said you wanted me to put people's heads in vises if I felt the need. Those were your words."

"Maybe in Boston it's literal, but up here, it's a figure of speech," Clay said.

"Mitchell Cline deserves to be dragged from the back of a crab boat," I said. "The law and the beautiful system isn't going to give us that."

"I know." He put his hands up. "But it'll give us *something* if we're patient and careful enough."

"I don't have any patience right now." I waved my hand. "Marni is dead. She's *dead*. Do you understand that? Do you feel it yet?"

"Of course I do. You're upset," he said. His voice was gravelly with emotion. "I am too. Everyone is. She was our little baby in the house, like Ange said. It's too quiet without her." The silence, like a fog, fell around us. Clay looked toward the stairs as though he thought he'd see her rushing down the steps to the front door. "But don't let the anger drive you to do something stupid."

"Whatever I do, it won't be stupid," I said. I turned to go, but his voice followed me.

"Don't stray outside the lines again, Bill," he said. "You know what happened last time."

CHAPTER FORTY

SQUID WAS SCARED of Dogtown.

It wasn't often that he acknowledged his fear. Living and working with Mitchell Cline had burned his nerves down to nothing, so terror was something abstract. He had enough difficulty just feeling the regular everyday emotions, and fear was an effort. Maybe the numbness had started earlier than Cline, under his father's fists or in the rattling cellblocks of juvie. Squid didn't know. He hadn't been forced to see a shrink in a long time, and anyway, he always lied to them.

But on his bike, pedaling through the dark woods of Dogtown, he felt the old familiar tingle of something like fear. The forest north of Gloucester was so dense, the morning light barely penetrated it. There were legends about this place, stories he'd heard from the locals of witches and ghosts and shit. There were weird rocks carved with words that appeared from between the trees like messages from someplace else, somewhere scary. He passed one that said USE YOUR HEAD, the letters green with moss. It made him think of the Druly woman, the sick, wet sound of the saw going through her spinal column as Turner heaved the tool back and forth. He swallowed hard, tried to shake off the feeling that someone was watching him as he rode. When Squid told Cline he didn't want to do the drop-offs out here anymore, the man had laughed and increased the number of people on his route.

Squid looked over his shoulder at the winding road. Nothing.

In the distance he spied safety. The double-wide trailer that served as a makeshift bar in the evenings sat nestled in the trees. Squid had passed this place a couple of days earlier in the car with Cline and the others, everyone in the vehicle silent with the weight of their dark mission. Vermonte, the bar owner, would be pissed they'd dumped the Druly woman's body out here, would probably bitch about it. But Squid wouldn't pass on the dissent to Cline. Cline's people looked out for one another, didn't snitch. They all knew the man's mood could turn on a dime.

Squid looked back, thinking he'd heard a car. Nothing again. His chest felt tight. There'd been what felt like a rock lodged in his throat since Cline had come to him the morning before and asked him to text Marni, a girl he'd known from school. The rock had grown as the ambulances and squad cars arrived at the house and people left the party and fled into the woods and surrounding streets. As he did with his fear, Squid pushed thoughts of Marni down. They would go away eventually. Nerves frayed. Emotions burned. There was no such thing as witches and no room in his life for guilt. He was a soldier who'd done what he'd been directed to do.

The car came out of nowhere, veering out of the on-coming lane and heading right for him. Squid jerked the handlebars and hit the slope on the side of the road at an odd angle. They seemed to be on him before he had even stopped skidding and rolling on the dirt and pine needles; they grabbed his wrists and shoved his face in the earth.

He thought it was cops until the hood came down over his head.

CHAPTER FORTY-ONE

THE PLAN ROLLED out almost naturally, as though it was our only available course of action. Kidnapping. Violence. I stood in the tiny, abandoned house in the dusty darkness created by the boarded-up windows and looked at the boy in the chair as Effie secured his wrists and ankles with duct tape. Nick, Effie, and I had come together in the forest in the early hours of the morning; it was as though we felt our plan would stain the house if we were to build it within its walls. Later that morning we had tailed Squid as he left Cline's house for a drug run into Dogtown. He had been a pitiful kidnapping victim, his body nothing but bone and taut sinewy muscle, as easy to pin and bind and pick up as a struggling lamb. From the old student ID I found in his wallet, I learned he was sixteen. He had cried nonstop from the moment we grabbed him to this moment, and now he sat hooded, waiting to know his fate.

Nick ripped the hood off the kid's head and he took in the sight of us, his surroundings. His face was wet with tears and sweat. I watched a hundred emotions flicker over his face. We'd bagged him too fast for him to know who we were, and now that he knew, he was confused. We weren't a rival drug crew who would kill him and leave him somewhere with his genitals in his mouth for Cline to find. We weren't FBI agents who would extract whatever they wanted from him and then dump him in a jail cell for the rest of his life. There was relief, but there was also terror. He knew we were Marni's people.

"Oh, fuck." Squid dissolved into sobs again.

"Yeah, *fuck*." Nick kicked Squid's chair, jolting the boy.

"Please." Squid looked at me, figuring for some reason that I was the friendliest of his three captors. "Please, man! You can't do this. You can't. This is kidnapping, man. This is serious shit. Let me go, okay? Please! Let me go. I won't say nothing."

"Squid." I held up the boy's phone. "Don't try to give me a lecture on serious shit. I've got your message here to Marni inviting her to the party two nights ago. Cline asked you to invite her because she knew you from school and trusted you. She's dead, and there are a bunch of photos from the party that put the two of you together."

"You can't prove nothing." Squid sniffed.

"Yeah, famous last words," I said.

"We just went to a party, that's all."

"That's all, huh?" I said. Effie took the backpack we'd

taken off Squid's shoulders and dumped its contents at his feet. Baggies of colored pills spilled out onto the bare boards. There was also, as the boy had promised us, another huge gun. The boy refused to look at the items.

"Did you know that when you die, your stomach becomes a kind of time capsule?" I folded my arms, sat on the edge of an old table a few feet away from Squid. "It immediately stops digesting whatever's in there. Addison Gilbert Hospital pulled a couple of pills identical to these out of an OD victim last week. I wonder if they'll find any in Marni's stomach."

"That's bullshit, man," Squid snapped.

"You better hope so." Nick was circling Squid like a wolf, every muscle in his body taut and ticking with desire for violence. "Because if it's not, we've got you, a drug fatality, and the lethal drugs that were supplied all together and wrapped up with a nice little bow."

Squid hung his head and sobbed soundlessly, shuddering with fear. He gave himself a minute and then let the rage take over, kicking in the chair, spitting as he exploded at me.

"You stupid-ass bitch! What did you expect Cline to do? The guy's a fucking psycho! He killed Newgate just for bringing his kid to a meeting!"

Effie and I looked at each other.

"He killed Mary Ann Druly too, didn't he?" I asked.

"That bitch made a fool of him in public." Squid wiped a tear on his shoulder. "You don't get away with that."

"We need to get Clay down here," I told Nick. "The kid's a murder witness."

"Dude, you dumb or what?" Squid sneered at me. "Listen

to what I'm telling you. Cline is gonna come and get you. He got Marni. That chick was dead the moment the fat cop brought her to the house in the squad car. Cline's gonna get me next, because he'll know you took me. Doesn't matter if he thinks I snitched on him or not. People are just things to him." The boy laughed suddenly, spittle hanging from his lip. "You think you're gonna put me on a stand? You hand me in and I won't make it to the jailhouse!"

In my hand, Squid's phone rang. The caller was identified only with the letter *C*. I walked to the door of the abandoned house and stood looking out at the pines as I pressed the answer button.

I kept quiet. Cline seemed to expect that.

"Robinson," he said. "I know it's you."

CHAPTER FORTY-TWO

"I'M SUPPOSED TO get a call from Squid telling me when the drop is made," Cline said, his voice languid, almost bored. "He doesn't call. Then Tricks, the bartender, finds his bike crashed by the side of the road. I put two and two together. I could probably be sheriff around here. I have instincts for this sort of stuff."

"Do you know anything," I managed, my teeth almost locked together, "about the person whose life you took at that party? Marni was a beautiful, intelligent—"

"Oh, I bet she was." Cline sighed. "People are always beautiful and intelligent and kind and generous when they die the way she died. Young, tragically, wastefully. I bet she lit up a room, didn't she? They always say that. 'She loved making people smile and she lit up every room she walked into.'"

"I suppose you'd know what they say," I said. "You've destroyed so many innocent lives."

"That sounds very grand, but I wouldn't call myself a destroyer of lives," Cline said. "These people do that themselves. You know what I am? I'm the master of pain. I have a monopoly on it. People like Marni come to me because they're hurting, and I take the hurt away. I decide who feels it and who doesn't."

"You seem pretty happy to deal it out. Squid is terrified of you."

"He should be," Cline said, "with the stuff he's seen. But you won't be able to use him for anything meaningful. He knows what happens when one of my soldiers allows himself to get caught. And that'll be your fault, Robinson. You've sealed his fate."

"You've got a real swollen head, you know that?" I said. "You talk about killing people like it's inevitable, like it's your right. You're not a god walking the earth, Cline. You're just a piece-of-shit drug dealer from a long line of lowlife assholes."

"Listen to you, motherfucker," Cline barked. "You think you can talk about my family like that? You don't know shit about my family, you punk-ass bitch!"

He'd lost it momentarily. I'd touched a nerve. I smiled as he dropped his sophisticated act and reverted to the trash talk he'd probably promised himself he would abandon the last time he left prison. There was a pause while he regained his composure.

"We don't have to do this," Cline said. "There's a way out for you. Give me the kid back, and I'll leave you and your people alone. It's what's best for everyone, man. You're a smart guy. You know it."

"Listen to *you*," I said. "You've got your speech prepared. When threatening me doesn't work, you switch to flattery. You're like a used-car salesman. 'You better get this deal now or you'll miss out. You'll hate yourself. You're a smart guy— let me sweeten the deal for you.'"

"There's no money in used cars," Cline sniffed. "And you don't know me, boy. But I know about you, Robinson. I know what happened in Boston."

Prickles, tingles, spread out from my chest and over my scalp; raw adrenaline unleashed. I should have seen this coming. People like Cline had cops, judges, and politicians in their pockets. He had drugs, and that brought him money, and money brought him influence, connections, friends in high places. I gripped the phone tight. "Yeah? What about it?"

"I've got contacts. I can make that shit go away," Cline said. "You can't tell me you were happy to give up the beat to clean toilets in a shitbox guesthouse full of losers."

"I'm guilty of the Boston thing," I said. "I got what I deserve."

"What about your roadkill wife?"

It took everything I had not to shatter the phone on the concrete steps to the house. I heard him shifting pieces of paper, probably Siobhan's accident report. More evidence that Cline had the local cops on his payroll. I closed my eyes and breathed while he continued.

"You're smart enough to figure, like I did, that the story the driver gave didn't add up," Cline said. "I can give you the people who were in that car. I can give you the real driver."

"Let me give you something," I said, my voice colder than I'd ever heard it. "Twelve hours. You have that long to turn yourself in to the police and not a second more."

Cline was laughing as I hung up the phone. I walked back into the abandoned house, and Effie jutted her chin at me, made an okay shape with her fingers.

You okay?

I didn't answer. Squid squealed with terror as I kicked his chair over and then stood above him, grabbed a handful of his shirt, and twisted it in my fist.

"Cline said we can't use you, but I think he's wrong." I yanked the kid forward so his face was inches from mine. "You're going to help me hit the master of pain where it hurts."

CHAPTER FORTY-THREE

SUSAN WAS STANDING on the porch when we arrived home. She watched Nick turn the car around after he had dropped off me and Effie, her eyes impossible to read. Effie went around the side of the house and I stood with Susan, surveying the holes in the siding. Though she kept her expression neutral, I could see her temple ticking with her pulse.

"There was a kidnapped kid in that car just now, wasn't there," she said finally.

"He's a contact of ours. Nick's driving him north to Augusta," I said. "He's got a cousin there. Cline's more likely to look for him at his mother's house in Boston."

"You've gone rogue." Susan shook her head.

"I haven't gone rogue," I said. "I'm not a cop anymore. I don't need to play by anyone's rules."

"Just because you're not a cop doesn't mean you get to snatch kids off the street!" She threw her hands up.

"I don't know what you're talking about."

"Yes, you do." She rolled her eyes. "Don't treat me like an idiot, Bill. Cline put a missing-persons report in with Clay, and he mentioned it to me. I heard about the crashed bike. You endangered that kid's life by making him flip on Cline."

"Oh, believe me, he was already in danger," I said. "It's a matter of time with these people. When the heat's on, they clean house. I've seen it over and over. Cline wants Squid brought in so he can kill him or locked up so he can get one of his prison contacts to do it. The kid will be safe with his cousin." I watched her shake her head again. "I needed information. This guy killed Marni, Susan. He had someone lure her there and he killed her. If his men had been better shots, he might have killed someone here at the house."

"I'm worried you're going to get in over your head on this," she said.

"Don't worry about me. I'm not your problem."

I turned to go but she took my hand. I couldn't look at her. From the moment Cline had offered to tell me exactly what had happened to Siobhan, to lay out for me the awful truth I'd been denying all this time, my nerves had been frayed. I didn't want to think about Siobhan. I didn't want to think about Marni. I didn't want to acknowledge the heavy desire now in my chest to hold Susan in my arms, to feel her hands on my neck, her lips on mine. Fighting back against it all seemed the only safe course of action. But then, without realizing it, I let her put her hand on my cheek. She was so close I could smell her sweet breath.

"Bill," she pleaded, "just don't—"

"I can't do this," I said. I pulled away and went inside.

Angelica was on the couch in the living room under the windows, one arm in a sling and the other lying across her forehead like she'd fainted; her left index finger was splinted. I went into the kitchen and stood at the window, felt Susan's presence without turning to look at her.

"What are you going to do?" she asked. I gripped the edge of the sink.

"I have a plan," I said. "But a part of me wants to throw it in. I keep thinking about just driving to Cline's house, dragging him down the stairs by his shirt, and kicking the shit out of him on his own lawn."

She was silent. The malice in my voice was frightening, even to me. Another being was speaking from a dark place in my mind. It was loss that did this to me, forced me down into my own deepest, most evil recesses.

"You're not that dumb."

"Oh, I can be pretty dumb," I smirked. I heard a *thunk* from upstairs, which I ignored. I turned to her. I wanted to tell Susan that I'd done this before. That I'd let the badness take me, stupid and filled with rage, and I both did and didn't regret what I had done. But the phone rang in my pocket, drawing us both out of ourselves. I answered without looking at the caller ID.

"Bill," someone said. A voice I hadn't heard in over two years. "It's Malone."

I barely managed to respond. "What do you . . . this is not a good time."

"Maybe it isn't," he said. "But I don't think we have a

choice. I'm a hundred yards from your house, and a black woman on the second floor has got me pinned with a big fuck-off rifle. She just blew a hole the size of a dinner plate in the tree right next to me."

CHAPTER FORTY-FOUR

EFFIE WAS SITTING on a wooden stool at the window, her eye on the scope and her finger on the trigger of a rifle even bigger than the one I'd pulled off Nick the other night. The silencer on it was as thick as my arm, which accounted for the *thunk* I'd heard when she'd fired a warning shot at my former partner. Effie turned and looked at me as I entered the bare room, then made a couple of signs I recognized from raid training I'd done as a young patrolman.

One target. Hundred yards.

"Does everybody in this goddamn house have an enormous rifle under the bed except me?" I asked. Effie looked like she was mentally reviewing the number of guests with large guns under their beds. I moved toward her, stopped when I noticed a tiny brown lump on the bedspread. The rat was sleeping, curled up in a ball like a cat, its pink tail tucked around its body. I knelt beside Effie and looked through the scope. Jerry Malone was indeed standing frozen in the forest, his hands out from his sides like he was prepared to either raise them or jump for cover if another shot came. He'd dropped the phone, probably not wanting to push his luck any further. There was a hole in the tree right next to him large enough for a man to put his head through. The scope of the rifle was so big I could see the individual splinters of wood from the shot that had fallen on his shoulder.

"He's an old buddy," I told Effie.

She rolled her eyes and threw her hands up. *Now you tell me.*

CHAPTER FORTY-FIVE

THE MALONE I approached in the forest in front of my house was much thinner and paler than the one I'd seen outside the commissioner's office in Boston. He'd grown a beard, but the dark hair only accentuated the rings under his eyes. I stopped ten feet away, saving us both the awkward silent negotiation about whether to shake hands.

"Great place." Malone nodded at the house. "Security system is a bit extreme, maybe."

"I'm having some troubles with the locals," I said. "Someone decided to use the house for target practice a couple of days ago. I'm expecting a slide in short-term rentals."

I wasn't showing any warmth, not in my body language or the tone of my voice, but I recognized that I wanted to. Despite what happened in Boston, what prevailed were the good memories of me and Malone catching babies falling off balconies and running through back alleys chasing thieves, sitting on the dock after the shift and watching the boats come in, talking about our wives and our houses, how lucky we were. He brushed the wood splinters off his shoulder and looked me in the eye for the first time since I'd approached.

"I know it was the anniversary of Siobhan the other day," he said. "It got me thinking..." He couldn't find the words, shrugged. I understood. I crossed the no-man's-land between us and hugged him, slapped his bony back. The walls crumbled like chalk. What we'd done seemed so long ago now, so unimportant. I felt him half laughing, half sobbing with relief.

"Come inside." I led him toward the house, my arm around his shoulders.

CHAPTER FORTY-SIX

IT WAS SUPPOSED to be a quick trip into town, but Effie knew that nothing was quick when Angelica was involved. The two had jumped in the car after Bill's friend Malone arrived to go get some supplies for a barbecue, but Angelica was treating the trip as an opportunity for some kind of philosophical lecture about writing. From the bright lights of the Stop and Shop, down the hill past the whale-watching and tourism stretch, and into the café on the edge of Harbor Cove, Angelica had droned on. Effie window-shopped, took in the sea air, and generally ignored her partner. Gloucester was settling down for the evening, pink light falling softly on the storm-blue sea. Angelica ordered coffees for the two of them, hardly pausing in her oration to address the waitress. A group of men came in and took the booth directly behind Angelica, big men who settled themselves loudly in the leather seats.

"I don't know about you, but I can't understand how the archetype of the muse has survived unaltered for as long as it has," Angelica said. She didn't wait for any gesture of an answer from Effie. "It diminishes the author's accountability for the successes and failures of the written work, and besides that, it banishes the creative act to the realm of the spiritual conduit, and—*oh my God!*"

Effie had been staring out at the harbor light but she snapped back toward Angelica, who was sitting bolt upright in her chair like she had been zapped. Effie put her palms up—*What?*—but Angelica flapped her hands at her.

"Shh, shh!" Angelica said. "Be quiet."

Effie sighed.

"These guys," Angelica whispered, leaning forward and adjusting her sling, "in the booth behind me. They just mentioned Mitchell Cline."

Effie discreetly leaned out of her seat, but all she could see were broad shoulders barely contained in expensive fabric. She pointed at her ear, the guys in the booth.

You heard them?

"I was eavesdropping," Angelica whispered. "I'm terrible, I know. I listen to everyone. It's in the writer's tool kit. C. S. Lewis compared eavesdropping to spying on people by magic. See? More elitist mysticism."

She listened. Effie waited. Both women looked out the windows of the café, and Angelica pointed sharply up the street.

"There," she said. "Look. An Escalade. Vinny said the car that did the drive-by was an Escalade. And that one's got a new windshield. You can see the plastic installation tab hasn't been removed from one side. Nick said something about Bill smashing the windshield of Cline's Escalade."

Effie raised her eyebrows. Angelica had transformed before her eyes from babbling author to armchair detective.

"What are we going to do?" Angelica asked.

Effie slammed her fist into her palm.

"I have a better idea." Angelica looked at the car, the reflection of the men in the window beside them, the hillside, and the harbor. "Cause a distraction in exactly ten seconds."

CHAPTER FORTY-SEVEN

ANGELICA STOOD. EFFIE scrambled, thinking fast. She watched, counting mentally, as Angelica approached the next booth.

"Excuse me, gentlemen. Could I just borrow this sugar? We're all out."

She saw Angelica leaning over. Effie shoved her coffee cup and saucer off the edge of the table. The china shattered on the floor, coffee splashing on the legs of a couple at the next table. Everyone turned to look, including the men in the booth. Effie shrugged, made an embarrassed face, and got up to assist the waitress who came over to clean up the mess.

"You know what?" Angelica turned and smiled at the waitress. "We'll just take our check, if you don't mind."

She flashed Effie a set of keys with a chunky black remote

before tucking them into her sling. Effie smiled, and the two women left some money on the counter and walked quickly out into the street.

"We'll need another distraction for cover," Angelica said, "in case they look out the window."

The evening winds were sweeping in across the harbor. The two women seemed to have the same thought. Angelica tossed Effie the keys and stopped a couple walking two dogs right outside the window of the café.

"Oh, dachshunds! Look at them! They're just gorgeous! You know, Radclyffe Hall had dachshunds."

"Who?"

Effie unlocked the Escalade parked at the top of the hill, put the keys in the ignition, put the car in neutral, and released the emergency brake. She gave Angelica a nod, and the two edged over to the wall beside the café window as the people with the dogs continued on.

Nothing happened. The car remained in position. At the bottom of the hill, by the harbor, a police cruiser parked, and two officers got out.

"Fuck," Angelica snapped. "We'll have to push it. It's not moving! Fucking, fucking shitballs!" She stomped her foot. Effie's eyes widened. She almost laughed. Angelica looked like she was about to throw herself at the vehicle and push it down the hill with her one usable but injured hand when the car began to move.

Angelica and Effie watched as the Escalade rolled down the hill, gathering speed, and then slammed into the police cruiser; the crash was so loud and thunderous that everyone in the street stopped and turned.

"Triumph!" Angelica whispered fiercely.

The two women leaned forward and saw the men in the café rise from their booth. People were running to the crash, including the two officers who had only made it to the edge of the park.

Effie tugged at Angelica. She resisted at first, seeming to want to stay and watch her work.

"Take that, you murderous bastards," Angelica snarled. Effie grabbed the sling and dragged her friend away.

CHAPTER FORTY-EIGHT

FAT PEOPLE REPULSED Cline. They always had. Unfortunately, he couldn't look at someone like Sheriff Clayton Spears without imagining the man naked, seeing the alien creases and folds of his figure beneath the tan uniform, the parts of him that excessively sweat or grew hair in unnatural biological reactions to his bulk. He reclined in his wing chair in the third-floor office and eyed the man perched on the settee before him scribbling notes in the stupid little notebook he held with his sausage fingers.

"And could you provide a list of the people who can vouch for your presence and activities at the party?" Clay asked. He sat back, making the settee creak. Cline was thinking how he'd dispose of the piece of furniture after the sheriff was gone. Perhaps he'd burn it. "Was there someone with you for a majority of the event?"

"I didn't sneak out of my own party, leaving my house and my personal property unguarded in the presence of hundreds of strangers, so I could go and blow holes in the house of a man I barely know, Sheriff." Cline rolled his eyes. "Everything in this house, everything in this room, is expensive. That lamp at your elbow is Baccarat Eye. It's worth twelve thousand dollars."

The sheriff looked at the lamp and seemed startled by its presence. He shifted his bulging body to the edge of the settee, apparently not wanting to make physical contact with anything in the room if he could possibly avoid it. "I can see you're a man of taste, Mr. Cline," the sheriff said. "You said you were in the importation business?"

"I did."

"What do you import?"

"Focus, Sheriff." Cline leaned his chin on his hand. "You're not here about me. You're here about the drive-by and the overdose. Don't lose track."

"Mr. Cline, I'll ask whatever questions I deem necessary for the investigation," the sheriff said. Cline smiled. He enjoyed a little pushback, flickers of power and protest in the fat man's eyes, but the sheriff's tone of voice hadn't sold what he was saying. He was the mongrel in the room, and Cline was the purebred Doberman.

"What do you make, Sheriff?" Cline asked.

"Excuse me?"

"Your salary. What is it?"

"I make a hundred and eighteen thousand, one hundred and thirty-seven dollars." Clay straightened on the settee. "That's the base."

"And that keeps you comfortable?" Cline let his eyes wander over the creature before him. "I suppose your living costs are meager. Your room at the Inn can't cost much, and you don't look like you blow wads of it indulging in the single man's footloose lifestyle. That watch. Where do you even get a watch like that? Walmart? Dollar General?"

Clay turned the plastic watch on his wrist self-consciously.

"Maybe you lost everything in the divorce." Cline yawned. Turner was on the phone in the hallway. Cline heard him murmuring, "What do you mean? How badly? A police car?"

"Now I'm the one who feels like we're getting away from the point of my inquiry here tonight, Mr. Cline," the sheriff said.

"Haven't you ever *dreamed,* Sheriff?" Cline asked, leaning forward, suddenly full of enthusiasm. "Haven't you ever fantasized about who you could *be* in the world? Before you started shoveling down Pop-Tarts and Miller Lite to drown your self-loathing, before you realized you'd be stuck here forever in Bumfuck Nowhere because your parents raised you as an unimaginative, codependent hick, didn't you at least flirt with the idea that you could be *something*?"

Clay struggled. Cline watched as the sheriff glanced at the men guarding the doorway of his office as though seeking their assistance. Always looking somewhere else for help.

"I'll give you a million dollars," Cline said, throwing a hand out as though he were tossing bills into the air. "I'll even tell you what to do with it so you don't blow it all on cheap hookers and a yellow Hummer. Go and get gastric-band surgery. Liposuction. A brow shave and some cosmetic dental work. Put some of the cash into fast rollover investments. Hire a personal trainer, a stylist, and a speech therapist and get yourself a decent watch, for fuck's sake. If you like law enforcement that much, get a cover job—consult for a private security firm, something that gets you into a suit every day instead of a Halloween costume with a toy cowboy badge. In twelve months, your life will be unrecognizable."

The sheriff's pudgy mouth opened and closed a few times. Cline waited, but the words that eventually came out were not what he expected.

"I like my life," Clay said. His face suddenly darkened, shifted. Cline was looking at a man for an instant. An equal. "And you've just offered me a bribe, sir."

The sheriff stood. Cline looked up at him, impressed and amused, yes, but mostly annoyed.

"I'm going to forget what you just said and bid you good night," Clay said.

Cline sat in the dark for a long time after Sheriff Spears was gone. Eventually Cline let a sigh escape his lips. He looked at Turner, who waited expectantly for a command.

CHAPTER FORTY-NINE

MIDNIGHT, WHEN WE would enact our plan, was approaching. I felt the hour coming on, though that didn't stop me from checking my watch every ten minutes, meeting Effie's eyes knowingly across the fire blazing between us in the pit. When we first started the Inn, the firepit in the woods by the house had been regularly in use, the rising gold embers drawing people out of their rooms to the old rickety benches Siobhan had bought and placed around the barbecue area. The warmth of the flames, Malone jabbering in my ear, brought back memories. Those great old times were mingling confusingly with the new as I followed the embers up toward the dark trees above and imagined Marni leaving us, so young, so unfairly, for whatever realm was next.

I gripped my bench hard when I thought of her, imagining her tiny form beneath the sheets on the gurney rolling by me, unnoticed. The hospital had insisted Marni's mother identify her, and I had followed the woman's direction not to go and view her body. The last time I saw the child was in the back of Clay's squad car when I'd promised her better things were coming.

"The guy was a monster," Malone was telling Susan, the two of them sitting on either side of me. "He used to walk into the break room and go, 'What's that smell? I thought this was a police station. All I see around me are pieces of shit.' He never approved overtime, personal expenses, sick leave. You can't work with a captain like that. So this guy here comes up with a *genius* plan." Malone slapped me on the chest, taking me away from my thoughts. Susan was watching me carefully.

"Tell her what you did." Malone grinned.

Despite everything, I couldn't help smiling. "I started sending him presents."

"Bill starts sending our asshole captain presents." Malone laughed. "He sends this cute little box with a big red bow and inside is a red lace thong in a size two. The note is from a secret admirer in the E-Thirteen District."

"I didn't think it would work," I told Susan, who was trying not to laugh. "But it did, really well. The captain comes around showing everybody this thong, twirling it on his finger and reading the letter about how the woman can't wait to wear it for him and the things she's gonna do."

"He's quite the erotic storyteller." Malone slapped me again. "You'd be surprised."

"So what happened?" Susan asked.

"I sent him the thong, then a box of chocolate body paint and a pair of those fluffy handcuffs," I said. "By the time the third gift arrived the captain had put in for a transfer to E-Thirteen District."

"That is genius." She laughed. "I could have used that tactic about a dozen times across my career."

Malone noticed how miserably Angelica was slouched beside him, watching the flames reflected in a glass of wine. He turned to her, and Susan turned to me.

"Are you okay?" Susan asked me. I hadn't realized I had that thousand-yard stare.

"I'm fine," I lied. "Old memories, you know. They stir things up."

"Want to go for a walk?" she asked.

We left the group at the fire and strolled through the trees to the beach. It was an unseasonably warm night, and the water was pale glass, the way it had been when Nick walked out here in the tangle of his own nightmares, reflecting an eerie gold moon near the horizon. Susan clutched her coat around her and watched the stones passing beneath her feet, the only sound the lapping of the water nearby and the horns of boats in the distance returning home.

I broke the silence reluctantly.

"You must know what we did," I said. "Me and Malone."

CHAPTER FIFTY

"WHAT DO YOU mean?" Susan frowned.

"The Boston thing. The reason I was fired. You must have checked me out."

Susan stopped walking and smirked almost bitterly at the horizon. I felt bad for accusing her of snooping into my past.

"I was married once before," she said. "Bureau guy, of course. A fellow recruit. We had been very competitive with each other at the academy, sort of rivals, until graduation, when we realized why we were so obsessed with each other. The relationship was always chaotic, but that was exciting to me, you know? We were sent on assignments all around the country where we had to pretend we didn't know each other, and it was electric. We'd rendezvous secretly in alleyways in New York and on beaches in Los Angeles at night, see each other in little hole-in-the-wall bars."

What she was describing sounded like a spy movie, and she knew it. She laughed.

"We got married too fast. Things changed. He was impossible to live with. Sarcasm became insults, which became shoving, then grabbing. Then he started talking about what he'd do if I ever left him. I got worried. I looked up a couple of his old girlfriends. He'd thrown one of them down the stairs and broken her hip, then later threatened to kill her if she said anything about it to the Bureau agents who did his background check. Another was so scared of him that she moved to Australia and changed her name."

"Jesus," I said.

"You'd think it would have made me more cautious." Susan looked at me. Her eyes were big and full of truth. "But it didn't. I don't look people up anymore. I'm afraid of what I'll find. Once I discovered who he really was, I knew I had to leave."

"He still works there," I said.

"He does," she said. "He's high profile. So was I. What I did, by leaving—it humiliated him. We had the perfect wedding. There were many important people there, people with power and influence, and I left him to explain where I'd gone. I just cut ties. So I try to avoid dealing with the Bureau as much as I can. I lost a job I loved and a lot of people who cared about me. But I'm . . . you know. I'm happy here." She straightened and shook herself in a way that made me think she was lying. Trying to wear the truth of her words.

"Are you just starting again here at the house?" I asked. "Or are you actually in hiding from this guy?"

She chewed her lip, looked as though she wanted to tell

me something else. Then she said, "I don't want to talk about it." She waved me off.

"If this guy has hurt you or if he's going to try to hurt you—"

"Then I'll deal with it myself," she said. "Like I did the first time."

"You . . ." I nodded. "Of course you will."

"You've got the white-knight mentality about you." She smiled. "Boston cop for a couple of decades. How could you not, right?"

I drew a long breath. "It's more than that. I know I'm too protective of women. It's old-fashioned, and I've taken it too far in the past."

"How?"

"Oh." I shrugged. "It's a long story."

"Well, don't let it get you into trouble with me," she said. "I can handle myself, and I can handle my business. And so can Effie."

"Is she connected to your ex?"

"No," Susan said. "She was a case of mine, sort of. She needed to get away, and so did I, so it made sense to go together. But I'm speaking out of turn now. I shouldn't have brought it up." She turned away and started to head back toward the house. But I took a deep breath, put an arm around her waist, and drew her to me.

"Whoa!" she cried.

CHAPTER FIFTY-ONE

"WHOA!" I RESPONDED, my face flushing. I let her go and she stumbled a little on the rocks, put her hand to her lips. We both laughed awkwardly, our faces burning.

"Were you going to kiss me?" Her eyes were wide, full of hilarity.

"Well, I just..." I cleared my throat, looked down at my feet, then up at the sky. "Oh Jesus. I just thought you might...I, uh, well, the moon and the water and..." I gestured. "You know?"

"No." She laughed. "I mean, yes, I get it! It—it was perfect. I just wasn't ready for it." She slapped a hand over her eyes. "I was actually hoping that you *would,* but I didn't think you were *going to,* and then you just *did,* and—"

"You were hoping I would?"

"Yes!"

"Oh no." I covered my face. "Now I've ruined it."

"No, I was definitely the one who ruined it."

We both put our hands in our pockets and looked at the stones beneath us. I thought it was over, and then she grabbed a handful of my shirt and dragged me to her. As soon as her lips were against mine, I was sealed in a moment so perfect, so long desired that I felt like crying. I held her against my chest, and she looped her arms around my neck, and all that I had lost and all the fear and fury at the threat of losing more dissolved.

We pressed our foreheads together, and when I opened my eyes I found she was smiling as wide as I was.

"Now, that—"

"—was perfect," I said. We looked at each other, and then out of the corner of my eye, I caught movement by the trees near the house.

Effie. She nodded at me, pointed to her watch.

It was time.

CHAPTER FIFTY-TWO

THE BOAT WAS exactly where Squid said it would be, about three nautical miles off Gloucester, cutting laps up and down the coast until it was time to come in. Nick was at the stern of our tiny tin boat, and Effie and I were huddled at the bow, as though by keeping low in the vessel, we might avoid the boat being seen on approach. The moon, high, white, and full, wasn't good for cover, but the three of us had decided to go that night before Cline got to thinking about what our next move might be. Nick cut the small engine a long way out from the vessel and let the bigger boat drift into our path.

Sweet Relief. The hand-painted letters on the side of the boat passed under my fingers as I climbed a rope ladder slung over the side. I helped Effie up and then hurled a rope I found coiled on the deck to Nick to attach to our boat.

The thrumming of the engine underfoot and the wash from the stern was a worrying sound screen; it could hide the approach of footsteps or the shouting of men who might have spotted us.

We crouched by a stack of crab cages. Nick had his lips almost at my ear so I could hear him over the sound of the engines. "Recon first," he said. "Meet back here in five. You take the bridge. Effie and I will take the lower decks."

I crept along the side of the boat, ducking under the porthole windows. The narrow stairs to the bridge wing were slippery, the rail crusted with salt. I was struck suddenly by the beauty of the silver path the moon was cutting across the sea and I wondered for a moment what the hell I was doing.

There was one man on the bridge. He was bent over the chart table in the red light, marking out his position with a pencil. A cigarette was clamped between his lips.

Effie and Nick were already back when I arrived.

"One man on the bridge," I said.

"Great." Nick grinned, his eyes shining with excitement. "There are two contacts in the galley, one asleep on the lower deck. Let's go down first, Cap."

He moved, but I grabbed his shoulder.

"Keep your head," I said. "Tell me if you're starting to lose it."

"I'm not gonna lose it." Nick shrugged me off. I followed Nick and Effie into the bowels of the vessel, my gun in one hand, the other bracing against everything as the world rocked around me. We passed a room lit with huge red lamps, and I glimpsed a big table cluttered with plastic tubs, a big machine with a crank handle, bottles, and buckets.

Two figures moved in the eerie light, gloved to the elbows and wearing full-face respirators. I kept watch in the hall, my pulse hammering, as Nick and Effie went into the sleeping quarters. I heard a thump and a yelp.

The need to retreat jabbed at me. I imagined aborting the mission now, dragging my friends back onto the little boat, cutting the rope loose, and letting us drift to safety, the big boat becoming a dark mass on the horizon. It wasn't too late.

Nick emerged from the sleeping quarters, tucking the duct tape into his jacket pocket.

"He's down," he said. "Three to go."

CHAPTER FIFTY-THREE

CLAYTON SPEARS DIDN'T mind the night shift. Once a week he got out into the quiet streets and roamed around Gloucester patrolling, responding to bumps in the night, breaking up drunken parties, and pulling over the occasional drunk driver. He took the night shift at least once a week to remind his team that he wasn't above them, that he was willing to fight fatigue and boredom and the disappointment of false calls like the rest of them. But the lamplit streets held a kind of security for him. No one stared at him, judged him, whispered about him as he passed by in his cruiser. At night he wasn't a tubby, shy, failing sheriff elected every year only because he was the devil Gloucester knew. He was a lone wolf protecting his sleeping pack.

The night shift would also keep him out of the office, away from the phone. He knew Marni's autopsy was being rushed through, and the results would be reported to go into her case file with the department. He didn't want to be there when the call came through. He wanted to be out, where he could see the stars.

It was one in the morning when Clay came upon the two young women crouched by the deserted roadside. Clay looked at the tire on the asphalt beside their car and tutted as he pulled over. The women, as they fumbled with the tire iron and read instructions from their phones, were a quarter of the way into the lane, and the spare was sitting maybe a third of the way in. He exited his vehicle and pulled up his gun belt.

"Morning, ladies," he said as he approached.

"Oh, wonderful," the younger one said, clapping her hands with glee. "Ronnie, it's the sheriff. Can you help us, sir? We're in big trouble here. Neither of us has ever changed a tire before. We're totally stuck!"

"Let's forget about changing the tire for now and get off the road." Clay pointed to the roadside and the women went where he instructed. "You're begging to get hit by someone coming up over the hill."

Clay bent down, grabbed the spare from the asphalt, and rolled it toward the women. His head was down, hands on the rubber, when at the corner of his vision a boot appeared. Not a woman's boot; a big, black, decidedly male one.

"Lights out, fat boy," a voice said.

Clay heard a *swish,* and then there was only blackness.

CHAPTER FIFTY-FOUR

NICK AND I sent Effie up to the bridge to take care of the captain and hold a gun on him until we were done downstairs. We stood in the darkened hallway, our guns hanging by our sides, and I watched as that strange light flickered in Nick's eyes, the same one I'd seen as we launched into an attack on Rick Craft at the Greenfish, the same one that lingered there as he stood in the freezing waters near our home. I wanted to ask if he was okay, but he sprang into the room before I did, his voice booming, the gun swinging between the two bewildered men in full-face respirators.

"On the ground! On the ground! On the ground!"

They didn't go down easily. Gloved hands went up, and then they reconsidered, perhaps acting on a lesson Cline had drilled into them from the beginning about their fates should they ever let him down. The man nearest me grabbed a canister of red powder and flung it at us; the glass burst against a porthole window. I could taste the dust in the air, burning and metallic. I launched myself at him, and the edge of the table jutted into my hip; a tub of pills tumbled and scattered as we hit the floor together. I clubbed him in the back of the head with my gun and he gave the heavy exhalation of someone losing consciousness. Nick had abandoned his gun and pinned his guy up against the low cupboards on the wall, his arm bent backward.

"You stupid fucks." The guy's voice was muffled by the respirator. "You ain't cops! Get out of here!"

"We're not cops, but we're not going anywhere." I took the duct tape from Nick and began binding the man in front of me. "Not until we're done."

Nick's guy watched me, realizing my mission as I finished binding my guy and then started scooping up the spilled pills from the floor. I stacked a couple of tubs, and his eyes widened behind the cloudy glass of his face mask.

"You don't want to do this, man," he said. "I'm telling you. I'm telling you, bro! You're making a big mistake! Cline will put you in a hole. He will put you in the fucking ground."

"Shut up, idiot." Nick forced him to the floor and put his knee into his back, then wound the duct tape tight around his gloved hands. I took three stacked tubs full to the brim with colorful pills and walked back outside.

The pills disappeared into the white moonlit surf as I emptied the tubs one by one.

CHAPTER FIFTY-FIVE

DIRT. THE SHERIFF tasted it as he came to consciousness, granular on his lips and strangely reassuring. He had the sense that for some time he'd been lolling around the back of his own squad car, heaped on the seat like a sack of bones, the acrid smell of the men's cigarettes making him gag. He could hear them now nearby, the small one complaining and the big one barking back at him like a dog.

"If I'd known we was gonna bury this one, we could have come out here earlier, Bonesy. It's fucking freezing, man! The ground is solid rock."

"He wants us to be more careful this time," the one called Bones said. "The Druly woman was fun and games. This is a cop we talkin' 'bout. Shut up and dig."

Clay tried to roll onto his back to take the pressure off his ribs, but as he moved, he found his hands were numb, his arms twisted behind him. His own cuffs were on his wrists. His head protested with the movement, pain branching out from the wound at the back of his skull like white-hot fingers running through his hair. He staggered to his knees with difficulty and then got to his feet, wobbling and groaning with the pain.

The men stopped digging and assessed him. He recognized them from Cline's house. Bones and Simbo, two of the sneering henchmen Cline kept ever at his side. It took a lot to make Sheriff Spears angry, but he felt the dull thump of anger hit him now. It crept up through his chest and neck, an old friend returned.

"Sheriff, you could make this easier on yourself by lying the fuck back down," the big one said, pointing to the soil. Clay looked around him at the forest. Moonlight streaked through the dense trees. For a moment he thought he might be somewhere near the Inn. Then he remembered the Druly woman's body in the depths of Dogtown, her headless corpse lying on its side, dumped like trash.

"This is not very nice," Clay said. The anger was taking over. Mean whispers and vicious sneers were flickering through his mind. The bad Clay inside, usually a solid sleeper, was up and knocking at the door of his heart. "I don't deserve this."

The men before him pulled enormous knives from their belts. Clay wondered if the plan was for his head to appear separate from his body, maybe dumped out here somewhere, maybe washed ashore weeks from now, covered in crabs and snails. The thought made his jaw lock with fury.

"You go first," the small one, Simbo, said to his partner. "Dude's four times my size."

"Stop," Clay said, his warning halfhearted, left over from his training. The good Clay calling back as he fled, leaving the bad Clay at the wheel. "Go now, and I won't hurt you."

"You . . ." The big guy grinned at his partner, laughed with surprise. "*You* won't hurt *us*?"

"You've got three seconds," Clay said. His speech was slurred, his head still foggy from the blow. The two killers in the dark considered their options, then advanced toward him.

CHAPTER FIFTY-SIX

CLAY DIDN'T LET them come. The distance between him and the big one was maybe twenty feet, and for every inch of that distance, Clay ground his feet into the dirt and then hurled himself forward with all his might. He slammed into Bones at full speed, his wide shoulder driving into his gut, not slowing until the man's back connected with a huge tree. Clay felt the breath leave Bones, felt his ribs crunching and muscles collapsing against his shoulder. Clay backed up a couple of steps, ready to kick the man when he hit the ground. But Bones was unconscious immediately, a shattered insect squashed in the dirt.

The smaller one, Simbo, wasted no time. He raised the knife, and Clay took the adrenaline surging through his system and swung his foot up and across Simbo's arm, knocking the blade away. The move threw him off balance, left him sprawling on the ground on his back. The small, stocky guy was on him, and Clay clenched every muscle in his body and snapped upward suddenly, aiming his head butt as best he could. It was a glancing blow off Simbo's mouth, but it was enough to shock him. Clay rolled, got up, stomped on the writhing figure in the dark again and again. He heard more bones crunching. Simbo's forearm snapped like a branch. Clay kept stomping until the man was still.

The sheriff stood in the dark panting. Muscles and tendons that had been inactive for years were now alive; sweat dripped down his neck into the collar of his torn shirt. The last of his courage burned low, the rest of it consumed by the fight. He moaned a couple of times with exhaustion and anger, searched with his trapped fingers on the back of his belt for the key to the cuffs. It was gone. He sighed and began the long trudge toward where he guessed the road might be.

CHAPTER FIFTY-SEVEN

WHEN I HAD emptied all six tubs of pills into the sea, I started carrying boxes and bottles of ingredients out. I grabbed a barrel and rolled it on its rim toward the door. The guy I had hit was waking slowly, moaning and sighing, trying to turn onto his side. His partner, held still by Nick's gun, was watching me carefully. Nick had dragged the respirators off both their faces, but they were sweating badly. These men were going to have to run from Cline after this, and Cline seemed like the type who could find a man no matter where he hid.

"Let's hurry this up, Cap." Nick's eyes were funny. Too distant, too wide. "We gotta meet the team at the point in oh-five."

"What?" I stopped rolling the barrel. "Nick, are you okay?"

He shook his head. "Hmm? Yes. What? I'm fine. Let's hurry this up."

"That's enough." I let go of the barrel. "We've done all we can. Time to go back."

Nick didn't hear me. His head was up; he seemed to be listening to some noise coming from the rear of the boat. The minor distraction was all his captive needed. I didn't see the knife he'd been working against the duct tape on his wrists until the blade cut through the last shred. He turned and jammed the blade into Nick's calf.

The gunshot was deafening in the tiny space; the bullet pinged off a pipe and shunted into the bulkhead before me. Nick's bullet hit the cupboards just inches above my head— his finger had jerked on the trigger. The man grabbed for Nick's gun and the two wrestled while I came around the big table to assist. My guy was more conscious than I'd thought. He kicked at my legs suddenly, tripping me into the cabinets against the wall. Nick's guy had his gun. He backed into the corner of the room and fired wildly at the two of us. It was only the boat lurching suddenly down a steep wave that saved us. The man slid, fell; the gun was knocked out of his hands as he hit the ground. Nick snatched up the weapon and pointed it at his opponent's head.

"Nick, no!" I cried.

CHAPTER FIFTY-EIGHT

VINNY SAW THEM coming long before they knew he was there. Two tall, thick men jogging quietly through the trees toward the house, guns out. He sat still in his wheelchair at the corner of the porch, his hands beneath the blanket on his lap. He'd never been a good sleeper. More nights than not, he wheeled himself out here to watch the silent forest and think. The journey to the porch had taken longer this time because his left wheel was held in place by an under-sized bolt Doc Simeon had found in a jar in the garage. The ancient gangster smiled as one of the men skirted around the house to check the perimeter while the other walked directly toward him, not seeing him until he was only feet away.

Vinny watched the man assess him in the moonlight. The wheelchair, the newly bandaged leg, the blanket on his lap, and the hat clamped on his withered head. Like people always did these days, the young man underestimated him. The pair were wearing balaclavas, but Vinny could see that there were tattoos on the man's hands. Some kind of insects—spiders, maybe.

The tattooed man said nothing until his partner returned to his side. The two looked at each other, assessed Vinny again, and then turned to go.

"What?" Vinny smirked. "You're not gonna kill me? You're not worried I'll roll up behind you while you're inside popping heads in beds?"

The men glanced at him, bewildered.

"Old man, you just sit there and feel lucky," the tattooed one said. "I ain't about shootin' pathetic old cripples in their chairs. You can be the one who tells the story."

"Pathetic old cripple?" Vinny laughed. "You think so, huh? Boy, I got ten inches of cold hard steel between my legs that might disagree with you."

The men laughed. Their laughter was drowned out by the roar of the gun from between Vinny's thighs; the blanket over his knees was shredded as the bullet passed through it. The tattooed man's kneecap exploded, sending him sprawling on his face on the gravel driveway. The partner fled. Vinny lifted the heavy Desert Eagle pistol and tried to grip the trigger, but his hand was strained from the first shot. He grabbed the knife from his shirt pocket, turned, threw it, felt a rush of satisfaction as it chunked into the partner's thigh as he made for the porch door. The guy stumbled and then wrenched open the front door and disappeared into the house.

CHAPTER FIFTY-NINE

NICK THOUGHT HE was back there, back inside the nightmare of his war again. That is the only reason I can give for the shot, a merciless blast from only four feet away that should rightfully have taken the life of the man on the floor in an instant. Whatever Nick was seeing, whatever fantasies he had about the threat to him from the unarmed man, they did not include the respirator still clinging to the back of his head. The bullet glanced off the steel canister on the respirator, deflecting it away from the man.

I lunged at Nick, swept him into a headlock, and pushed the gun away in time to direct the second bullet into the wall. My partner's strength was furious. He dropped the gun, turned, and palmed me in the face so hard that my head snapped back into the wall.

"What the fuck, Cap!" he said.

"We've been ordered back to base!" I yelled, struggling for words. "We gotta go. We've been called in. Go! Go! Go!"

Nick seemed to take the bait. We ran for the door, swaying into the wall as the boat lurched again. On the deck outside the galley hatch, I spotted Effie on the bridge holding a gun on someone, presumably the captain, her attention torn between him and us.

"Come on!" I called, my voice almost drowned out by the sound of yelling from inside. "Let's go!"

Effie dashed down the stairs; a man appeared from behind her and fired a gun. Bullets pinged off the rails and lobster traps as we ran for our boat.

It seemed safe to speak only when the dark shape of Cline's boat had disappeared into the night. I tried to calm my thundering, sinking heart by telling myself that we had destroyed all of Cline's product on board. Probably millions of dollars' worth of stock. But the shaking in my limbs wouldn't quit, and dark thoughts swirled of Marni on her stretcher, of the man Nick had almost shot dead cowering against the cabinets. We had nearly murdered a stranger in cold blood to avenge Marni. It wasn't what she would have wanted, not at all.

When the red and gold lights of Gloucester Harbor lit my face, I turned and saw Nick sitting at the back of the boat with his head in his hands.

"You almost killed that guy," I said. It was perhaps cold and unnecessary, but I wasn't just talking to Nick. I was talking to myself too.

"I did bad things over there, in the war," Nick said. He heaved a heavy, shuddering breath. "They won't go away."

CHAPTER SIXTY

SUSAN SNAPPED AWAKE at the sound of the gunshot from the front of the house; she rolled off the bed and into a crouch in the corner of the room, out of view of the window, before she was even fully awake. For a moment her mind reeled, struggling to locate herself in time and space. Arkansas, 2012. Daseri's men had made her and were on their way up the dingy hotel stairs. No, wait. Gloucester, 2018. Cline's people, the Inn in the woods. She took her gun from the desk and crept to the door. Across the hall she spotted Malone, his high cheekbones and wild eyes illuminated by a silent television screen behind him. They locked eyes wordlessly and slipped out into the dimly lit hall.

A howl of pain from the front porch. Someone swearing, begging. Malone and Susan moved into the dining room, eased their way to the bullet holes in the wall.

"Stop your whining, you little pussy," Vinny growled as he wheeled slowly past. There was a man on the driveway clutching his knee, curled up in a ball in pain. Ten feet away from the man, probably flung there in the blast, a pistol lay on the pale gravel.

When Susan turned, Malone was gone, and there was a gun in her face.

"On your knees," the man said.

Susan put her hands up slowly, keeping her face neutral. She started to go down, waiting until she could see the tension in his body shift as he anticipated her surrender. That's when she struck, batting the gun aside, punching out as hard as she could. She was aiming for his balls but went a little high; her knuckles collided with a belt worn low, but the force was enough to shock him, double him over. She turned and felt his arms come around her and now the gun was in both their hands, the aim wavering over the walls, the ceiling. Malone slammed into them, wrenching the man's head back so that Susan could grab the weapon. Her mind was a constant hammering of half-formed thoughts, panic she had once been taught to keep at bay now unleashed as soon as it was triggered.

How many are there?

Is anyone in the house already dead?

CHAPTER SIXTY-ONE

SUSAN SWUNG THE pistol, tried to pick out the shape of the balaclava she had glimpsed in the dark, but before her was a tangle of shapes as Malone and the intruder wrestled. They crashed into the dining-room table, crushing a bookshelf, spilling books and ornaments. Someone got free— she heard the crunch of bones and a gasp of pain, and her heart sank as a silhouette appeared in the doorway, not Malone but a bigger, stronger man who glanced back as he headed down the hall.

"Stop!" Susan pointed the gun, but he was already gone. "Stop right now!"

He was in the kitchen. Susan ran and pushed the swinging door open, and almost immediately it swung back and hit her awkwardly, the shock enough to jolt the gun from her hands. His hands were on her wrists as he dragged her into the dark, and she twisted, planted a foot in his gut, and wrenched herself free. The knife block tumbled under her hands, spilling blades, but there was no time to get them. She grabbed a pot on the stove, turned, swung, and landed a solid blow to the side of a face. She heard what sounded like a tooth rattling as it hit the floor.

He was outnumbered and outmaneuvered and he knew it. Before Malone was fully through the door, Susan saw the shape of the intruder skirting past him. Susan and Malone rushed to the doorway in time to see the man run up the stairs, a desperate move, the intruder trying to hide in the house in the dark. He reached the second floor, and Susan's eyes were flooded with visions of who lay there sleeping and what he could do to them—stab them in their beds, bash their heads in, take them hostage. For a split second she could see all the atrocities she had witnessed over the course of her career, the howling mouths of the dead frozen, protesting their last violent seconds, in beds, in doorways, hanging over banisters, trying to claw their way out to escape.

Susan didn't make it to the second step. As the man reached the top of the staircase, Neddy Ives's door slammed open with tremendous force and smacked the intruder with as much power and desperation as he was using to get away. The collision seemed to shake the house.

Susan and Malone parted as the unconscious man tumbled down the stairs between them, a rag doll who came to a twisted stop at their feet.

Neddy Ives surveyed his work for a moment, gripping the door, his eyes hollow in the dim moonlight spilling in the second-floor window.

"Would you mind keeping it down?" he said quietly. "It's late."

Malone and Susan watched as he went back inside his room and closed his door.

CHAPTER SIXTY-TWO

I SAW THE flashing red ambulance lights from a long way off, and I slammed my foot down on the accelerator even before I could tell they were at the Inn. Having dozed off almost as soon as we left Gloucester's harbor, Effie jerked awake in her seat, like a robot suddenly switched to standby mode.

Almost all of the crew was on the porch in the eerie blue predawn, coats or blankets pulled around their shoulders, watching as two men were loaded into ambulances. Doc Simeon was briefing two paramedics, his hands covered to the wrists in blood. I leaped out of the car and silently counted my people like a parent counting kids, my heart hammering in my chest.

On the stretcher, a man I recognized from Cline's house was sucking oxygen and howling with pain, one knee swathed in thick bandages already soaked through with blood. Another man was cuffed and sitting up on a stretcher, looking mildly dazed as he was wheeled toward the vehicle. Blood dripped from his nose and mouth.

"You didn't tell me it was this serious," Malone said as I got to the porch. "Vinny stopped the first guy but the other one got inside."

"Vinny didn't just stop the guy," Doc Simeon said, walking past us toward the house. "That man will never walk properly again. His kneecap was shattered. Felt like eggshells in there."

Everyone looked at Vinny, who had a blanket with a large hole on it on his knees. His old hands were clasped on the fabric and his eyes were on the trees; he looked like a man watching a football game, half listening to us.

"I don't know what everybody's complaining about." He shrugged. "Guy's got another one."

Susan explained what had happened as the ambulances rolled on into the night. Angelica was leaning against a porch column, one hand on the back of Vinny's wheelchair.

"Maybe Doc doesn't approve of Vinny's violent approach," Angelica said. "But I think it was warranted. We've shown them that they can't come at us with force. They've shot at us. We've, uh . . . done some things to them too. Now I think the only course of action is to invite this Mr. Cline over here to discuss the issue of his leaving town. We could put together a nice lunch."

Vinny started laughing, a gravelly, hacking sound.

"What?" Angelica stroked the sling on her arm consolingly. "People of your ilk have them all the time in the movies. *Sitdowns,* you call them. With the, uh . . . the *consiglieri*?"

"All that time you spend making shit up in books has given you a real interesting perspective on life, Ange." Vinny nodded appreciatively.

"This whole event is like an allegory." Angelica looked around, her voice wistful. "The gunmen in the night. The porch here is like a theater stage, the silent trees beyond an army of judgmental yet silent souls."

"Dear God." I massaged my brow.

"Hey, innkeeper," Vinny said as I turned to go inside. "You want a real laugh, go talk to the sheriff. He's in the kitchen."

Susan followed me through the dining room and across a scattering of broken glass and splintered wood it seemed we had cleared away only a day earlier. I stopped in the hall and put my hands on her shoulders.

"I'm so lucky that you were here," I said. A stirring deep in my chest had begun, terror at the reality of the situation, the danger my guests had been in, the awful possibilities. "I might have come back and found them all dead in their beds."

"The people here can take care of themselves," she said. "It was actually Mr. Ives who dealt the finishing blow."

I didn't know what to make of that. The man with no past who dwelled in the room next to Marni's was emerging, and I had to admit I was feeling a shift in my perception of him. He'd always made me uneasy, like a monster that lives under the stairs, a shadow I crept past like a child. But I was starting to appreciate the guy who lingered in the dark, who could take out a fleeing suspect with a rickety old door and go back to sleep like nothing had happened.

Clay was in his usual position, leaning into the refrigerator, loading a plate in one hand with sandwich fixings. I saw in the gold light that at the back of his head, a patch the size of a playing card had been shaved and a mean-looking gash stitched closed. When he turned to us, I could see the beginning of two black eyes. He limped to the table and sat down, eased a heavy ice pack onto his crotch.

"Look at this, would you?" He sighed, gestured to his face. "I have to have a meeting with the school-district woman this morning. I'm gonna look like a panda."

"Christ." I sat down, put my head in my hands as he made his sandwich. "What happened?"

Clay explained about the abduction, the fight in the woods, half his story muffled by bites of an enormous sandwich and slurps of Miller Lite. Despite everything, a smile played on Susan's lips as she listened.

"So let me get this straight," she said. "Two days ago, a housewife nails you in the face with an encyclopedia, and tonight you fight off two guys with your hands cuffed behind your back?"

"It was a dictionary." Clay held the cool beer bottle to his forehead. "And I wasn't ready for her. These guys at least gave me a second to get my bearings."

"He's the *definition* of surprise." I elbowed Susan in the ribs but she just rolled her eyes. "See what I did there?"

"Any permanent damage, Clay?" Susan asked.

"No, they did all the scans at the hospital," Clay said. "I got to see pictures of my own brain. I've never seen it before. It looked good, I thought. The nurse said she had never seen a skull as thick as mine. Said it was like a coconut."

"You're amazing." Susan reached up and slicked down a

cowlick on the side of Clay's big head like she was patting the ear of a St. Bernard. "I'm just so glad you're home. I can't imagine dealing with…"

She was going to say "another death." I could see it in her eyes, the way she lowered them, almost with guilt. We'd lost Marni, and the loss of Siobhan lingered everywhere in the house, like the walls were painted with it. Clay let the pickle-chaser for his beer linger on his tongue a couple of seconds before he swallowed, savoring it like wine.

"So what's with the ice pack?" I jutted my chin toward the ice the sheriff was shifting carefully between his thighs.

"Weren't you listening?" Clay winced. "I *kicked* a knife out of a guy's *hand*. Must have been four foot off the ground. My body ain't built to move that way. I think I've strained something in"—he glanced at Susan—"in a man's most tender region." I smiled when something passed over his features as he went back to his meal, relief or perhaps some long-awaited, well-earned pride.

Though I might have sat forever watching Clay and Susan reveling in the triumphs of the night, I couldn't share their feelings of security. As soon as I turned away from them, I heard my phone pealing in the basement and I went to get it. Though the number was blocked, I knew exactly who it was.

CHAPTER SIXTY-THREE

WHEN CLINE SPOKE, there was a new edge in his voice. Though he tried to maintain his usual cool, smooth tone, I could hear the razor in his words.

"I bet you're celebrating," he said. "I bet you think you've done the right thing."

"I'll celebrate when you're exactly where you belong— behind bars or in the ground." I did not try to disguise the hatred in my voice. "You know, I met a few people like you when I was a cop. One of them told me that anyone who's killed will see their victims in their dreams. People who say they don't are lying. I hope Marni gives you every- thing she's got. I hope you wake up screaming for the rest of your life."

"I'll let you know." He laughed.

"You tried to come at my house and my people, and hopefully you realize now that you can't fuck with us. This is not your town, Cline."

"What should I do?" he wondered. "Shuffle on to the next little seaside shithole? Shall I tell them who sent me? I'm sure they'd be very grateful."

Cline had hit me right where it hurt. He knew that an enemy in plain sight was far less frightening than an enemy who suddenly disappeared, maybe taking his evil elsewhere or maybe waiting and biding his time nearby. The people who lived in whatever town Cline went to next wouldn't be ready for him. I had the measure of him. Or so I thought.

"You don't want me to go anywhere," Cline continued. "Face it, Robinson. This is the most alive you've felt since someone painted the road with your wife's entrails. I'm your purpose now."

I steeled myself against the guilty thoughts. No, Cline was not my purpose. My people, my house, my town—they were my purpose, and Cline was threatening them.

"You have a very inflated sense of your role in my life, Cline," I said. "You need to think less 'God walking the earth' and more 'Indistinct mass of crud in someone's boot tread.'"

"That sounds like a thing someone who's won would say," Cline said. "But I've got to remind you—you haven't won here tonight."

"You don't think?" I scoffed. "Your product is at the bottom of the ocean. Your guys are in the hospital."

"Yeah," he said. I could hear a mean smile in his words. "So what does a guy do when all his men have proved to be useless to him?"

I opened my mouth to answer, but the line went dead. I jumped at Susan's hand on my shoulder. She had crept down the basement stairs without my hearing her.

"Was that him?" She must have been able to tell it was from the look on my face. "What did he say?"

"I..." I drew a deep breath. "I think he's bringing in reinforcements."

CHAPTER SIXTY-FOUR

THERE WERE THINGS to do. There are always things to do when you have seven people under your roof and a rickety old house. But the events of the evening sent me into a kind of mental paralysis, and I could only wander around, looking out the windows, half expecting to see more of Cline's guys on their way to slaughter the people I loved. In time I managed to throw together one of my characteristically terrible breakfasts, this one watery scrambled eggs, deflated roasted tomatoes, and burned toast. I cleaned up the mess in the dining room and sat through the brief and uncomfortable interviews of all my residents with a couple of Clay's trusted officers, gold columns of morning light streaming through the bullet holes in the dining-room wall.

Clayton called at midday to tell me what I already knew:

Marni's tox screen showed she'd had enough fentanyl in her system to kill a horse.

When the sun was just climbing over the tops of the pines guarding the sea, I went to my car, which was parked at the edge of the woods. I figured I'd drive into town and run some errands, try to take my mind off things. I slid behind the wheel, looked over, and saw a backpack I didn't recognize on the seat beside me.

Thinking it must belong to one of the members of the house, I grabbed the bag to move it to the footwell so it didn't slide as I drove. The zipper wasn't closed, and thick stacks of cash spilled onto the floor of the car.

CHAPTER SIXTY-FIVE

THE HOUSE HAD fallen quiet again. I went to my bedroom in the basement and emptied the contents of the backpack onto my bed, stood staring at the heap of cash for a minute. I jogged up the stairs and shut the basement door, then pulled the small blind down over the window to the backyard.

I counted the cash. Eight hundred thousand dollars. There was a short note written on a piece of fine cream stationery. Cline didn't do anything cheaply. The note read simply: *Think carefully*.

I sat on the bed beside the cash. There was no need to think carefully. My whole body shook with fury. Cline thought he could buy me off after he had killed Marni, destroyed my house, threatened my friends. I began snatching up the bills and throwing them back into the bag.

I stopped to look at the cash in my hands, wondering what my next move should be. The only course of action, I supposed, was to give the money to Clay. There would be no proving Cline sent it to me. It would sit in an evidence locker until the State of Massachusetts claimed it as proceeds of crime. I fanned the bills with my thumb. The cash remaining on the bedspread was more than I had ever seen in one place in my life. This was what Cline paid in shut-up money. There would probably be more cash, keep-shutting-up money, if I accepted it and backed off. How many people was he paying to look the other way, surrender their turf to him? For the first time, the magnitude of his operation hit me.

A brief fantasy, like a flash across my eyes: A car. A house. Booze, parties, beautiful women. Sure, I wasn't the booze-parties-and-beautiful-women type, but money could make me that way. Fat stacks of money could do anything. Change my life. Change my *mind*. The guilt rippled through me as the seconds ticked by and the money stayed in my hands. No bad fortune immediately came crashing down on me. The money made me feel strangely good, even though it was just sitting here, stacks of paper sizzling with power and potential.

I was drawn out of my reverie by a gentle knock at the basement door. I shoved the cash and the backpack under my bed. At the top of the stairs, above the labyrinth of unpacked boxes and stacks of paint cans, ladders, and toolboxes, Susan opened the door. She hadn't been at breakfast, but she had showered and changed and looked fresh and ready to work. She didn't usually wear her hair up, so I had never noticed how perfect her ears were. Or maybe I had. Maybe in the fog of the past couple of years, I'd always known how beautiful Susan Solie was but had simply shut my mind to it, and all the trauma of the past few days had thrown open that door.

"I knew you'd be down here in your dungeon," she said, rubbing her arms. "I don't know how you stand it. It's freezing!"

"It's easier to sleep at low temperatures," I said.

"Come here," she said. "I want to show you something cute."

I followed her to the laundry room, where she pointed out the window. Angelica was sitting on a picnic table by the edge of the woods; Vinny was in his wheelchair on the other side. Vinny was describing something, maybe a scene from his past, pantomiming throwing open a door, pointing a pistol. Angelica's face had an unfamiliar expression—rapture and intrigue. She was actually laughing at the story.

"Man," I said. "Are those two interested in each other?"

"I don't know, but I'm glad to see her smiling. She can't write with her right arm in a sling and her left finger broken, and she's been totally miserable, like she's being starved or something." Susan grinned. "The two of them? It's crazy," she said, watching the couple. "But it could be great."

In the closeness of the laundry room, both of us leaning toward the window, I could feel Susan's body beside mine, the warmth of her hand by my thigh. I was struck by the same feeling I'd had on the beach, as if I were enclosed in a protective sphere, sealed off from the chaos of the world. My mind was twitching with temptations. I suddenly wanted to drag her to me, squeeze her, push her against the wall. I wanted to lie in bed with her and tell her everything—how lonely I felt in the dark hours without Siobhan beside me and how guilty I felt when I looked at Susan and hope and happiness flooded through me. I wanted to let it all go and admit to Susan that I liked her and that I didn't know what that meant. The two of us—it would be crazy. But I wanted to know if she thought it could be great. I was just about to ask her if she was still thinking about that kiss on the beach when I heard Doc Simeon clearing his throat behind us.

"Can I have a word with you, Bill?" he asked. Susan left us, and the doctor put his hands in the pockets of his immaculately ironed slacks, took a deep breath, and let it out slowly.

"I work for Cline," he said.

CHAPTER SIXTY-SIX

"YOU..." I SHOOK my head, tried to clear my mind. "You *what*?"

The old man walked past me and out onto the porch. I followed, and we sat together on the wicker chairs there, his back bowed as though under the weight of his confession.

"I've been retired for eighteen years," he said, staring down at his wrinkled hands. "That's a long time to feel like you have no purpose. Sure, it was my decision to retire. I couldn't keep up with all the new developments and the paperwork, and sometimes people would come to me with problems and my mind would just go blank. I'd have to look up treatments in medical journals. It wasn't right. But I've had nothing to work for in my life for so long now. No dreams. I went into a real depression maybe a year back and for a long time I wasn't able to shake it. I used to watch the clock all day just waiting for it to be a reasonable time to go to bed."

Vinny and Angelica had disappeared from the picnic table in the distance. The wind had risen, and the pines by the water stirred as the doctor talked.

"Mitchell Cline and his guys approached me at the town library," he said. He laughed a little bitterly. "I think perhaps they were prepared to threaten me. But they didn't need to. I accepted their offer. I was happy to do it."

"What do you do for them?" I asked.

"I write prescriptions for painkillers," he said. "Though I'm retired, my DEA license is still active. That's an identifier that the pharmacies need to distribute controlled substances, and the Drug Enforcement Administration uses it to keep an eye on narcotic prescriptions. Cline probably has plenty of physicians and pharmacists on the payroll."

"But who do you prescribe the pills to? Cline and his crew?"

"No," the doc said. "He brings me names and details. I don't know who the people are. They're probably stolen identities. Homeless people, maybe. I've never seen anyone in person. I prescribe whatever they want. Oxycodone. Vicodin. Fentanyl. Sometimes I just get a prescription pad, sign my name on every page, give it to them, and let them do the rest."

"You let them prescribe whatever they want?" I turned, clenched my fists, tried to resist the urge to scream. "This is why you wanted me to back off them."

I took a step toward the doctor, telling myself not to hurt him. I felt my resolve failing.

CHAPTER SIXTY-SEVEN

I GRABBED THE air right in front of the doctor's face but held myself back. I growled with fury and turned away.

"You've got every right to be angry with me," he said.

"Angry?" I snapped. "You acted like it was the people of this town you cared about when you asked me to walk away from Cline. You were just trying to save your own skin!"

"I still think you should look at the people who go to Cline for help," the doc said. "You don't understand what they go through."

"You would know," I said. "You're a part of all this!"

"I am." He nodded. "I'm a fundamental part of Cline's business. He and his crew take the pills they get through me and mix them and cut them with other things, then that goes into those little colorful capsules they sell."

The doc fell silent. I couldn't respond. It felt as though

Cline himself had reached inside me and was twisting my organs, laughing in my face. He had done more than send his guys to pepper my house with bullets, execute my people in their beds. He had been in my house the whole time. In Siobhan's house. His evil stink lingered in the halls, billowed through the rooms.

"Did he tell you to confess to me?"

"No," the doc said. "I don't think he knows I live here. I can't be sure. He hasn't mentioned it, and I saw him only two days ago. I have always dealt directly with the youngest member of his crew, a boy they called Squid. He's gone now."

"I can't believe this," I said, rubbing my eyes. I was suddenly exhausted.

"Neither can I," the doc said a little sadly. When I didn't respond, he opened his hands, trying to make sense of it. "I wish I had some reason to give you for doing it. Some understandable justification. But I don't. I'd been bored and lonely for almost two decades. I had enough money to survive comfortably but soullessly. And then someone came to me and said he'd pay me seven thousand dollars a week to sign meaningless little slips of paper. That first night, my head was filled with all kinds of dreams. I've been saving for a boat. I'd like to try to sail to Italy. Maybe see the Greek Isles."

I went to the corner of the porch and breathed slowly and evenly, trying to dissuade my body from reacting as it wanted to. I felt like punching the wall. Picking up the chair I'd been sitting in and smashing it to pieces.

There was also a burning for violence against the doctor

himself slithering like poison in my veins. He'd been dreaming of sailing around the Greek Isles while doling out the drugs that had helped kill Marni and countless others. But when I turned back to look at him, all I saw was a good, kind old man who'd done a terrible thing. The same guy who had leaped in to help a would-be assassin bleeding to death on my driveway, a man who had been a slave to his loneliness and purposelessness, just like me.

"What's your plan?" I asked. "You've told me the truth, and you must know I can't have you living here and doing what you've been doing."

"I'm going to leave." He nodded. "If Cline doesn't know I'm with you now, he'll find out soon enough. I'll be in danger. I've got plenty of money. Give me a couple of days to make arrangements, and then I'll be out of your life."

He started to leave, and I turned away, not wanting to watch him go. All that I wanted to say was left unspoken, just like it had been with Marni. Another person I cared about had been stripped from me by Cline's hand. I made a silent promise that he would be the last.

I'd thought the doc had gone inside, but then I heard his voice behind me as I stood looking out at the water. "For what it's worth," he said, "I'm sorry about your friend Malone."

"What do you mean, you're sorry about him?" I turned, and the old doctor looked surprised, uncertain. He shrugged a little sadly.

"If you don't know yet, I shouldn't be the one to tell you," he said. He left me standing there, my head full of questions I wasn't sure I wanted the answers to.

CHAPTER SIXTY-EIGHT

CLINE WAS POSSESSED by a level of rage that was so hot and wild, he felt like his brain was swelling, like his eyes were bulging from their sockets. He stood in his office looking out over the water, trying to calm himself. Below him, the gardener was just wrapping up for the day, throwing tools into the back of his truck with heavy clunking sounds. Downstairs, some of the clingy idiots drawn in by his money and power were blaring their lazy rap music. The pressure in his skull collected at the top of his spine.

Four of his best men were in the hospital. Bones and Simbo had apparently been beaten silly by the moronic local sheriff. Cline couldn't believe that. Unless the man had cornered his soldiers unexpectedly and sat on them, Cline didn't know how to account for Bones's ruptured kidneys and Simbo's skull fracture and broken arm. Then there were

Turner and Russ, who had approached a houseful of deadbeats and dropouts in the middle of the night and somehow wound up in the back of an ambulance, even though both of them were experienced killers. They'd been foiled by washouts and crazies sleeping in their beds. It was unthinkable.

Cline tried not to let his mind linger on what he had lost on the lobster boat. The fury was making his jaw ache. Between bursts of anger, he had tiny moments of fear, the unmistakable fingers of panic flicking and stroking wires inside his brain. News of a loss this horrendous, this complete, would get around. If Cline didn't recover quickly, someone would come for him. Cline had men, territory, respect, and he had built his business carefully, but now others might assume he was all fluff, easy prey; everything he had was lying exposed, one of his kingdom's walls shattered.

Cline walked down the stairs to tell the idiots in the yard to turn off their music. He was going to send them away, this little posse of sycophants Squid had brought to the house months ago who never seemed to leave. There were two girls who were always there, high-school dropouts like Squid most likely, wannabe gangsta bitches Instagramming themselves in his Jacuzzi while drinking his champagne and flashing gang signs. Cline liked having easy pussy around, but he hated their music. In Cline's day, rap had been about something. The song they were playing as he walked toward the French doors was just a sonic squealing and the word *juice* whispered over and over.

He stopped just outside the doors when he heard what the girls were discussing.

"...he was like nothing, man. Like some old cop dude from down Boston way. I seen the fool out here. He was the one put a plant through Cline's windshield, yo. The crew at his house is all like homeless people and women and retards and shit."

"And *they* fought off Russ and Turner? How did they do that?"

"Yeah, man. I don't know! I heard Russ's leg was, like, disconnected. Like detached. Some fucked-up cripple, one of the cop's guys, blew it off with an Uzi."

"You're shittin' me."

"Nah, man! Doctors had to sew it back on and all."

"Fuck. This old cop dude sounds ripped."

"Hell yeah. He some badass motherfucker."

Cline opened the door and saw the two girls on the couch, curled up together, their knees up and their feet on the cushion. One of them had shoes inset with lights that flashed different colors. He grabbed that one by the neck.

"What's that you were saying?" Cline asked as he marched the girl toward the fountain in the middle of his yard. She managed a squeal before he thrust her head under the water. Her friend followed them but she didn't know what to do; she stood nearby pleading and crying, wanting to reach for Cline but not having the courage. *Tough little gangsta bitch, huh?* he thought. Cline let the girl in his hands up for a second and then plunged her back under. He pressed her against the edge of the concrete fountain, his crotch against her cute little ass, pushing her head down hard until he could feel it scraping against the bottom of the structure.

He let her up. "The old cop, what did you say he was?"

"Nothing. Nothing! I didn't say—"

Cline plunged the girl under the water again. Her flashing shoes twisted on the pavement; her fingers clawed at his hand. He looked at the friend and counted the seconds off, the pain in his head easing considerably. The friend kept begging, but he couldn't hear her—there was only a warm, pleasant humming in his ears. He let the girl up and she coughed and vomited.

"What did you say?"

"He's nothing!" the girl blubbered. "Please! Please, man! I said he's a loser! He's...he...he ain't—"

Cline dunked her head. Lifted it. "What did you say?"

"A badass. I said he was a badass."

Cline dunked the girl again, held her under until she was spasming violently against him, urine mixed in with the water soaking them both, staining her white jeans. When he thought she was just about to go limp, he released his grip and let her slither down the side of the fountain. After a moment, she crawled away from him, a loathsome, soaking-wet creature, shivering and whimpering. He watched the girls hugging each other and sobbing, and he stretched his neck until he heard a crack, the tension and pain melting like butter.

"Who's the badass now?" he asked, and he turned back toward the house.

CHAPTER SIXTY-NINE

I NEEDED TO get away from the Inn, from the house where my friends were recovering from their wounds, where blue and red lights had flashed in the night and gunshots had shattered the windows. It was too emotional there for me to properly plan my next move. I invited Malone, Nick, and Susan out with me to the Greenfish and sat with them at a high table near the windows looking out on the street.

Nick and Malone went to order at the bar, and Susan sat close to me, turning a coaster over and over. I had told them about the doc on the way here, and it weighed heavily on everyone's shoulders.

"I just can't see that in him," I told her. "He's someone I thought I knew, and that scares me. It makes me feel like I don't know anyone in my house—that my house is full of secret keepers and liars."

I thought of Nick's words on the boat, of his claim that he had done bad things on his deployment. How bad were we talking? Why hadn't he, my best friend, ever confided in me?

"The doc's been in the house maybe . . . a year and a half?" I said. "He told me he hit a crisis point in his life a year ago. He was that low, low enough to accept Cline's offer, and I couldn't see it."

Guilt and rage picked at me. The words of fury at Doc Simeon rolled off my tongue so quickly and easily, and yet under my bed there was a bag of Cline's cash that I had not yet disposed of. I was one of the liars too. One of the secret keepers.

"Maybe Doc didn't want you to see it," Susan said. "You ever think of that?"

"But why not?" I asked. "I'm a good listener. I could have talked him through it."

"That's just the thing. You would've wanted to help him." She put a hand on mine. "You know how difficult it's been for you to let people help you with your grief over Siobhan."

I thought of Marni, of the memorial she had organized with the others only days earlier. Marni had poked a hole right through the cone of silence I had erected around myself about Siobhan. I'd thought that if I simply closed my ears and my mind to the memory of my wife, the pain of her loss might go away. But it turned out that Marni's intervention had been exactly what I needed. Cline had come into Doc Simeon's life when he was low, breaking through his inactivity and loneliness with sudden promises of purpose and adventure. The master of pain had offered to take the hurt away, and the old man had accepted.

Nick put a beer down in front of me and he and Malone sat down. "This guy is going to come at us again," Nick said. "We need to be ready."

"I don't know." Malone looked at me. "What can he do now? I mean, how many guys can he have? We put two of them on stretchers, and your local sheriff took care of two others. His little running boy Squid is under a rock somewhere in Augusta. Cline has got to be feeling threatened, at least for now."

"He'll have other guys," Susan said. "He might have to reach out to other distributors to get them, but there are always soldiers who are willing to make a name for themselves by doing the dirty work for a boss as powerful as Cline. The guys we took out just leave open spaces for these men to prove themselves. If you ask me, the first order of business for Cline will be getting rid of those men who are holed up and injured."

"He's going to kill his guys just because they got hurt?" I looked at Susan. I remembered Cline's words: *So what does a guy do when all his men have proved to be useless to him?*

"I think you can bet on that," Susan said. "When your men fail you, you clean house."

CHAPTER SEVENTY

"DRUG LORDS DON'T offer health insurance," Susan said. "While the injured men are out of action, they'll need to be paid to keep quiet or they'll be easy pickings for cops who want to question them, make offers."

I gripped my head, squeezed my eyes shut. Cline was right. I hadn't won; I'd just put more people in his firing line.

"You don't know this for sure," I said to Susan. "You're just guessing."

"Think about it." She shrugged. "We've got Turner and Russ approaching the house in the middle of the night, armed and hostile. If we can't prove attempted murder, we can at least go for weapons charges, assault, breaking and entering. With their records, which are likely to be extensive, they'll do serious time. Then there are Bones and

Simbo, who will be charged with kidnapping, assault, and attempted murder for what they did to Clay. Some or all of them will trade what they know about Cline for a better deal."

"They could get a lot of time off for being helpful," Malone mused. "They could argue that Cline intimidated them and coerced them into coming for us. They might get by with no jail time, or they could make a play for a minimum-security prison and witness protection after."

"But surely Cline's not going to come for them himself," I said. "He's a coward. He hasn't stepped out from behind his thugs since we've known him."

"He hasn't had to," Nick said. "But if we're right, these guys are just liabilities now. They better have security on their hospital-room doors. And not the local cops either. We know they're dirty."

The table fell silent. A group of young women were crowded around the old jukebox nearby, laughing and play-fighting over the music choices. Their happiness stood in stark contrast to the mood of the people around me.

"There are going to be more deaths," I said. I felt the truth of it in my bones. "Unless we stop Cline ourselves somehow, those four men are on the chopping block."

CHAPTER SEVENTY-ONE

NICK AND SUSAN ordered dinner, but I couldn't eat. I stood on the deck outside the bar and looked at the lights of Gloucester and the soft slope of the hill toward the water where the blinking port lights guided men home from the sea. I thought about Doc's words, his warnings about me suddenly removing the master of pain from the town and leaving the addicts who relied on him in the lurch. There would be men on the boats who used Cline's products to get through the relentless hours and backbreaking work of lobster and crab fishing off the coast, the brutal life they led trying to feed their families on the shore. How many people would be left desperate and sick if I took Cline out of the equation? And how long would it be before someone else took his place, preying on the young, the hurting, the hungry of our town with his deadly cocktails? I was deep in my thoughts when Malone appeared beside me, his face a welcome light cutting through my brooding.

"I don't know what you're doing sulking out here," he said. "I'd be in there with that lady if I were you."

"Who? Susan?"

"'Who? Susan?'" he repeated, imitating me. He laughed. "I've seen you looking at her, Bill. I've seen her looking at you. I've been dodging fireworks across the table all night."

I felt heat creeping into my collar. "Is it really that obvious? I guess Nick must know, then. Maybe they all know."

"Is it serious?"

"I don't—" I laughed, feeling stupid. "I don't know! I've kissed her once. With everything that's been going on, I haven't even had the chance to ask her if... if it was just a random moment or..." I opened my hands. "She said she'd wanted me to. But what does that mean? Was she talking about right then or has she been thinking about it for longer?"

"Look at you." Malone grinned. "You can't even talk about it!"

"I can't talk about it," I agreed, trying to cool my cheeks with the palms of my hands. He leaned on the rail beside me, and for a moment we looked just like we had years ago, two patrol cops marking time at the end of a night, watching boats in the city harbor.

"You remember that bomb threat we caught at the Meritage?" he asked, already grinning at the memory. I did. Malone and I had been newly assigned partners on patrol, tasked with assisting the Secret Service for the visit of an ex-president to Boston for Veterans Day. The president had been rushed out of the restaurant halfway through his spaghetti marinara when someone spotted a brown paper bag another diner had left under one of the nearby tables. A bomb threat had been called in to the president's hotel that morning, so the Secret Service agents were taking no chances. The entire building and half the waterfront were evacuated. Malone and I were told to go up to the restaurant and check that everyone was out, and like an idiot, I got curious about the package and decided to see if I could get a glimpse of what was inside the bag.

"I don't know what I was thinking," I said now, watching Malone as he tried not to laugh his ass off. "Maybe I thought I might have been able to hear it ticking or something."

"You were a hero." Malone laughed. "A true hero of the people."

I'd gotten very close to the bag on that fateful day, and I was so young and brazen that I'd reached out to see if I could open the bag and see inside. When my fingers were mere inches away, the bag moved.

"When that bag moved—" Malone was slapping the deck railing, laughing so hard he couldn't finish his sentence.

When the bag moved, I'd fallen back with a terror so sudden and all-consuming I'd almost fainted. The bag contained not a bomb meant to assassinate the president but two huge live Dungeness crabs that someone had obviously bought at the local market and planned to take home for dinner. When I'd recovered enough to stand, Malone and I had taken the crabs, their pincers bound, down to the waterfront to show the former president. The papers got a shot of me kneeling on the dock, clipping the creatures free of their bindings before I released them into the harbor.

While the *Globe* had been quite mature about it, other newspapers had a good time with the story. One headline read "Cops Catch Crabs; President Scuttles Away." I still had the newspaper clipping somewhere.

"I wonder if those crabs are alive now," I said as Malone tried to recover from the hilarity. "How long do crabs live?"

"I don't know. But if they're alive, they're probably still telling that story."

"Over drinks at their underwater crab bar," I said. "The Claw, it's called. I went there once. Nice place. A bit wet."

"Jesus." Malone sighed, watching the lights in the distance. "That was so much fun. We had a good time, didn't we? We were a great team."

"We're still a great team." I nudged him in the ribs, feeling how hard and prominent they were beneath his shirt. As though he could sense my concern, Malone turned to me.

"Look, there's something I've got to tell you," he said. He took a deep breath. "I didn't just come up here to hang out, to see the place. I wanted to know you'd forgiven me, because if you hadn't, I wanted to fix it before it was too late. I've got cancer, Bill. It's terminal."

CHAPTER SEVENTY-TWO

I LISTENED TO Malone tell me about his illness for as long as I could, then I crossed the bar to the restrooms to wash my face. I looked over at Susan, perhaps an involuntary reflex, my mind seeking comfort. She seemed to notice my distress, but I waved her off. I knew that if she asked me what was going on, I wouldn't be able to put it into words. Malone was leaving me and there was nothing I could do to stop it. Just like Siobhan had. And Marni. And Doc. I needed a minute to close my eyes and think.

I turned the corner to the hall where the restrooms were and saw a man with sweat-slick hair and grimy clothes carrying a stack of boxes toward the back door of the pub. He turned and caught my eye and nodded his head toward the door.

"Dude," he said. "Could you . . ."

I already had my hand on the doorknob of the men's room. In my sadness, my stupor, I didn't see the danger lurking.

"Sure thing," I mumbled. I pushed past him and opened the door. As I stepped out into the dark, he set the boxes down, came out, and slammed the door closed behind us. Another figure emerged out of the night and shoved me into the wall.

"Don't move, shitbird!" a voice snarled.

CHAPTER SEVENTY-THREE

I SHOVED BACK at the second figure, who was just a silhouette in the dark. In a moment I realized it was a woman, and I felt a pang of regret as she stumbled away from me.

"Hey! Hands off, asshole!" the guy who'd been carrying the boxes said.

"Hands off?" I pushed him. "What the hell is this?"

The moon emerged from behind a cloud and I caught a slice of his face. I recognized him now—it was the gardener I had seen at the side of Cline's house the day Nick and I confronted him.

"This is a thank-you." He stuck his finger in my face. "My partner and I have been on Mitchell Cline for three months. You and your idiot friends cost us the biggest drug bust in Massachusetts history last night."

The realization of what was happening was like a punch to the gut. "You're undercover cops?"

"Boston PD," the woman said. She was stocky and square-jawed and had small, mean eyes. "We've been brought in because the locals are on Cline's payroll."

I struggled to comprehend what they were saying, my mind still reeling from Malone's revelation and the sneaky maneuver the two of them had used to get me outside the bar. I supposed they knew one of Cline's men could be inside watching me and they didn't want to blow their cover. Someone tried the door behind me, but the male cop butted it shut with his shoulder.

"What's your goddamn problem with Boston PD, Robinson?" The male edged closer to me, his face now just inches from mine. I could smell nicotine gum on his breath. "You trying to fuck up our operation as revenge for getting canned by the commissioner?"

"Back off." I shoved him away. "I didn't know you geniuses had an undercover operation going. Are you seriously posing as Cline's gardeners? What are you doing, peering in his windows and watching him eat breakfast while you prune his rosebushes?"

"That's as close as we've been able to get," the woman said. "Cline handpicks his crew from the streets, and they sweep the house daily for bugs. He never interacts with anyone but his soldiers, and when they're outside the house, they never talk shop."

"We've sent in potential crew members, prostitutes, corrupt cops looking to get onto his payroll," the man said. "We even flipped the guy's cousin and sent him in for a friendly family visit wearing a wire. Nothing. This guy won't even discuss his business with his own flesh and blood. Just to get in as gardeners, we had to construct foolproof fake identities, and all we get to listen to day in and day out is the shitty music his people play in the backyard while we pull up his weeds. We can't get anywhere near Cline."

"The drug boat was going to be our big payoff." The woman poked me hard in the chest. "And *you* fucked it up."

Nick, Malone, and Susan came running around the side of the bar; they must have sensed something was wrong. Nick and Malone were reaching for their guns, causing the two cops to reach for theirs, but I stepped between the two sides, my arms out. "Stop! Stop! It's okay."

"Who the hell are these pricks?" Nick got right up in the male cop's face; they were nose to nose, as if they were two wolves fighting over food.

I explained the situation as both parties stood glaring at each other.

"If you knew the drug boat existed, why didn't you just hit it?" Nick shook his head.

"We had a tracker in one of the tubs of product," the female cop said. "We had another one on Cline's car. We were waiting for the two to meet. We were going to jump on him then, but you idiots dumped it all into the sea."

"We were trying to protect our town," I said. "We want this guy out of here as much as you do."

"Yeah, well, you just did him a favor," the woman said, taking a pack of cigarettes from her back pocket and sticking one in her mouth. "And you—" She looked at Susan. "I'd have expected more from a fed. You let these guys go running around like vigilantes while you sit back and write stories about circus hamsters for the local rag?"

"Circus hamsters?" I looked at Susan.

She rolled her eyes. "A local kindergartner taught his hamster to walk a tightrope he made out of shoelaces. I needed a feel-good filler." She turned to the undercovers. I could see a new tension in her face. "You shouldn't have that information," Susan said. "Who gave you approval to do a background check on me? I'm not a part of your investigation!"

"You became a part of it when this guy"—the woman gestured to me—"turned up and put a potted plant through the windshield of Cline's car. We wanted to know who we were dealing with. Turns out it's a bunch of renegade dumb-asses."

"These dumb-asses have done more damage to Cline in two days than you have in months," Susan said. "Take a look at yourselves before you go insulting them."

The female cop came toward me. Though she had to look up at me, she was still intimidating, her features hard and taut.

"Stay off Cline." She poked me again. "Or you'll find yourself sharing a jail cell with him."

CHAPTER SEVENTY-FOUR

SIMBO COULDN'T BELIEVE it had come to this. He sat on the edge of the motel bed and looked at his hands. They were still trembling. This was not how it was supposed to go. He'd been with Cline for three years and never slipped, never gotten himself tangled up in a felony arrest that would be worth betraying his boss to squeeze out of. Cline had made it clear from the beginning: If you go down for serious time, you're dead. It didn't matter if Simbo decided to trade Cline in. The man was going to come for him in any case.

The police had come after him, of course. Within minutes of Simbo arriving at the hospital with a concussion due to the door inside the Inn opening in his face, there were two cops standing at the end of his bed. They were Boston undercovers who looked familiar, for some reason, a man and a woman with the keys to his handcuffs. Simbo had told them what they wanted to hear, made them promises, waited until their backs were turned, and split. He wouldn't turn Cline in. Maybe that would help when the man came for him.

Maybe he'd make an exception as he had before.

Cline never hired users. It was another one of his policies. Simbo went to the filthy motel bathroom now and stared at himself in the cracked mirror, tried to breathe through the nausea. He remembered the first time he'd laid eyes on Cline, a face in the back seat of a shiny black Escalade watching through the window as Simbo beat a homeless man half to death with a tire iron. The man had come for Simbo's stash, which Simbo had spent the whole day getting, kneeling between the legs of men in business suits in expensive cars, using his body and his mouth because he had nothing else to offer. Simbo had thought Cline was just another one of these men indulging their secret desires on the way home to the wife and kiddies. But instead, Cline had been the one offering something—a way out, a use for the violence and fury Simbo was so accustomed to.

Simbo washed his face, tried to stay calm. He went and opened the bottle of Jack Daniel's he had brought with him, drank half of it in nervous, jittery gulps, watching the television without really seeing it. After a while, he pulled back the curtain at the front of the motel room, checked the parking lot. Empty. He crawled into bed and lay wide-eyed in the dark, twitching at sounds in the street.

He didn't know he was asleep until he felt the man land on him. Simbo tried to roll over, but Cline had braced his legs on either side of him. He felt the scratch of something plastic coming down past his nose and then a loop pull tight around his throat. "You knew the rules," Cline said.

Simbo grabbed at the zip tie, buried so deep in the flesh of his neck that his fingers could only scrabble at the band impotently while the pain rushed to his head. Sounds were coming out of him that he didn't recognize, but the noise of his choking was soon drowned out by the blood screaming in his ears. He fell off the bed, thrashed and kicked, his limbs out of control, refusing to pull him toward the door. Cline flicked the light on and stood there watching, his arms folded. Simbo's whole body was convulsing violently. The seconds ticked by. Cline got bored and glanced around the room at the peeling veneer of the particleboard cabinets, the moldy floral curtains. In the street, a homeless man was yelling at someone; an ambulance rolled by, sirens wailing.

Cline's gaze returned to Simbo as he spasmed and flailed violently on the floor, taking his time to die. "Look at this place." Cline smirked. "You didn't end up very far from where you started."

CHAPTER SEVENTY-FIVE

SUSAN CLIMBED INTO my car when we left the bar. Malone wanted to get some supplies for home, and he and Nick headed into town. My thoughts were so tangled as I drove along the wooded roads toward the Inn that I couldn't keep track of what Susan was saying. Had I done the right thing in starting all this with Cline? People were dying, and he remained in our town in his castle on the hill, like Dracula preying on the villagers below him, trying to decide whose blood he wanted next. Susan put her hand on my leg and I found myself squeezing it, the way I had done with Siobhan so long ago.

"I'm sorry." I glanced at her. "I'm a million miles away."

"Talk to me," she said. "What did Malone tell you? When you came in from the deck, you looked devastated."

I told her about Malone's diagnosis, what little I knew. It

was stage four, inoperable. Chemo and a spate of experimental treatments hadn't worked.

"He has about two months," I said. "Maybe less. I thought he could just stay with us at the Inn. He doesn't have anyone else."

"We'll take care of him," she said.

"He came back to reconcile with me before it was too late. About Boston," I said. She was silent, waiting, probably not wanting to say anything that might tip me one way or the other about telling her. I focused on the road ahead, gripped the steering wheel, and for the first time since it happened, I told the terrible story of my downfall.

CHAPTER SEVENTY-SIX

"MALONE CAME TO me at the end of our shift one night,"
I said. Susan settled back in the passenger seat to listen. "He
said he had a problem. A good friend of his, a woman he
went to college with, needed help. Her daughter had gotten involved with a real psycho, a violent, abusive guy, and
while they were together, they made a sex tape. It was stupid, of course. The girl was young and she'd been trying to
make her parents mad, so she went for the typical bad boy.
She broke up with him, but now the guy was saying he was
going to put the tape on the internet unless she got back
with him, and once it was out there—"

"It's out there forever." Susan eased air through her teeth.
"Shit."

"Yeah," I said. "Exactly. All this boy had to do was click
a button. He said if she brought cops into the picture, he'd

post it. So Malone came to me with this plan all worked out. He wanted to go to the boy's apartment while he was out and steal the computer that the girl said had the video on it. I said I was in."

On the road ahead of us, a mother deer and two fawns sprang onto the asphalt, danced in the gold light, then leaped into the trees. I watched them go, feeling a weight ease off my shoulders as I spoke.

"The night we show up at the guy's building, Malone's got an empty backpack with him. I didn't ask questions about it—hardly noticed it. He says all he needs me to do is guard the lobby, so I do just that. He goes up to the apartment, and after a while he calls me in a panic. The guy is there. Malone was sure he wasn't, but he came out of a back bedroom and Malone's holding a gun on him. I go up there and..." I took a breath. The words were tumbling out of me, bottled up for too long. "I just lost it."

"What did you do?" Susan asked.

"Look, I had a case when I was a brand-new officer. Boston cops are walk-around cops. The brass like you to be seen out there on the streets, you know? Out of the cars and talking to the people. Well, one day, Malone and I are running down the street responding to reports a guy and his girlfriend are fighting outside a café. As we turn the corner to break up the fight, he's got her by the hair. She frees herself and runs away from him—right into the path of a city bus." I exhaled slowly. "I didn't see a lot of bad shit in my time on the beat. I was pretty lucky. But that was bad."

Susan reached over and held my hand. I squeezed her fingers.

"So, in the apartment with Malone, I beat this guy up," I said. "I admit it. I mean, I broke bones. I thought he had been whaling on his girlfriend and he'd put the icing on the cake by threatening to ruin her life. Malone tried to stop me, but I really did a number on him. And then as we're leaving, I see Malone's backpack is full."

"Oh no," Susan said. Her voice told me she could see ahead, into the depths of my downfall.

I continued. "In the hall I say to Malone, 'What's in the bag?' and he says, 'I don't know which device the kid's got the tape on. I took laptops, tablets, hard drives, everything. I'll find the file, delete it, and send the stuff back.' Already I'm fuming, because this is not what I agreed to. We go our separate ways that night, and the next morning Malone's on top of the world. I figure the girl and her mother must have thanked him, and the boyfriend had taken the beating and maybe learned from it. It must have all gone perfectly."

I gripped the steering wheel hard, trying to shut down all the screaming voices in my head, the thoughts about what I could have and should have done to stop what happened.

"Turns out there was no girl," I told Susan. "No sex tape. It was all lies."

CHAPTER SEVENTY-SEVEN

"THE APARTMENT MALONE robbed—*that I helped him rob*—belonged to Ivan Pilkos, an illegal arms dealer in Boston," I said. "Malone took a quarter of a million bucks from the guy, and then I go in there and bash his head in about some girlfriend and some tape that never existed. Pilkos was just some low-level scumbag Malone had heard was all cashed up. He'd never even met the guy. He was asleep on the couch when Malone walked in."

"Oh my God." Susan covered her mouth. I nodded.

"What Malone didn't realize," I said, "is that across the street from the apartment building was a private storage facility. A *big, expensive, highly exclusive* private storage facility. This place has storage boxes and vaults for rich people who don't trust banks, and it has cameras all over the front of the shop."

"But surely he looked for cameras," Susan said.

"There were obvious ones and hidden ones," I said. "Malone thought he was taking us in at the right angle so the cameras couldn't see us, but he didn't know about the hidden ones. The firm was so paranoid, they had cameras all over the street. Sure, they wanted to get video of the robbers when they were inside the facility, but they also wanted video of their car, their escape route, their getaway driver. The cameras got Malone and me outside the apartment building. They got video of us in the lobby. They even got a shot through the apartment window of Malone stuffing his backpack with stacks of cash. A rooftop camera. Clear as day. It was unbelievable."

I sighed, exhausted.

"The people who worked for the secure facility thought we were common burglars, and they turned the footage in to the department," I said. "We were fired two weeks later."

"Did they take back the money Malone stole?"

"The department wanted to keep it quiet," I said. "Keep it away from the press. A story about dirty cops in Boston would have been front-page news for a month. They asked Malone where the cash was, but he clammed up. He was fired anyway, and he knew they wouldn't prosecute him. Pilkos wouldn't press charges on the beating. There was a search of Malone's place for the cash, but nothing was found."

"Why did he take it?"

"He said back then it was because he was in debt," I said. "I knew he'd bought his apartment at the wrong time, and the market downturn had left him in trouble. But tonight he told me that he came up with the plan just after his diagnosis. He wanted to get experimental treatments that insurance wouldn't pay for. He gave twenty years to the city and he wanted something back. I mean, I understand where he was coming from. That money would have been used for a good cause. Who knows what Pilkos was planning to do with it?"

I shifted uncomfortably in my seat. It seemed, for a moment, that Susan could read my mind. That in the closeness of the car, she might have sensed my secret, the cash under my bed. When she spoke, it was a relief.

"You didn't try explaining what had happened to the commissioner?" Susan asked. "Telling her why you got involved?"

"There was nothing to explain," I said. "I was guilty. I'd robbed and beaten a man. Just because I thought what I was doing was right didn't excuse it. And turning Malone in would have been serving my best friend up on a platter." I looked at her. She was watching me, her eyes dark and thoughtful. "Whatever wrong I've done in the world, I'd never turn in a friend."

"Has he apologized?" Susan asked. "I mean, I don't want to be judgmental. I don't know what was going on in this man's life. But you were his partner. He betrayed you."

"What can the guy do? He can't take it back."

"Well, he owes you," she said, sitting up in her seat. "Big-time."

I drove in silence, thinking about Susan's words. After a while, I began to pick out a familiar stretch of road from the darkness, the trees and hedges that I knew led me past somewhere I did not want to go. I spotted the house in the distance and saw that a light was on in one of the windows.

I made the decision and latched onto it, afraid that if I questioned it at all, I would change my mind.

"What are we doing?" Susan asked as I pulled the car over outside my wife's killer's house.

CHAPTER SEVENTY-EIGHT

CLINE LIKED A purge night, liked to get all his business taken care of in one hit, before his targets could scatter like roaches from a kitchen light. The first time he'd cleaned house, he'd wiped out his whole crew only weeks after assembling them. He'd found out he had a rat in his pack when a cop had dragged him in and told him about it; the cop wanted half Cline's stash for the favor. Cline had called the crew in, told them there was a last-minute job on, and driven them to a field in a big van. Then he'd turned around in the driver's seat and said nothing while he sprayed them all with an automatic like fucking Tony Montana. Made them dance in their seats. He'd sat in the field afterward and watched the van burn, the coiling smoke and embers rising into the night. He'd felt pure.

Now he closed the door of the Escalade quietly, put his

gloved hands in the pockets of his coat, and counted off the street lamps as he walked toward Addison Gilbert Hospital's parking lot. He pulled his cap down low on his brow as he crossed the lot and opened the back door that Dr. Raymond Locke had left unlatched for him.

There'd be no playing around with Russ the way there had been with Simbo. He'd knelt by Simbo's body after the thrashing stopped and looked at the red starbursts in the whites of his eyes, the colors still leaking in the last stutters of his heart. Cline walked the halls of Addison Gilbert and took the stairs to the second floor, following the scrape marks in the paint of thousands of gurneys passing.

Cline found the curtains pulled around bed fourteen. He checked his weapon, nosed the gun between the curtains, and shoved the fabric aside suddenly. The skinny white guy in the bed jolted awake.

Cline recalculated quickly. Let the gun waver just an inch. "Who the fuck are you?" he snarled.

The guy didn't answer. Cline lifted the chart from the bottom of the bed. Russell Hamdy. Right name, wrong target. Cline walked down the hall, swept the curtains back from all the other beds, checked the vile snoring and moaning creatures he found there.

In the parking lot, sweat seeping into the arms of his coat, he saw a black blob lumbering between the vehicles. He recognized her from the ER. Cline walked up behind the woman and stuck the gun in the back of her neck. She froze against her flamingo-pink coupe, the cardboard box of fluffy, shiny treasures in her hands pinned against the window.

"Russell Hamdy," he said. "Where is he?"

She turned, and Cline stepped back. Yes, this was the one he'd seen at the triage desk once when he'd come to speak to Locke in the ER; he remembered her ridiculous yellow claws and regrettable pink eye shadow. Bess was her name, he thought. A big buffoon in a clown outfit. She didn't even look at the gun.

"I thought you'd come." She smiled, shifted the box in her hands. "When they brought Mr. Hamdy in, I knew it was connected to you. That's what happens when someone like you comes into town. First you get the overdoses, then you get the suicides, then you get the kneecaps blown to dust. And people like me who won't shut up about it, who won't stand by and let you keep on killing—we get sent packing."

Cline looked at the box she was holding. He could see a novelty mug with a little crown on it that said SASSY SINCE BIRTH.

He thought about asking her again where Russ was stashed, but the defiance in her eyes told him he was wasting his time.

Cline raised the gun in both hands.

CHAPTER SEVENTY-NINE

SUSAN SEEMED TO know my purpose, though to my knowledge she had no idea where Monica Rink lived. I exited the car without waiting for her and started walking up the pebble driveway. Cline had offered to tell me what happened the night Siobhan died, and I'd refused to hear it. But his words had started a fire in me, one that was threatening to consume me. I couldn't wait any longer.

An orange cat fled out of my way, leaping into a hedge, as I advanced toward the door.

"Bill, stop." Susan grabbed my hand as I went to knock. "You don't know what you're—"

I knocked. We waited, Susan still holding my hand. I looked at her and realized she was scared, frightened for me, perhaps, and the heartache I was about to put myself and Monica through. A figure in a green T-shirt, maybe expecting someone else, bounced to the door and opened it.

I recognized her from the photographs in the paper after my wife's death. Her mouth was big and expressive, turning before my eyes from an expectant grin to an uncomfortable grimace. She knew exactly who I was. Monica grabbed her flame-red ponytail as though for comfort and glanced back into the empty hall.

She couldn't speak, so I did. "I'm not here to cause trouble," I said, putting my hands up.

"I can't—" She tried to shut the door, but my foot was in the way. Susan tugged on my arm.

"Bill, this isn't a good time," she said. "You're upset about Malone. It's been a rough week. You need to just—"

"No, *you* need to just." I pointed a finger at Monica. "Just tell me the truth. It's been long enough. I can't take it anymore."

The young woman hesitated, looked back into the hall again. I wondered if there was a boyfriend or some friends there whom she was mentally begging to call the police. I could imagine them, a posse of twenty-somethings slumped in beanbags waiting for pizza or more friends to arrive so they could watch a horror movie and cuddle together. Generally enjoying their lives, the way Siobhan had once. Siobhan had been a twenty-something, and then she had grown, matured, married me, created a dream of running an inn by the sea and falling asleep to the sound of waves on the shore and wind in the leafless trees. I held the door just in case Monica thought she could kick my foot away.

"It *has* been a rough week," I said, locking eyes with the

woman whose very house made my stomach shrink. "I've lost some people I love, and I've learned that not only are there terrible things behind me, but more of them are coming my way. I'm taking this moment to cut the bullshit." I squeezed Susan's hand. "I want answers. What happened that night? What happened to my wife?"

Monica drew a deep breath. Her lips worked around silent, agonized stutters. "I h-hit your wife accidentally. Siobhan Robinson. I was alone in the car. There's nothing more for you to know except that I'm...I'm...I'm so sorry."

I looked at the girl before me and knew she was lying. Susan pulled on my arm again, and I almost let her lead me away. I was telling myself that I had all the answers I was going to get when a figure stepped into the hall behind Monica Rink.

She was smaller than Monica. Same fiery hair and lean, waiflike frame. A little sister, seventeen, maybe a touch older. She yanked white earbuds from her ears at the sight of me. I looked at the young girl across the miles between us and knew the truth. Monica took advantage of my shock and slammed the door in my face.

Susan put an arm around my shoulders and led me toward the car.

"That young girl—" I began.

"I know," Susan said.

"She was the driver," I said. I could feel that my eyes were wild as I tried to take in everything about this moment, not thinking of the horror or comfort that it might bring. I looked at the stars as we reached the car. "The younger girl was the driver. She'd had a couple of drinks. The vodkas open in the footwell of the car. She hit Siobhan and called her sister for help. Monica Rink covered for her little sister."

"That girl couldn't have been old enough to drink." Susan gripped me by the shoulders, her dark blue eyes square on mine. "She did something incredibly reckless and stupid. She killed a woman on the side of the road. Monica probably covered for her to save her from the stain on her record or . . . I don't know. The shame. The stories. Bill, you saw that little girl's face as well as I did. She's never going to escape what happened."

"I want to go back." I turned toward the house. "I need to tell her it's okay. I'll tell them both it's okay. That I forgive them. They didn't mean to do it."

Susan pulled me to her and pressed her lips against mine. I put my arm around her waist and drew her closer, sought that safety in her embrace that I'd experienced once on the beach, that sealing-off from the world. There were tears on her cheeks or possibly mine; I couldn't tell. I held her to me and breathed her in.

"Let's go home," she said.

CHAPTER EIGHTY

SUSAN AND I walked around the side of the house, knowing we were probably being tracked by Effie's gun, and sneaked up onto the end of the porch in case Vinny was camped out near the dining-room windows. Like naughty children, we crept through the hall and the kitchen, pausing at the sink to push and grab at each other, moaning between kisses, her hands fumbling at my belt. Someone came halfway through the kitchen door, saw our tangled silhouettes, and backed out quickly. We froze and listened to the retreating steps, laughed guiltily.

I didn't want to rush things. We were hot in each other's arms, sweating with anticipation, shivering with excitement. There was a strange relief tingling in my body at Susan and I finally knowing, at least in this moment, what we wanted from each other. Maybe I was high from having looked my wife's killer in the face, knowing after so many nights worrying that it had all been an awful accident, a mistake. I took a bottle of cold water from the fridge, and we both drank from it, looking at each other in the golden light, smiling.

We went to her room and I shoved her onto the bed, listened to her laughing in the dark.

CHAPTER EIGHTY-ONE

A FOREIGN BED. The unfamiliar pattern of Susan's soft breathing. Creaks and groans in the house that I did not recognize from my time sleeping in the basement. I lay awake for hours thinking about Cline, about how he had crept into my life and taken it over. There was no doubt in my mind that for all the terror and heartache he had inflicted on the people sleeping in the rooms around me, I was the one who'd allowed him through the door to our world. I had been the one searching for a purpose. Wanting a fight. If I'd just stopped Winley Minnow trashing his family's house and not taken things any further, Marni might still have been alive. As would the men Cline had taken out for failing him. When my stirring seemed to be drawing Susan out of her dreams, I crept down to my room in the basement.

I took the backpack full of cash out from under the bed

and heaped the stacks on the coverlet. Looked at the note Cline had left me.

Think carefully.

People had died in my selfish pursuit of Cline. Would it be selfish now to leave the battle? The money before me was offered on the condition that I walk away and leave Cline to his own business. I picked up a stack of cash and flipped through it, felt the electric pulse of the power tied to what the simple pieces of paper represented.

"Oh my God."

I jumped. Susan was standing in the dark behind me, tying the belt of her robe.

"What...what is..." She looked at the money. At me. I watched emotions flicker across her face, confusion and hurt.

"I got it yesterday," I admitted, and I handed her the note from Cline. She took a stack of money from my hand and looked at it.

"You didn't tell me."

"I didn't tell anyone," I said. I let her take in what that meant. A coldness came over her features and she dropped the stack and the note back in the pile.

"You son of a bitch," Susan said softly. Her eyes were two pinpoints of light caught in the dim blue flooding through the window. "You're not thinking of—"

"That's exactly what I'm doing," I said.

CHAPTER EIGHTY-TWO

"I'M THINKING," I said. "Listen to me. I've been lying awake thinking all night. We're relying very heavily on the idea that we're going to stop Cline. That eventually he'll wind up where he belongs, in a prison cell or at the bottom of a six-foot hole. But how many more losses are we willing to accept before that happens? Marni's gone, Susan. And it's because of me."

"It's not because of you." Susan shook her head. "You couldn't possibly have guessed what Cline would do to her."

"But what if I'd just walked away in the first place?" I asked. "What if I'd just turned my back? She'd still be alive."

"This isn't about what-ifs!" Susan yelled.

"It is," I said. "That's exactly what it's about." I turned and sat on the bed, picked up a stack of the notes. The admission came slowly, eased through my tight throat.

"There's . . . there's something I didn't tell you about Siobhan and me. The night she was killed, she had gone into town to get things for dinner. That's what we did after we had a big fight. We'd make a nice dinner, have a couple of glasses of wine. Reconnect with each other. She liked the walk into town and back, but she also wanted that time alone to think through what we'd said to each other during the fight."

"What did you fight about?" Susan sat down on the bed beside me.

"This house, this town," I said. "This was her dream, not mine. And I guess when I lost my job in Boston, I was too shocked and numb to really think about what we should do next. We sold our house and found this place and bought it before I'd really stopped to ask myself what I wanted. I missed my job. I missed the city. I didn't feel like I belonged here, and I blamed her for not realizing that I hadn't been ready to make big, world-changing decisions."

Susan leaned into me. Her shoulder against mine was warm.

"I ask myself all the time—what if? What if I'd put my foot down? What if we'd stayed in Boston? Or what if we had come here and I'd just been stronger, taken the change in stride, hadn't fought with her that night? She'd still be alive. This cash? It's not just cash. It's another what-if. We know what Cline is capable of. What if we back off now?"

"I can see what you're looking at when you look at this money." Susan nodded. "You're seeing yourself selling this place. Taking the cash. Setting yourself up comfortably back in Boston. Forgetting Cline. Forgetting what happened here."

"Maybe. I mean, there are other things I could do with the money. Share it. Give it to someone who needs it."

"Whatever you do with it, it would be a way for you to stop fighting and pretend everything's okay," Susan said.

"Maybe it *would be* okay, after a while," I said. I looked at her, and I saw one possible future realized so perfectly. Susan and me in an apartment in Boston, just like Siobhan and me, the circle of time closed and everything that had happened in Gloucester conveniently erased. I could find some kind of law enforcement job in my city. The police department wouldn't hire me, but someone would.

Susan took my hand and rested her chin on my shoulder. The feel of her and the smell of her was not my lost wife, and I realized I was an idiot to think I could go back in time. I looked at the cash and the backpack and suddenly thought of Malone. Had he been seeing his future when he opened the safe at Ivan Pilkos's house and started shoving stacks of bills into his backpack? Malone had wanted to take the money, start again, pretend everything was okay. I understood now what had made my friend cross to the dark side. It was his actions and mine on that fateful night that sparked all the tragedy and pain that had happened since.

I put the stack of money I was holding back into the bag. Susan met my eyes, and she knew I had made a decision. She smiled at me in the dark.

We had lain on the bed in each other's arms, our heads together on one pillow, for only a second or two when I smelled the smoke.

CHAPTER EIGHTY-THREE

SUSAN AND I couldn't find the source of the smoke anywhere inside the house, so we crept to the front door. The night was still and silent, silver and blue in the light of the moon. The smell of burning wood was unmistakable. I looked at the clock in the entryway; it was 4:00 a.m. I ran to the basement to get my coat and gun while she ran up to her room to get hers.

We met at the door, and the air misted at my lips as we crept across the porch and down the stairs. The eeriness of the stillness before me set my teeth on edge. My mind turned a hundred shapes into the silhouettes of men with guns. I wanted Susan to follow me, to let me guard her, but she walked ahead, her gun out, following the smell of the burning. I looked up as we passed beneath Effie's window and saw her thrust open her curtain, the smell having reached there, her enormous rifle tracking me as she identified my shape in the dark. I waved at her to stay where she was. She nodded.

In the darkness, I spotted the firepit on the east side of the house. The fire was lit. On the bench in the light, a man sat with his arms resting between his legs, his head down. Shadows picked at his shoulders and the dark pattern on the front of his dress shirt.

Susan stepped to the side and we stood before the man, our guns trained on his head.

"Don't move," I said. I kept my voice low. All I needed was for the household to wake in panic at another attack in the dark hours. I didn't know who else was out there in the night watching. Had this man come alone, or was his presence and the fire a decoy for an ambush? I noticed Susan's pulse was hammering in her neck.

"What do you want?" Susan asked.

The man didn't answer. I stepped closer and realized the dark pattern on the front of his shirt wasn't a design.

It was blood.

CHAPTER EIGHTY-FOUR

"HE'S DEAD." SUSAN shuddered. Her hand fluttered near her mouth, but she regained her composure quickly. We rounded the fire on opposite sides and went to the man. He was small, thickly built. His head was bruised and scabbed with wounds at least a day old, but a huge, smiling gash across the front of his throat was new, still wet. I looked out into the dark forest, saw no one. There were drag marks in the dirt and leaves leading up to the bench. I fished in his back pocket and drew out a small leather wallet.

"Stanley Turner," I said. "This is one of Cline's guys."

"What is this?" Susan was out of breath, on the verge of panic. "A sick present?"

"He's been dead a little while." I ran a hand over the body. He was cold in the back and warmed in the front by the fire. "Killed somewhere else. There's no blood on the ground." I looked back at the house, thinking, oddly, of Angelica. The sight of a body with a gaping neck wound propped up a few yards from her bedroom would send the fragile author into conniptions. A strange, detached consideration in the peak of my terror; I supposed my mind was seeking safe ground.

"What do we do?" I dragged Susan out of the light of the fire in case we were being watched. "Is Clay here?"

"No, not that I know of," she said. "I think he was going back in tonight to work on the case."

"We'll do a lap of the grounds, see if—"

"Hey!" A voice in the blackness. Susan and I turned, training our guns on a figure emerging from the dark. Nick put his hands up. He held a pistol in one of them. "It's me. It's me."

"Jesus," I said. I wanted to grab Susan to me, shield her, shove her inside the house. But that was more of my overprotective bullshit. She had told me she could take care of herself.

"I smelled the smoke, saw the stiff, and did a patrol of the area." Nick glanced toward the forest, his eyes wide. "There's no one out there. Not that I can see."

I was so angry it was hard to unclench my jaw. "He's trying to intimidate us. Scare us. Dropping one of his guys on our fucking doorstep. He's a coward."

"Are we absolutely certain this is one of Cline's guys?" Susan asked.

"He'd had his head bashed in pretty bad, and not tonight. This is probably the guy Clay stomped on in Dogtown," I said.

"Cline hasn't even stuck around to watch us freak out."

Susan was breathing deeply, trying to calm her nerves. "I don't understand."

"It's not about watching us be scared," I said. "I think it's about sending the message. *These guys, they're just commodities. They're disposable. If I can do this to my own men, imagine what I can do to you.*"

We stood, all of us lost in thought. Nick was tapping his gun against his thigh, his eyes searching the ground. I looked at him. The muscles in his shoulders were ticking with tension.

"I'm going to go inside and call Clay," Susan said. "This is a crime scene."

"Yeah, you report in," Nick said. "We'll take care of things here."

Susan frowned slightly at the comment, then jogged back toward the house. Nick walked a few paces away from me, turned to the forest, and murmured something. He shook his head as though telling someone no.

"Nick, are you all right, buddy?"

"He's not going to give us anything. We'll have to find out ourselves. Tell Rickson to load up and you cover the door. I'll take care of this."

"Tell . . . who? What are you talking about?"

Nick raised his pistol and shot the body on the bench twice in the chest.

CHAPTER EIGHTY-FIVE

MY EARS WERE ringing. The shock I had already been experiencing suddenly ramped up, the volume cranked high,
all my nerves electrified. I snatched the gun from Nick, but
he was in a dream state, yawning, rubbing his head, turning and murmuring to people who weren't there. The body
had bucked twice as the bullets entered it and now slowly
flopped to the ground before the fire like an oversize doll. I
felt a wave of nausea, the lifelike twitch of the body for an
instant making me think of zombies, monsters, dark things.

Susan came running out from the house at the sound of
the gunshots. I ran and grabbed her before she could get to
the body.

"No, no, no, no." I turned her around. "Stop them coming
out. The others. They'll have heard the shots." I grabbed the
body and dragged him out of the light of the fire. In the

searingly cold night, I could hear Angelica's frantic questioning in the wind, Susan's placations. I saw Nick's tall, straight frame walking around the side of the house.

It seemed an age before Susan joined me. There was blood on my arms, my hands. I stiffened to try to stop the shaking in my limbs, but that only made matters worse.

We were both thinking the same thing, but neither of us wanted to say it. In time it was she who broke the silence.

"The shots—they'll know they're postmortem," she said. "But they'll want to check every gun in the house, and that'll mean any registered to Nick."

"There's blood all over the firepit area now," I said. "Drag marks in the dirt. They'll know he was here and that he was already dead."

We looked at the body. Without speaking, Susan took Stanley Turner's arms and I took his legs.

CHAPTER EIGHTY-SIX

DOGTOWN. OUR HEADLIGHTS picked out the winding roads. Now and then the gold beams flashed on an ancient stone foundation of a house long gone. On huge boulders by the roadside, carved and painted with black letters. They were supposed to be motivational slogans for the unemployed and desperate in the failed town, but their meanings changed as I watched them roll by.

Never try, never win.

I shouldn't have tried to stop Cline. I would not win against him.

A local vandal had spray-painted a boulder with his own words: *Save yourself.*

"Cline wanted us to come into his world," I said. Susan glanced at me. She looked sick. I couldn't blame her. In the trunk of the car, a body lolled and shifted as we drove through the night.

"What do you mean?"

"If we'd reported the body, we'd have had the house searched. Our people would have been questioned and our home invaded again, not with his men this time but with cops. If we didn't report the body..."

She looked out the windshield at the night.

"This," she said. "The night. Dogtown. Cline's own dumping ground. His guys were out here only days ago dumping a corpse, and now we're here. He must have known we'd be forced to choose the same spot. It's the best place for a mission like this, isn't it? We already know it's been scouted out!" She laughed, a crazed, angry sound. "He wants us to sympathize with him. To understand we're not that different. He's sure pulling out all the stops to get us to back off."

"I'm not backing off."

"Look at us." Susan jerked a thumb toward the trunk of the car. "That's someone's son back there. We're Cline right now. We've become him."

"We're not him," I said. "We're nothing like him. He did this to us. We'll move the body and then call it in. There's no sense in sacrificing Nick because of what Cline did. He'll never pass a psych evaluation, not in his current state. He'll be implicated in the shooting, and who knows where it will go from there?"

Susan was quiet for a long time. "We have to do something about him."

"Cline will—"

"I don't mean Cline," Susan said. "I mean Nick."

"What exactly are you proposing we do with Nick?"

She didn't have an answer. "He's not safe to have around the house."

"He's not a dangerous dog, Susan. He's a person."

"I get that," she said. "Don't you think I get that? I'm here, aren't I? Doing . . . doing this. Nick needs treatment. He needs to talk to someone about what happened over there, on his deployment. He can't keep it locked away anymore. It's killing him."

We drove on in silence. I watched the roadside as I drove, looking for a discreet trail to dump our evil secret.

CHAPTER EIGHTY-SEVEN

I HADN'T SLEPT after Susan and I returned from Dogtown. The former FBI agent had lain awake beside me, the warmth and love and security of our connection at the beginning of the night soiled and forgotten. At sunrise I gathered up our bloody clothes and bagged them, and she stood watching, numb.

"We had no choice," she said. "But I'm still disgusted with us."

"You and me both," I said. I had walked to Nick's room and knocked on the door, found him sitting on the bed. We agreed to meet on the porch later that morning and go to the psychiatry clinic at the VA hospital.

I made coffee in the kitchen. Vinny and Angelica were at the dining-room table together, Vinny's leathery cheeks glowing pink as he jabbed at the laptop between them.

"Not there, *there*," Angelica said, pointing at the screen with her broken finger. She tried to move the laptop mouse but Vinny swept her hand away. "The little envelope symbol. Mail. Sign in."

"Don't tell me you've got a new job, Vin." I smiled, blew the steam off the coffee I'd made. "Angelica's personal assistant. Are you going to take dictation of the novels?"

"I'm trying to check this vegan-activist-bullshit-provocateur's e-mail for her," he growled, swiping Angelica's hand away again. "You ask for my help and then you don't want it. What's wrong with you, woman? I know how to use this piece of crap."

Angelica let her hand fall, rolled her eyes at me. There was something comforting in the bickering of the two people at the table. Susan had told them that last night's gunfire was due to Nick getting a little confused again, shooting in the dark. With all that was happening with Cline, they seemed to take the incident in stride. This was what my household had become.

"It's *i-c-a*, not *i-k-a*." Angelica sighed. "Angelica. Like Angelica Garnett."

"Who the fuck is Angelica Garnett?"

Angelica slumped in her chair and stared morosely at the carpet while Vinny tapped on the keyboard. I looked out the window and saw Nick waiting for me on the porch, his big hands gripping the arms of a wicker chair like a man on the witness stand. He was watching something across the driveway—a couple of squirrels tussling on the grass.

"You've got renewals for a bunch of subscriptions to crappy literary magazines," Vinny reported. "And there's an e-mail here from the Richmond-Sotherbury publishing house."

"Oh." Angelica picked at the lace on her skirt. "What's that one say?"

I sipped my coffee while Vinny read silently.

"Says they tried to call you but you didn't answer." Vinny yawned, scrolling through pages. "They want to make you an offer."

Angelica's back straightened slowly. She looked at the screen, then she pulled the laptop toward her. Vinny and I watched as she read the e-mail he'd opened. She seemed to read it a few times, looking away and then looking back, blinking. Her eyes narrowed, then widened, and then her mouth turned down and opened until it was a dark cave.

She hung her head down and burst into loud, heaving sobs. Vinny and I looked at each other.

"Oh my God." I put my coffee down and went to Angelica. Vinny tried to turn his broken wheelchair, making the poorly fitted bolt clunk. "Is it bad news?"

"No, no, no." Angelica sobbed, grabbing my shoulder as I crouched before her. "It's—it's—it's—I'm be-ing published!"

"Huh? I don't get it." Vinny's lip curled. "I thought you *were* published. Ain't you some kind of *New York Times* ... fucking ... award-winning ... whatever-whatever?"

"I lied." Angelica wiped furiously at her eyes with her left hand, but the tears kept coming. "No one ever asked to read my work anyway. I started telling people I was a writer a long time ago, and then I just ... I just stretched it and stretched it."

"You're not a writer *at all*?" My mouth was hanging open and so was Vinny's.

"I am a *writer*," Angelica cried. "But I just . . . I'm not a published *author*. Or I haven't ever been. I was speaking to some people once and I told them I wrote novels, and they just assumed I'd been published. And then once I'd let that lie go unchallenged, it seemed easier to maintain it than to explain. And then perhaps I . . . I let the fantasy go a little more. I added some awards. What's the point in being a pretend author if you're not going to be a successful pretend one?"

I didn't have an answer for that.

"Writing is all I think about. It's all I talk about!"

"We noticed," Vinny said.

"It has been my dream since I was a little girl, and . . ." Angelica broke into fresh sobs. "No one cared, so I could say what I wanted. I was just pretending."

Angelica kept crying, and Vinny and I stared at each other, trying to take this in.

"I've submitted manuscripts, of course," Angelica said. "Siobhan used to read my work. But they . . . they always failed. I've kept all my rejection letters. There are four hundred or so."

"*Four hun—*" Vinny roared. I cut him off with a look. Nick came to the window to see what the wailing was about, and Susan appeared at the door to the hall, clutching her satin robe, looking alarmed.

"Richmond-Sotherbury." Angelica moaned, covering her face with one hand. "*Richmond-Sotherbury!*"

"Is that good?" I asked. Vinny shrugged.

"They're the best." Angelica nodded. She gave a long,

loud wail that could have been pure misery or unbridled joy. "They're the best!"

She turned and fell into Vinny's arms, and he patted her back as she cried, looking at me for help, but I didn't have anything to offer.

I was still trying to decide if I should console or congratulate Angelica when my phone buzzed in my pocket. I answered, and Sheriff Spears spoke before I could say a word.

"There was a killing spree last night," he said.

CHAPTER EIGHTY-EIGHT

NICK DROVE TO the VA hospital while I sat in the passenger seat and talked to Clay. The sheriff sounded colder, less emotional than I had ever heard him. I sympathized with his plight—he was unable to trust his men, and his little patch of New England was steadily growing nightmarish. I followed Nick into the foyer of the hospital. The muscles between my shoulder blades were tight and hot with tension.

"You remember that woman from Addison Gilbert, the one with the crush on me?" I asked. Nick looked like he wanted to smile at the memory but my expression forbade it. "They found her dead in the hospital parking lot last night. She was shot walking to her car."

Nick reached for a stand of information booklets but managed to stop himself before he grabbed it and smashed it to the ground. The veins in his arms rose beneath his brown skin.

"She didn't even know anything," Nick snapped.

"Cline might have been looking for one of his guys," I said. "He found Christopher 'Simbo' Jackson in a shitty motel in Amesbury and took him out. They don't know where Russell Hamdy is."

"Has Clay picked Cline up?"

"He can't," I said. "All they've got is a shadowy figure on the security camera in the hospital parking lot, and they know the area has been the site of a few assaults and robberies lately. The footage is not good enough to be connected to Cline. Simbo left a suicide note. The guy put a cable tie around his own throat, or that's how the Amesbury cops saw it."

"What about the other guys?" Nick asked.

"Tray 'Bones' Ramirez has disappeared," I said. "He and Stanley Turner split from the ambulance that picked them up after Clay beat the shit out of them. The paramedic at the scene thought Bones had internal injuries, and he was pretty sure Turner had a skull fracture and a broken arm. Bones is probably being seen to by one of the doctors on Cline's payroll, and we both know where Turner is."

Nick exhaled. I tried to shake off visions of Susan and me dragging Stanley Turner's corpse out of the back of my car. If Clay didn't find him that afternoon, I would have to call in an anonymous tip.

"What about the big guy?" Nick said. "The one whose kneecap Vinny blasted out."

"That's Hamdy. He went to Addison Gilbert and then they lost him," I said.

"They *lost* him?"

"They literally lost him." I nodded. "He had checked in and was waiting for surgery when he disappeared. He's either hobbling around somewhere with a shattered knee or Cline got him too."

Nick walked away from me, rubbing his neatly shaven head, blowing air out in angry huffs. We took the elevator to the psychiatry clinic on the third floor. Nick signed in, and then we stood in the empty waiting room. The tiles were sticky and the magazines on the low table offered exclusive pictures of Brad Pitt and Jennifer Aniston's wedding.

"I can't do this, man," Nick said, turning to leave. "Cline's coming for us next. Once he's gotten rid of his old crew, he'll assemble a new one, and we're the only loose ends in this thing. We gotta go."

I put a hand on his arm, stopping his progress. "You're not going anywhere. An hour or so isn't going to make a difference."

"You kidding me?" Nick pushed away my hand. "Cline wrapped up half his business last night. We're—"

"We're fine without you for the moment," I said. "Malone and Effie have got the house. Clay's on the murders. I'll stay out of trouble until you talk to the people here. Nick, you're doing the right thing. You need this."

"Mr. Jones?" The woman behind the front desk stepped out, holding a clipboard. Nick looked at me like he'd just been shut in the gas chamber and I was the guard about to turn the lock and walk away.

CHAPTER EIGHTY-NINE

I WASN'T WORRIED about Nick. He was doing the right thing. I was sure he had PTSD, and now the veterans hospital would take care of him, schedule therapy, maybe put him in a support group. That had to be the hospital's bread and butter. But as I wandered the halls, I began to feel an aching concern in my stomach. There were elderly men in wheelchairs staring out the windows at the parking lot; one was sleeping with his head at an awkward angle, the front of his shirt soiled with food stains. At a counter on the second floor, an exhausted-looking nurse was having a shouting match with a patient on crutches. She stopped to bat away a fly that had been buzzing around her face. I watched the fly go, strangely disturbed by its presence in the hospital. The smell of this place wasn't the same nostril-tingling, disinfectant freshness of Addison Gilbert.

It was faintly sour and tainted with something unmistakably biological.

I wandered the corridors, thinking about Cline, my head down, tracing the smudgy footprints of others on the linoleum. After a while I came into a hallway and witnessed another argument, a nurse trying to reason with four very large men standing outside a darkened ward.

"You have to respect visitor protocols," she said. "We have a system here, and you have to have approval."

I watched, my hands in my pockets. The four men were obviously military. They had the functionally muscular bodies of men who worked out several times a day, but in addition to the muscles that looked pretty, they had well-developed muscles in their hands, forearms, and necks, the kind of muscles you get only by picking up and moving heavy equipment across long distances. They were dressed in civilian workmen's clothes that had never been worked in. Flattops you could rest a beer can on. Two of them were backing the nurse toward me without touching her, their big hands up, a moving wall of hard flesh.

"Thanks for your concern, ma'am," one of them said. "We got it from here."

Something seemed to tell the nurse that whatever *it* was, their having it was set in stone, and her protests were useless. She turned and brushed past me as she left, bringing me to the attention of the men. The nearest one met my eyes as the four of them walked back to the door, and I saw recognition flash there.

"Is there a problem, sir?" he asked.

"No problem." I noticed a restroom door behind the wall of men. "Just want to use the restroom."

"There's one on the second floor."

"I want to use that one." I pointed. "It's my favorite."

"It's out of order." The meathead squared his shoulders. "Move on."

Now I knew what I was dealing with. I smiled and nodded toward the door.

"Cline's guy," I said. "Russell Hamdy. Tell him I want to see him."

CHAPTER NINETY

RUSSELL HAMDY TOOK ten minutes to decide whether or not he'd see me. The recognition I'd seen in one of the guys probably meant they had been briefed on people who might approach the room, and I was one of them. Russell's military friends watched me silently from the doorway, looking from their charge to me, their eyes mean and their mouths hard. In time I was beckoned in, although no one moved to let me through, which forced me to slide between tautly stretched fabric and clouds of strong antiperspirant.

Cline's man was sitting upright in the bed, a complicated apparatus around his bloodied and bandaged knee. His face was pale and drawn; an oxygen tube was under his nose. Russ had his hands beneath a blanket on his lap, and I knew that he was holding a loaded gun that was pointed at me.

"This is one hell of a disappearing act," I said, looking

around at the curtain pulled tightly over the window and the four empty beds. "How do the nurses feel about you giving yourself a private room?"

"They'll do what they're told," he said. His words were slightly slurred, probably an effect of whatever painkiller he was on. "They don't want my blood all over the floor any more than I do."

"So you're ex-military," I said. "What's Cline doing with an ex-military guy on his crew? I thought he only took losers and jailbirds."

"I was a loser and a jailbird." Russ gave a lopsided smile. "After two tours in Iraq, I was deployed to help out after the Boxing Day tsunami in Indonesia in 2004. We were pulling bodies out of the water for six weeks straight. Kids and all. That kind of shit fucks you up pretty good."

I nodded.

"I did some things I'm not proud of, and Cline stepped in when I hit rock bottom," Russ said. "But before all that I was a Marine. And once a Marine, always a Marine."

The guys in the doorway stirred, wanting to give an *oo-rah*, perhaps, but not wanting to drop their menacing cover. I admired the setup. Russ must have called the team of military thugs from his past when Vinny popped him, knowing that if his old friends didn't swoop in and rescue him from Addison Gilbert, Cline would come creeping in before dawn. Even if Cline knew Russ was ex-military, he'd be safe from the drug lord behind his wall of human steel, at least until he was charged and incarcerated for attacking my house. I wondered if Bess, the nurse at the triage desk, had helped the men secure a way out for this damaged soldier turned gangster. She'd have known, looking at his injuries and the state of affairs in her hospital, what she was likely dealing with. Her assistance of the man before me might have cost the woman her life.

"Have the police been here yet?" I asked Russ.

"Two undercovers." He shifted painfully against the pillows. "And I told them the same thing I'll tell you. I'm not talking about Cline."

"Are you serious? You'll go to prison for that merciless prick?" I said. "You've got these beefcakes standing guard to protect you from him. You know he's coming to kill you. Why don't you put him where he belongs and save yourself?"

"Because if I stay quiet, he might give me a chance," Russ said. "All I can hope is that after a while he'll see that I'm still loyal and give up trying to get at me."

"Look at you." I gestured to his mangled leg. "Cline did this. It's your service to him that got you into this fix. You'll never walk properly again. And you want back in with this guy?"

"Man." Russ shook his head. "You've still got no idea who you're dealing with."

"So enlighten me," I said.

"Cline's not one of these everyday dealers who is happy to lawyer up and do a small amount of time when he gets backed into a corner," Russ said. "He'll kill to make sure he doesn't ever do time."

"Why?"

"Because he's got more to lose than just his business," Russ said.

"What is that supposed to mean?"

Russ just glared at me. He knew he'd said too much. I looked at his leg, fantasized about grabbing the apparatus supporting it and giving it a shake to get him to open up more. But I knew the guys at the door would turn me into a human pretzel at the slightest wrong move.

"Tell me how I can get to Cline," I said. "I'll solve your problem for you."

"You won't get near him." Russ shook his head. "He's cleared his house. He's vulnerable until he gets a new crew. Cline will go to ground for a while, get some new soldiers, pop back up again. Maybe here. Maybe somewhere else."

I felt the fury rising in my throat. "That's bullshit. He doesn't get to just come into my town, threaten and kill my friends, and then disappear."

"He won't disappear completely." Russ smiled. "He'll wait. In a few months, a year, maybe, he'll come back into your life so silent and so fast you won't know he's there until he's got his gun in your mouth. That's what he does."

A chill prickled through my body, making the hairs on my arms stand on end. I knew that the man before me had seen Cline do this, reappear in his victim's life like a curse, never letting anyone escape him. If Cline hadn't taken care of all his crew now, he would get to them in time. The most that Russell Hamdy could hope for was that the man would change his mind.

I realized my best chance to grab Cline was to do it now, before he disappeared and reemerged stronger than he had been before.

My phone rang in my pocket. We had spoken of the devil, and he'd heard himself being discussed.

CHAPTER NINETY-ONE

I DIDN'T LET him speak this time. I went out of the room before I answered and took the call in the hospital hallway.

"It takes a special kind of asshole to cut down his own men at the first sign of weakness," I said. Cline wasn't ready for my attack. He paused, and then he laughed.

"My uncle," he said. "He bred racing greyhounds. Have I told you this?"

I was taken aback by Cline's friendly, reflective tone. He sounded refreshed and bright, like someone waking from a long, deep sleep. Killing had done this to him, made him cheerful. I grunted.

"I forget who I've told things to sometimes," he said. "But my uncle, yeah, he had these greyhounds. I was always curious about them, being as I was a kid and an animal lover. I wanted to pet the dogs, but they were vicious, hysterical, easily spooked things. He made them that way. A good dog will run fast primarily because it wants to catch and kill the rabbit up ahead, but if you add a terror of what's behind it, the motivation is double. These dogs spent their lives trapped between what they wanted and what they feared. You could see the whites of their eyes all the time."

I thought about Cline's guys standing outside his house, so ready to jump at anything that threatened their master. They were vicious purebreds trapped between fear of him and desire for the life he provided.

"Are you telling me this for a reason?" I snapped.

"My uncle chose the best of the breed. He mated only exceptional dogs. But sometimes things happen. A dog overstrains a tendon. It gets lazy. The inbreeding, it sometimes causes problems. When he had dogs that started underperforming, my uncle would take them and bash their heads in on a concrete block in front of all the other dogs. He had a wooden mallet especially for the job that he would carry around on a string attached to his belt. Usually it took only one blow."

"So the Cline family is full of psychopaths," I said. "I think that's the least surprising thing I've ever heard in my life."

"I had to cut my numbers down," Cline said. "Replenish my stock. You demonstrated for me that I didn't have performers in my collection—I had pretenders. You, Robinson. You forced me to reevaluate. This is all on you."

"Is that what you tell yourself? Is that how you sleep at night?"

"You know I'm right," Cline said. "You've got the guilt.

I know you're thinking of walking away now, Robinson. That's why you haven't handed that money back yet."

"Of course I thought about taking the money," I said. "It's a lot of money."

"There's more where that came from."

"Well, I hope you drop the rest of it at the police station in Gloucester," I said. "Because that's where I dropped mine this morning. I wonder what the state will do with it. I hope they put it into rehab clinics. You might have just contributed to the demise of your own business, Cline."

"I don't think so, chump. The Gloucester police department was exactly where you shouldn't have taken that money."

"Why, because all the cops there are on your payroll?" I asked. "That's the very reason I chose to go there. I sat down and made them count it all out. Watched them enter it into the evidence logs under the cameras. The whole station came to take a look. They'll know that's your money, Cline. They'll know your bribe didn't work."

An announcement calling for doctors to respond to a code on the eighth floor blasted over the PA system above me. I covered the phone mike with my hand, adrenaline dumped into my veins.

"Don't panic," Cline said. "I know exactly where Russ is. He can recover there with his bodyguards. I'll get him when the time is right."

I wondered if Cline was bluffing. It made me decide to try it myself.

"Let me tell you something that *I* know," I said. "I know why you won't do prison time."

"Really?" he asked.

"Yeah," I said. "Really."

There was a pause while Cline assessed my words. I hoped my tone was convincing. I could hear nothing in the background on his end. He was somewhere quiet, collecting himself before he went into battle again. The seconds ticked by, and I bit my tongue, waiting for him to call or fold on what I'd said.

"They need me," he said. "You might think you're doing them a favor, but they need me."

I smiled. Nick was walking down the hallway toward me. I hung up on Cline and grabbed his arm.

"Let's go," I said. "I think I've hit on something."

CHAPTER NINETY-TWO

NICK WAS SILENT as we walked from the hospital to the car. He sat with his feet on the dash and his seat reclined as I drove close to Cline's house, then stopped in the street beyond his. I could just make out a slice of Cline's driveway beyond the neat hedges, but as I watched, the man appeared; I saw a flash of black trousers, shiny shoes, a pin-striped shirt as he headed for the Escalade parked out front. I'd spooked him.

"I knew it," I said. "I knew it."

Nick didn't respond. I did a slow U-turn and waited for Cline to get out into traffic, then followed him at a distance.

"So what did she say?" I asked. "The shrink?"

"How do you know it was a woman?" he said.

"Because they're smarter than us." I kept my eyes locked

on Cline's big black car. "Susan makes me feel like a dope with a single sideways glance."

"You're talking about her like she's your girlfriend," Nick said, putting his arms behind his head. Maybe it was the excitement of being on Cline without his knowing I was there or the rush of trying to obtain the upper hand, the gathering hope that I could bring him down, remove him from my life, my friends' lives. Whatever it was, I wasn't paying attention to Nick's mood. I gripped the steering wheel, took a deep breath.

"We..." I glanced at him. "Before everything that happened last night. You know. We might have taken things up a notch."

"That's nice. So sorry a psychopath leaving us a corpse and me being a crazy freak ruined it for you."

"You're not a crazy freak," I said. "And no number of corpses could take the shine off Susan Solie."

"That should be on your Valentine's Day card to her," Nick said.

"It just sort of happened. I'd been wondering if... if it was going to happen. We'd kissed. But I didn't know if it was just the moment and something that struck us both. We were on the beach and the moon was over us and I'd been so consumed worrying about everyone and the plan with the boat," I said. "But I think there's something there with Susan. Something between us. I mean, *I know* there's something there, at least on my side. But maybe she—"

I looked at Nick. He hardly seemed to be listening.

"Sorry," I said. I burned through a yellow light to keep on Cline. "So what did the shrink say?"

"It was bullshit." Nick snorted. "Total bullshit. I don't think I'll go back. You sit with a person for more than an hour and they can't even give you a solid diagnosis. Can you believe that? She wants to consult with her supervisor. Why would you license someone to be a shrink if she can't even give you a proper diagnosis without having to run to her teacher? 'Congratulations, madame. You sort of know how to do your job but not really.'"

"She has to talk to her supervisor to decide if you've got PTSD?" I asked.

Nick licked his teeth, watched the cars ahead of us.

"Nick?"

"She knows I've got PTSD," he said.

We sat in silence. Nick took his feet off the dashboard, clasped his hands, and looked at them in his lap. I listened to him taking a deep breath, trying to find the words, failing, and trying again.

"I'm pulling over."

"Don't pull over," he said. "We need to stay on Cline. We need to get this guy." He folded his arms, a barrier of muscle and bone over his heart. "She thinks I'm also schizo-phrenic."

CHAPTER NINETY-THREE

THE CAR AROUND me seemed to shrink. Suddenly it was hard to stay on the road. I looked at my friend.

"What do you mean, she *thinks* that?"

"You can't just diagnose it in an hour," he said. "See, this is the bullshit I was talking about. She needs to get her supervisor to sign off on me having *schizophreniform disorder,* which is what you have if your schizophrenia symptoms haven't been going on longer than six months. And then when the supervisor signs off on that, that becomes your day one. So you have to be observed for six months like a fucking rat in a lab until they can figure out if it's the full version or one of the sub-versions. I mean, what the fuck? It was all so wishy-washy. She wasn't listening to me properly. Most of the time she was just taking notes. She's the one who's nuts if you ask me."

"So you don't think she really got what you were saying?"

"No." Nick straightened in his seat. "I mean, one of the symptoms she was talking about was catatonic stupor. I know what that is. I've read about it. That's what she didn't get—I'm not an idiot and I checked out this stuff before when I was trying to figure out what was wrong with me. *Catatonic* is when you're there but you're not really there, like you're a robot. In a trance. I've never experienced that."

I thought about the sleepy, dreamy state Nick went into after his episodes, the almost automatic way he moved and talked. Like someone who wasn't fully present. I opened my mouth to say something and then closed it.

"She wanted to know about my delusions." He shrugged. "That's when you're imagining rainbow elephants prancing around the fucking sky and lizards crawling on your skin and shit."

"Well." I cleared my throat. "Those might be hallucinations, which are different from delusions, I think."

"Whatever."

"I mean last night..." I cleared my throat again, glanced at him. "You seemed to be sort of...reenacting a scene, maybe? Talking to people who weren't there. Someone named Rickson?"

Nick turned away from me to look out his window.

"You said you did bad things over there while you were deployed. You said to Rickson that this guy wasn't going to give you anything, and then you shot—"

"I don't want to talk about this. It was my mind playing tricks. It means nothing."

"Yes, but were they memories you were reliving, or was it just—"

"Cap, fuck!" Nick said. "Would you listen to yourself? You have no fucking idea what you're talking about!"

"That's the point!" I said. "Look, I know war is hard. But I'm starting to wonder whether there was...maybe there was more to it. Who was Rickson? Were you asked to do things that were..."

Nick didn't answer.

"You can trust me, Nick," I said.

"It was just the regular stuff," he said slowly. "Just the fucked-up nature of war. I don't know any guys named Rickson from back then. I didn't do anything criminal."

I didn't say you did, I thought.

Silence fell between us, hot and heavy. He sniffed, then spoke again in a softer voice, trying to ease back into the conversation. "So maybe it is hallucinations." He shrugged. "Whatever. Fine. But if I'm having hallucinations, how am I supposed to know they're hallucinations? What are we saying here? Like, is Cline not real? Are we not following a dude who's been messing with us, who killed Marni, who sent guys to our house? Are *you* even real?" He poked me in the shoulder, too hard to be a friendly jab.

"I'm real," I said. "And we'll figure it out together. Whether it's PTSD or schizophrenia or whatever the hell it is."

"Well, she thinks I've got both, which is just fantastic," he said. "Whoo-hoo! What a catch I am. A crazy, messed-up freak who doesn't even know what's real and what isn't."

"You're not crazy," I said. When he didn't answer I put my hand on his arm. "You're *not* crazy."

"She thinks the PTSD kicked it off." He shrugged my hand away. "It can bring out symptoms of schizophrenia you might have had lying dormant under the surface. She said it was like the thunderclap that sets off the avalanche. She was full of stupid metaphors like that." He snorted, clumped his big boots up onto the dashboard again. "See, these people at the veterans hospitals, they diagnose you with whatever condition because they need the funding. Putting me on a program of observation, feeding me pills, x-raying my brain—that all costs money. Someone has to pay for that, and they charge whatever they want. They're as bad as Cline." He gestured out the windshield. "It was all bullshit, Cap. I'm not going back."

"Nick," I said. "I just want to say that I—"

"I know, I know," he snapped. "You're *here* for me. Well, if you're here for me, Cap, you better go get yourself a crowbar or a fucking metal file or something, because they're going to lock me up. That's how it works. They say you're crazy, that you're a danger to yourself and others. Then they commit you to an institution, and they keep you there and rake in the insurance money."

"No one is going to commit you, Nick."

"If they do, you're going to break me out. You said it yourself. You're here for me. Well, if you're here for me, that's what it's going to take, man." He snorted angrily. "How ironic. Just when we get Cline behind bars, they'll stick me there too. Only it'll be padded walls for me."

I watched the road, tried to think of what to say. "I—"

"I don't want to talk about it anymore." Nick waved at the car in the distance. "Speed up. We're losing him."

CHAPTER NINETY-FOUR

NICK AND I had followed Cline to a quiet street in a neighborhood north of Boston but not far from the central business district. The brownstone building had three floors; flowerpots bursting with red flowers hung in every window. It looked like there was a kid's bedroom on the second floor because a teddy bear was sitting in the window and a hockey stick leaned against the glass.

I took in all these meaningless details with my mind consumed with Nick's problem. It sounded to me as though his psychiatrist knew exactly what was going on, but I didn't want to try to convince my friend of this. He was in pain, and pushing him right now would only add to that.

Cline sat in the car texting someone, and then he went to the red-painted front door of the home.

"See? See?" I nudged Nick. "I had a hunch he was coming

to meet his boss. He must have a partner or at least a distributor, someone who handles the business on the Boston end."

"How did you know he'd come to see him?" Nick asked.

"Cline's guy told me he wouldn't go to jail. It didn't matter who stood in his way, he'd stay out of prison at all costs. I told Cline I knew why. It's because he's just a puppet. He's working for someone more powerful, someone who will clean *his* house if Cline is ever arrested."

I tapped the window beside me, anxious. I knew I'd spooked Cline with my bluff, that coming directly to Boston after my call must be connected to his business. The fearful, razor's edge to his words as he'd spoken told me there was something at stake here, and I thought it meant there was a boss in play. Maybe there was more than one. *They need me. You might think you're doing them a favor, but they need me,* Cline had said. But what did that mean, exactly? Could *they* be his bosses?

"You think he's come here to warn the guy?" Nick asked.

"Yeah. I'm almost sure of it. He's come to tell the boss that he's gotten in over his head with us." I nodded, folded my arms. "It's probably hard, admitting he needs help. But we've got the upper hand now. The element of surprise. We're going to find out who this guy is, what we're really dealing with."

Cline knocked, and the door opened. I don't know what I expected to see. Cline in an older form, harder, more scarred, a kind of father figure sending my nemesis out into the world to spread the virus he'd created.

But when the door opened there wasn't a man but a very beautiful woman. Two children rushed from behind her and into Cline's arms.

CHAPTER NINETY-FIVE

"WHAT THE HELL is this?" Nick asked.

"I...have no idea," I said. The woman on the stoop seemed angry with Cline. She held a hand up, palm out, like she was trying to keep him from entering. But Cline picked up and carried the two boys, five or six years old, under his arms and barged his way in. I had been wrong about Cline. He was not working for someone else. *They need me,* he'd said. He didn't mean his bosses; he meant his family.

"I don't understand this." Nick shook his head. "The guy has kids? He spends every ounce of his energy poisoning other people's kids. Giving them free samples. Trying to get them hooked. How does he do it?"

"Same way he wipes out his whole crew after saving them all like rescue dogs," I said. "He can turn the care on and off like a faucet. He cares when it's convenient." I popped my door as soon as Cline's clicked closed. "Let's go," I said.

"What? Where?"

I jogged across the street and ducked down the narrow alleyway beside Cline's house, squeezing between two large garbage cans. Nick was close behind me, gripping the bricks as he crouched by my side. There was another flowerpot hanging from a low kitchen window, which was open. Nick and I watched each other as the voices from outside reached us.

The sound of the children was like happy dogs barking, their small feet stomping on the boards.

"Daddy, I want to show you my class project!"

"No, I want to show you my—"

"Come to my room, Daddy. Come to my room first."

"Frankie, Jamie, I want you to go upstairs to your room," the woman said.

"But we—"

"Go upstairs to your room!" the mother snarled. I recognized immediately the terror, fear, aggression in her voice. Women had turned on Malone and me as patrol cops when we came knocking after we got reports of screaming in apartments. They snapped at us, pushed us out of their homes, but I'd heard the fear rattling through their words, seen the relief in their eyes at the presence of another focus for their husbands' rage.

There were small, mournful footsteps on the stairs and then a long, hard silence.

"The court order says you have to give me forty-eight hours' notice before you come here," the woman said.

"Teri, I did give you notice. You just never answer your phone."

"A text from the fucking car thirty seconds before you knock on the door is not notice!"

"I don't like that tone," Cline said quietly. His voice was low, coiling, like a snake about to strike. "You know I don't like it, and you use it anyway. I come to my own house and you treat me like a criminal in front of my own sons, my blood."

"I just want a warning. That's all I'm asking for. The judge said you have to give me that."

"All *I* want is a bit of respect," Cline said. Something clattered on the kitchen counter. "You wear the clothes that I paid for. You live in the house that my hard work built. I gave you those two beautiful boys. I can take all of those things away from you in an instant, and you don't even have the decency to look me in the eye. Look at me. You understand what I'm saying?"

His voice was closer to hers now, inches away from Nick and me, on the other side of the window. I heard a whimper, and Nick flinched at the sound of it, his eyes distant and wide.

"Someone's giving me a problem," Cline said. "I don't know what he's going to try to do next. I want you and the kids out of the house."

"But—"

"*But?*" Cline snapped. Another clatter, a cry of pain. "But *what,* Teri?"

Nick had heard enough. He tried to rise but I dragged him down.

"Nothing and no one is going to take me away from those boys," Cline said. "Until I've tied up all the loose ends, you pack your shit and get out of here. I'll call you with the hotel reservation."

I heard his footsteps on the floorboards. The boys calling to him from the stairs. Cline's wife, or ex-wife, started crying from the kitchen beyond where Nick and I hid.

"Do we go inside and help her?" Nick whispered. I thought for a moment, listening to the little boys going to their mother, asking her what was wrong. The helpless confusion of tiny children living in the shadow of a monster.

"There's a way we can help her," I told Nick. "And it's the same way we help ourselves."

CHAPTER NINETY-SIX

SUSAN KNEW WHAT I had decided to do. She stood with me in the kitchen looking worriedly over my work as I massacred some vegetables and then laid them out on a tray, spice-rubbed a shoulder of pork. A day had passed since Nick and I stood idly by while Cline made his ex-wife squeal in terror. The sound of her frightened voice had kept me up all night, Susan tossing and turning as I failed to settle down. Before dawn I'd crept to my basement bed, knowing I'd need her, at least, sharp and ready to be my ally against the man who had come unwelcome into our lives.

In the end, I decided that I had to finish Cline. One way or another, I had to remove him like a cancer from his ex-wife's life, from my neighborhood. I had to release the choke hold he had on the addicts and hurting people of Gloucester and make sure that what happened to Marni didn't happen to anyone ever again.

"Is there something a bit strange about preparing dinner for everyone when we're about to do..." She paused, shaking her head. "What we're about to do?"

"I'm finding a weird comfort in it," I said, wiping my hands on a dish towel. I tried to explain to her and myself that, somehow, knowing the people in my house were fed, even with my subpar culinary offerings, gave me some consolation. "It's a job. I have to do it. We've got a couple renting the front room tonight. But I'm also doing it because it's a relief, and I think we'd better grab hold of whatever relief we can get right now."

She seemed to take the suggestion literally and put her arms around me. There was an exhilarating rush that shuddered through my body every time she touched me and also a warm, familiar sensation that I knew came from the feel of Siobhan in my arms not so long ago, the smoothness of her cheek against mine.

"We might never come back here," she said. I gripped her shoulders. "Do you get that? We might put this dinner on and leave here and it might be the last time we walk out the door."

I thought about Siobhan and the dinner she'd been coming home with, the last time she would walk out the door already having occurred without my knowledge. I hadn't said goodbye properly. But even if I'd had the chance, I reminded myself, there'd have been an impossible amount of things to say.

"I don't mean to be morbid." She laughed, pulling away

from me and wiping a tear from her eye. "It's just been a while since I was in the thick of it. A couple of years writing about circus hamsters and yarn sales will do that to you. Make you realize that there are things at risk, important possibilities you might be about to destroy."

She gestured to me as she said that. I wondered if I was one of those "important possibilities." She was certainly one of mine. As I'd lain awake the night before, I'd watched her sleeping and known just how deeply I'd fallen for her already, how difficult it would be to climb back out of my desire for her. I was indeed risking Susan in my plan. I was risking everyone I cared about.

"But we have to do something," I said, finishing my thought for her.

Doc Simeon came through the kitchen door and stood near us, frowning. I knew from the paleness in his cheeks and the tremble in his old hands that he'd done what I'd asked of him.

"Did he buy it?" I said.

"I think so," the doctor replied. "I think we're on."

CHAPTER NINETY-SEVEN

SQUID SAT IN the passenger seat next to me looking slightly disheveled, thinner than I'd last seen him, with bags under his bloodshot eyes; he looked like a cat who'd escaped into the wild and been found after a couple of weeks of hard living. Nick had left him in the care of his cousins and aunt in Augusta, but the boy hadn't wanted to endanger his family and he'd wandered out into the night. Nick told me he'd found the boy hanging out with a menacing bunch of people in the parking lot behind a popular bar. He reeked of cigarettes and sweat.

Doc and Susan sat in the back seat, silent, as we followed Nick and Malone on the highway down to Boston.

"Something's going to go wrong," the boy said, watching the tall pine trees whiz past us on either side of the road. "I can feel it. Something bad's about to happen."

"I know what that feels like," I said. The fever, hot and heavy, had been nesting in my chest since we left the house. I told myself it was just memories of Boston and my fall. Trepidation about what lay ahead on the road.

"You don't trick Cline like this," Squid said. "He reads minds. He's like a fucking vampire or something." The boy's eyes were a little too wide. I let him rattle off the words, getting it out of his system. "That's how he came into my life, you know. Like a vampire. Like he'd always known I was there and now it was, like, time to come get me. Bring me into the family. Make me one of his own."

"How did you meet him?"

Squid rubbed his nose, laughed a little.

"I was stealing bags at the airport," he said. "I had a good scam going. I'd go in dressed really nice with a suitcase full of magazines, make like I'd just gotten off a flight. I even had one of those neck pillows that I'd dirtied up so it looked like I traveled all the time. I'd find a flight that had just come in, so there were only a couple of people down in the baggage area. I'd watch the first bag come along, and if no one jumped at it, I'd grab it and walk out."

I heard Susan give a little laugh behind me. Somehow, even with all that was ahead of us that night, Squid's story lightened the tension in the car. We crested a hill, and I saw the cluster of lights on the horizon that I knew was Boston.

"Anyway, one day I picked up the wrong bag," Squid said. "It had two bricks of heroin in it. The guy had been dumb enough to check the bag with all his personal stuff too. I worked out who he was, bought a burner phone, and texted saying he could have the bricks back for ten grand. The guy didn't show up. Cline did. And not at the meeting place. At my house. He knew my name, my mother's name, everything." Squid shuddered. It wasn't cold in the car, but he rubbed his arms. "Maybe it wasn't the wrong bag," Squid said. He drew a pack of cigarettes out of his pocket, extracted one, and rolled down the window slightly. "Maybe it was the right one."

"What do you mean?" Doc asked.

"Cline will give you everything you want." Squid shrugged. "You want money? He's got money. You want girls? He's got girls. He'll tell them to be in love with you and they'll be in love with you. It's like magic. You can have everything you want—all you got to do is stay out of trouble. Because if you trip once..."

The car fell silent. Squid smoked his cigarette too fast, leaning and blowing the smoke out of the crack in the window with shivering breaths.

"What happened to the guy who lost the drugs?" I asked. "The one whose bag you stole?"

"He's in a drainpipe off the highway," Squid said. "Cline stabbed him in the head with a letter opener in his nice big office."

CHAPTER NINETY-EIGHT

COMING HOME. RETURNING to where it had all begun, the happiest and the most horrific days of my career, when Malone and I had walked the streets with no idea of the downfall that awaited us, the cliff edge about to crumble beneath our feet. We'd been untouchables in uniform, hunting down the drunk, violent, careless on our streets, two faithful dogs rounding up wolves and driving them away from our flock of innocent sheep. Now I drove and watched the wide streets rolling by, the windows of grand old hotels where we had responded to weddings gone wild, the banks where we had stood guard with our brothers foiling brazen stickups. Every corner had a memory.

Here, outside the Union Oyster House, we had stopped to examine Malone's trooper badge in the sunlight when he finally made rank, the clash and clatter of the bar's patrons on one side of us, press of tourists celebrating St. Patrick's Day at the other.

Here on the steps of the courthouse, we had elbowed aside journalists huddling around accused murderers, fraudsters, and priests caught up in the Catholic archdiocese scandal. I'd copped a microphone in the eye from a Fox News reporter here once. Just one block down, Malone had nearly tripped on a DVD player tossed over the shoulder of a meth addict running for his life across a parking lot.

All of that was lost to us now. The two of us had thrown in everything one night when we'd decided to take the law into our own hands, Malone for one reason, me for another, more than two years ago. Tonight, I was doing the same thing, driving toward the fateful street where we had crossed the line into that dark territory, knowing in my heart that what I was doing was the right thing and maybe being horribly, irreversibly wrong about that.

We drove around the block, passing Malone and Nick in their car as they pulled into a space directly across the street from the apartment building where Malone and I had sealed our fates. I met my partner's eyes and hoped he knew that I forgave him for what had happened here, what his actions had taken from us both. I desperately missed this city, these streets, the way the people had looked at me in my uniform, some lovingly and some hatefully. But what was happening to him, the disease that was eating at his bones and slowly taking him from whatever remained of his life, was not what he or anyone deserved.

I parked my car at the other end of the street, in view of Nick's vehicle and the apartment building's door.

"Okay," I said in the heavy silence of the car. I looked at my watch. "Make the call."

CHAPTER NINETY-NINE

I WATCHED THE plan unfolding before my eyes. Everything had gone perfectly so far. Doc Simeon had called Cline that evening and told him that Squid, the boy he had been giving prescriptions to for more than a year, had come to him for help. Squid was desperate and afraid, having run from Cline after getting himself taken down by Bill Robinson's team and interrogated. He wanted to make good with Cline and knew the Doc was outside the business, someone disconnected who didn't have a reason to pick sides. Doc told Cline that Squid had sworn he hadn't spoken to any police, wasn't trying to come back into the fold because he was wearing a wire or hoping to lead the cops to his boss. The doc said he was willing to act as an intermediary, to present Squid to Cline and make sure no harm came to either of them. The boy in the car beside me stiffened in his seat as

Doc dialed Cline's number now. I watched the gold-lit street, impossibly still and crossed with menacing black shadows, as the line connected. In the silence of the vehicle I could hear every word from Cline's end.

"Yeah."

"I'm here," Doc said. "I want you to promise again that you won't hurt the boy. He said he had no choice but to run from you. But he's loyal. He wants to work this out. He's got nowhere to go."

"Squid knows he can trust me," Cline said. I looked at the boy, who gave a tight smile. We both knew what was going to happen tonight. Cline was going to take Squid from the old man with one intention: to kill him. To *tie up the loose ends,* as he had told his ex-wife. But Squid wasn't going to die tonight. Nick, Susan, Malone, and I would make sure that didn't happen. In the most heavily surveilled street in Boston, we would capture Cline taking custody of the boy. We would follow and intervene, recording everything on Squid's phone.

As Doc gave Cline the street address, Squid took out his phone.

"All right," I said. "You call me. I'll set off a recorder on my phone and I'll listen in while we follow you. If anything goes wrong, I'll hear it. Nick and Malone will be ahead of you, and Susan and I will follow behind. Don't worry."

"Stay close, man," Squid breathed. He gripped the door handle as he pushed the buttons on his phone. "He'll be packin'. Cline could pop me in the fucking car and drive me out into the marshes. You better be ready."

"We're ready," I assured him. My phone buzzed, and I answered it, listening as Squid and Doc got out of the car.

The old man and the young, gangly boy walked into the light of the apartment building. I pressed the record button, looked up and down the street for Cline. Susan reached forward from the back seat and put a hand on my shoulder, and we watched the silhouettes of Doc and Squid standing still, waiting, as the painful seconds ticked by.

Squid reached into his pocket, probably for another cigarette. I heard his voice over the phone as he spoke to Doc. "You scared?" he asked the doctor.

"A little," Doc admitted. "You?"

The boy didn't answer. I felt my stomach twist. "Your man thinks he got Cline all wrapped up, huh?" Squid said.

"I think we're good," Doc said. "This is going to work."

"Famous last words." Squid laughed.

I watched as he drew a knife from his pocket and plunged it into the old man's stomach.

CHAPTER ONE HUNDRED

I HAD ONLY seconds to witness the horror of the old man collapsing as though sucker-punched, the boy's shoulder dipping and surging upward as he thrust the knife expertly into Doc's rib cage. The windshield before me exploded. I felt the seat I was sitting in thump as a bullet tore into the headrest right beside my ear. Cline was striding up the sidewalk, his gun in both hands, the pistol bucking as he pumped bullets into the car. I glimpsed a devilish smile. Squid had warned him. They'd orchestrated this together.

Susan didn't scream. She popped her door just as I did, and we fell out onto the road together and crawled on the asphalt scattered with glass as bullets zinged off the cars around us. I couldn't tell when Cline's gun ran out of ammunition and when Nick's and Malone's firing began. I heard them shouting from the end of the street, saw Cline swivel and try to shoot in that direction, his gun clicking uselessly. He ejected his mag and pumped another clip in as a bullet tinked off a lamppost right by his face. He didn't flinch. This was his city now too, and these were his streets, and the slices of darkness and cars and concrete edges seemed designed to protect him. He fired, and I saw Nick spin as he caught one in the shoulder.

Susan brushed past me, straightened up a bit so that she could steady her aim on the hood of the car. She fired twice at Cline. One bullet hit the wall behind him, alerting him to the coming second round. He whipped his head left, which made what would have been a fatal shot in the face a graze across the temple by his ear. The shot spooked him, and he fell into the shadows.

He was gone, ducking between the cars, a flash of black coat between a car that had turned into the street and stopped at the sound of the firefight. Gunshots roared between the buildings overhead, clapping and echoing like thunder. I grabbed my gun from the car and followed Susan to the other side of the road, where we crouched by Doc Simeon, who was pointing in the direction that Squid had gone, coughing blood onto his cheeks and shirt.

"It's going to be okay," Susan told him, pulling his coat closed over the wound in his stomach. Her hands were instantly drenched in blood that looked purple in the gold light of the apartment building. "You're okay. You're okay. It's nothing."

Sweet lies from a beautiful woman. There were worse ways to die, I thought. The old man's feet scraped against the sidewalk. I looked down the street and saw Malone and Nick running toward us.

"Are you all right?" I grabbed Nick. His jaw was clenched, and he was panting hard. Malone tossed me an extra clip for my gun. Nick's shirt was wet with blood, but he hardly seemed to notice the wound, that strange manic electricity taking hold of him quickly, making him shiver under my grasp.

"We've gotta go! We've gotta go!" He tried to drag me down the street. "They ran that way!"

"I'll stay here." Susan knelt over the doctor, pressing hard on his wound. Every cell in my body was telling me to stay with her, to be here for the moments that my friend lay dying on the ground, to somehow try to stop the life from draining from his worn body.

"Go, Bill." Susan pushed at me. "You've got to stop Cline."

CHAPTER ONE HUNDRED ONE

MALONE WAS AHEAD of me. He turned the corner of a closed and silent bank and a gunshot clapped overhead; the concrete corner of an ornate pillar just by his face exploded, forcing him back. We ran into each other, then pressed against the wall. I saw movement to my side and noticed a couple who had been out for a late-night walk cowering between two cars, their big spotted dog twisting and tugging on a leash, terrified. Malone rushed forward into the alley between the streets, but when I looked back to find Nick, who I thought was following us, he was nowhere to be seen. Cline rose from behind a dumpster at the end of the alley, fired off a couple of shots, and sprinted into the dark.

"Nick's not with us!" I grabbed Malone's arm. "I have to go back."

"He'll be fine!" Malone dragged me forward. "We've got to get this bastard off the street!"

We ran across the road, causing a car to slam on its brakes, the hood halting inches from my knees, the head-lights blinding. In a courtyard, the water in a large square fountain set into the pavement was so still that Malone didn't see it; he sprinted in, tripped, and splashed to the other side. We crouched against a post as bullets popped into a low garden wall beside me.

Across the courtyard, Cline and Squid met, two frantic silhouettes against the reflective glass of an office building.

Cline turned, and for a moment I thought it was his re-flection that stepped out and raised the gun and pumped Squid's frail, lean frame full of bullets. But it was a bigger, stronger man, a shape I recognized, gunning the kid down with the precise motions of a machine. Nick didn't even seem to see Cline, who shot out the glass door beside him and ran into the dark. Nick looked down at his victim, then up at me as I ran to his side.

"Jesus," he said. His eyes were wild, flicking between re-alities, over Squid's body and then to the gun in his hand. "I killed him. I killed a kid."

CHAPTER ONE HUNDRED TWO

NICK DROPPED HIS weapon and gripped his head, trying to blink away whatever he was seeing. He flinched at a noise or a movement that wasn't there, grabbed his weapon, and pushed it into my hands.

"I can't...I can't...I can't do this. Is...is this real? Did I—"

"He's dead." Malone had his fingers against Squid's motionless carotid. He looked at me. "Cline's alone. This is our chance."

"I can't come with you." Nick backed away from me. "I'm sorry, Bill. I don't know what's...I just shot a kid! Christ!"

I thought about going with Nick. But Malone had run through the automatic doors beside me. One friend was facing Cline alone, and the other was facing his nightmares. I stuffed Nick's pistol down the back of my jeans and ran into the dark building.

CHAPTER ONE HUNDRED THREE

IT WAS AN unfinished office building of some sort, belonged to a big corporation. Expensive chrome and marble, light fixtures hanging from their housings, and transparent plastic sheets draped over furniture. Malone was covering the elevators, where a bloody smear on the up button was as stark as a brushstroke of black ink against the white wall. A ruse. Cline wouldn't wait for the elevator. He wouldn't put himself in a box with only one way in and one way out no matter how fast it moved away from where his enemies were. Malone crept to the stairs and I followed. In the eerie green light of an exit sign hanging over the fire door, he pointed to a nickel-size drop of blood on the floor.

Time circling, looping back. I remembered days earlier, before Marni, before Doc, before I really knew what darkness had come into my life, Nick and I breaching Winley

Minnow's house together. Malone and I going through apartment buildings like this, floor by floor, a hundred or a thousand times across the years. My brothers in arms. It had been a mistake for Cline to think he could come back to our city and best us. We knew this place. Even if we'd been thrown out as guardians of these streets, these buildings, we had never put down our shields.

Floor by floor, we followed the dark spots in the deep green light, a blood trail Susan had started when she grazed Cline's temple and ear with her shot. She was with us as we followed, round and round, floor by floor, chasing the wolf up the stairs.

We were sweating as we reached the seventeenth floor, panting, every muscle ticking with tension. Only minutes had passed, but I felt like I'd followed Cline out of the depths of hell and up to the surface of the earth. We couldn't let him get out among the people again. He was our curse to contain.

Malone stopped me at the eighteenth floor, his eyes searching the ground for the spots, finding nothing. The hand that pressed against my chest felt strangely cold. Malone was so thin I could see the tendons in his neck and shoulder moving as he worked his jaw. He dried his hand on his jeans and tested the door handle—it was wet with Cline's sweat. Malone stepped back, and I kicked the fire door open from the side.

Gunshots ripped through the door as it swung, showering me in splinters. Malone fired into the dark and I threw myself into the room, rolled, fired wildly as Malone came in with me. I felt like Cline had fired from the north end of the huge room, but I couldn't be sure. The space before me, outlined against the city lights, was a complicated maze of cubicles with desks and chairs and more furniture shrouded in plastic wrap.

All was silent save for the ringing in my ears and the whistling of the night wind through bullet holes in the distant windows.

Then Cline spoke.

CHAPTER ONE HUNDRED FOUR

"ROBINSON!" HE ROARED my name, the word trailing off into an exhausted, angry laugh. "You should have just moved!"

I locked eyes with Malone. He was huddled behind a desk across a short aisle. In the ticking seconds, my heightened senses registered strange, disconnected details. People had started to move into the office, even though it wasn't finished. There was a pink afghan draped over a chair beside my partner. A framed photo on a desk. I saw a panel of lights on the wall, thought about turning them on. I knew I couldn't trust what the reflections against the huge windows would reveal of me to Cline. Malone signaled, and we started moving slowly and silently toward where the voice was coming from.

"Why didn't you leave town if you didn't like what I was

doing?" Cline shouted. "You stupid prick. You dug in. Now look at you. You're drowning, boy. When the big bad storm rolls in, you head for the hills. Don't you know that, you dumb fuck!"

I didn't want to let Cline know where I was, but I couldn't help myself. "You're the one who better run, Cline!" I shouted. "This ends here!"

Predictably, my voice was met with a hail of bullets. I crouched between the desks and fired, caught a flash of Cline by the windows, a streak of shadow. I waited until the shooting stopped, then crawled on my hands and knees toward the last place I'd seen the man. I could see the icy white lights of Fenway Park in the floor-to-ceiling windows.

"I'm not scared of you, Robinson." Cline laughed. I could hear him reloading his gun again. "You're a good man. You're a protector. You got caught up in that bullshit with your partner only because you thought you were protecting some girl."

Malone's sharp breath came from quite close to me. He was working his way along the ground in the next aisle of cubicles. Our eyes met, and I saw the pain in his face through the darkness.

"You're not going to hunt me down like this. You'll walk away and let me go. You know what you are, Robinson. You're not a killer."

Cline's sales tactics again, trying to tell me what was good for me, trying to bring on the guilt and the pain. Because wasn't that what I wanted to do? Of course I wanted to turn away from the horror that he had brought into my life. For-get it all. Leave town. Ignore the suffering of others. Let the people I loved defend themselves. I knew that if I had not pursued Cline in the first place, Marni might still be alive. Maybe Doc. I'd taken this mission on myself. Cline's sales pitch was good. He was outnumbered two to one, so he was giving it all he had. I could let him go, save myself and my friends additional bloodshed. Hope someone else would bring him to justice.

But Cline was right. Another man might have headed for the hills when Cline moved into town. I was not that man.

"I'm not going anywhere," I yelled. "And neither are you."

I crept along the base of a cubicle divider and heard a shuffle near me; I peered through a crack and saw Malone taking aim.

He fired, blasting out one of the windows. The wind howled, lifting sheets of plastic, making them sail like ghosts through the air. Malone had been near the target, but not on point. He must have fired at Cline's reflection, because the man popped up perpendicular to where Malone had hit, his shots flashing off the ceiling. I was so close that a cartridge from Cline's gun sailed over the top of the cubicle beside me and bounced, red hot, off my shoulder.

Cline had been overzealous, firing where he was sure Malone was, in the cubicle next to me. But he was out of bullets. His gun clicked impotently, and as I felt a smile spread over my face, a sound rose up in the distance. It was a sound I had heard almost constantly for two decades, a sound that once filled me with excitement and now was like a cold hand reaching into my chest and gripping my heart.

The wail of police sirens.

CHAPTER ONE HUNDRED FIVE

CLINE'S LAUGHTER BARELY reached above the rising and falling sirens of three or four squad cars on the street below. I heard his gun clatter to the carpet. He kicked the weapon, and I watched it sail soundlessly across the carpet and over the edge of the blasted-out window into the night. It would fly downward toward the street, empty of bullets, and land on the windshield of a car or on the pavement for the police to find. Cline's gun, with Cline's prints, empty and useless, leaving the cops to conclude that he was unarmed and at our mercy when we did whatever we were about to do next.

Cline rose to his feet and stepped backward toward the wall of windows. The bullet holes in the glass behind him brought a breeze that ruffled his hair. He grinned as Malone and I rose and stepped out from the cubicles.

"Don't be stupid, now," he told us, his tone light and

sweet, like a parent gently chastising a child. "You know how this could end. You're already on the wrong side of the Boston PD. Committing a cold-blooded murder wouldn't end well for the two of you."

Cline eyed Malone, getting his first good look at my partner. Malone's gun was held out like mine, an extension of his body, straight and high and pointed at Cline's chest.

"Cold-blooded murder suits you perfectly," I said. I was trembling all over with rage. "If we let you go now, there will be more teenagers who take a pill of yours at a party and die lonely deaths in the woods. There will be more soldiers strangled in their beds, more doctors ruining their good names by taking your dirty money."

"Maybe." Cline shrugged. "But you can hear the sirens, Bill. They're coming for us. You're not going to do this. Think about those people at the house. They need you, and you need them. You're happy there, aren't you? You've got a good life. You've got too much to live for, Robinson."

Malone looked at me. There was a mixture of sadness and resolve in his features; his eyes hardened and then emptied.

He turned to Cline.

"He does," Malone said. "But I don't."

CHAPTER ONE HUNDRED SIX

MY LIMBS WERE frozen, though I could see what was about to happen as soon as Malone's gaze turned from mine. He dropped his gun, bent low, and threw all his body weight into the sprint, his shoulders and long arms out, ready to catch Cline should he try to run. Cline saw it coming but seemed as immobile as I was, his eyes full of the awful breathless terror of a man already dead before his heart had stopped beating. Malone slammed into Cline, the momentum carrying them both toward the window that was already weakened by bullet holes. The deafening crunch of Cline's shoulders meeting the glass was like a gunshot, quickening my heavy limbs. It seemed like I watched them falling through the splintering, shattering glass, the window collapsing like a curtain, the two men hanging almost in the dark air beyond the bounds of the building. I ran for them as fast as I could.

I dropped, slid in the glass, was close enough to touch Malone's boot as the two fell. I gripped the edge of the floor as the icy wind raked my hair, a scream shuddering out of my lungs as they disappeared into the darkness.

For a second before they were consumed by the night, I saw Cline's bulging eyes over Malone's shoulder, heard his scream carried by the wind. He was reaching for me. I covered my eyes, rolled away from the edge, and curled into a ball, as though the motion could drown out the sickening sound of my friend and my enemy thudding to the pavement eighteen floors below.

I was saved from that horror by the noise of a team of officers crashing through the door to the office, shouting, guns drawn, flashlights winding over the room. Lights swept over me. I didn't get a good look at whoever reached me first. I was shoved onto my stomach and cuffed in the darkness.

CHAPTER ONE HUNDRED SEVEN

THE OFFICERS WHO had responded to reports of a shoot-out in the Boston CBD were young, fit, crisis-squad guys. They were the heavily tattooed and worryingly muscular types who had joined the force for the sole purpose of making the chaotic, fast-paced, high-stakes special response team. Black tactical vests, big guns. They knew who I was by my ruined reputation only. These guys were used to being over the top, and I didn't take it personally. Two gripped my arms as we rode the elevator down; another stood by the door with his gun hanging in his gloved hand, barking questions at me.

"Are there any other shooters?"

"No," I said.

"What is this? A drug thing? You and Malone taking out your dealer? Your partner? We've got reports of four casualties in the street. Two from the building. You push those guys from that window? Who's the kid on the sidewalk? You shoot that kid? Who's the old man?"

Four casualties. Doc hadn't made it.

"You're not giving me enough time to respond to these questions," I remarked calmly to the head guy. "You're just asking questions without waiting for answers."

"What are you, some kind of smart-ass? Is that it? You a smart-ass, Robinson?"

I sighed and stared at the door.

The street was a wash of red and blue light; there were dozens of officers rigging cordons, crunching through the glass on the foyer floor in their heavy boots, making radio reports. Half the people present had their guns drawn. It wasn't every day in Boston that men fell from skyscrapers and civilians took cover from bullets. I was marched past Squid's body, already covered with a sheet. I spotted Nick sitting cuffed in the back of a police car.

I was being pushed toward another police car when Susan ran out of the crowd toward me. She was somehow beautiful even then, maybe because I was so relieved at seeing her unharmed. She was flushed and didn't slow as she approached, so she knocked the wind out of me as she wrapped her arms around me in a desperate embrace.

"I saw them fall." She was shivering, gripping my shirt as though we'd be wrenched apart at any moment. "Jesus Christ, Bill, I thought it was you. I heard a scream and I looked up and—what the *fuck* happened?"

I didn't answer. Over Susan's shoulder, I saw another familiar face in the crowd, a woman approaching with her characteristic stiff-legged walk and unflappable expression. Commissioner Rachel McGinniskin was in full uniform, as if she wore it to bed and had been roused in the early hours and come right here with perfectly polished buttons and her hat perched like a crown on her curls.

"Robinson," she said by way of greeting. "Why am I not surprised?"

CHAPTER ONE HUNDRED EIGHT

"RACHEL," I CALLED her, because I could. A tiny, mean-spirited joy in my evening, making the squad guys bristle at my disrespect of their gold-striped queen. She licked her teeth and looked Susan up and down, raising her eyebrows at the blood—Doc's—that stained Susan's clothes from neck to knee.

"I got a call a half an hour ago saying guys were shooting at each other in the street," she said. "I thought, *What a dangerous, irresponsible, cowardly thing to be doing.* A witness looking out her apartment window at the fray reportedly recognized one of them as a former Boston PD officer, and I thought, *Ah. Our old friend is back.*"

"I try to make an entrance wherever I go," I said.

Rachel hadn't told the thugs flanking me to get rid of the cuffs. I guess she deserved a tiny, mean-spirited joy in her night too. She nodded at them to leave us. I took a couple of steps back and sat on the warm hood of a squad car. Exhaustion and shock were setting in. Susan put a hand on the nape of my neck, firm and calming. McGinniskin made a get-on-with-it gesture, rotating her finger like she was spinning a wheel, and in a low voice I told her what had happened on the street and in the tower and in the days before Cline and I came together for the last time.

"You really are a piece of work, you know that, Robinson?" McGinniskin said. I couldn't argue.

Commissioner McGinniskin folded her arms, glanced away, seemed to try to take in the story. She looked like she was struggling to decide how to say what she had to say next. In the end, she just laid it on me straight.

"A letter from Malone came through my office on Monday," she said.

I just looked at her.

"He explained what the two of you did a couple of years ago," she said. "He took full responsibility. Said he tricked you into it. Some story about a girl who needed help and a sex tape."

I glanced at Susan. She put her arm around me, kissed my head.

"Of course, how can I believe him?" McGinniskin mused. There was a softness to her voice I'd never heard before. Though her face remained hard, all the fury had suddenly left her. She took a handcuff key from her pocket and tossed it to Susan.

"Malone knew he was dying," McGinniskin said. "Could just be that he had been planning some kind of big fuck-you like this all along." She gestured to the building above us, the site of my partner's fall. "And why not save your skin in the process? One last favor for an old friend."

"Could be," I said. I wasn't up for fighting for my cause now. But for some reason, I felt like I didn't have to. Susan unlocked my cuffs and I handed them to the commissioner.

"Malone returned the remaining stolen money with the letter," McGinniskin said. "Seventeen thousand dollars. I guess that was all that was left after his treatments. Makes me wonder why, if you were indeed his willing partner in crime, he didn't just give it to you. But in any case, what could I do with it? The guy you both robbed never made an official report, of course. The department suspects the funds are a result of his criminal activity."

"So what did you do with it?" I asked.

"I donated it to a homeless shelter," she said, giving a dismissive wave.

I didn't know if I was free to go and was too tired to ask. I stood and started walking off, but the commissioner called my name and I turned to look back at her standing by the squad car, her arms still folded defensively.

"Stay in touch," she said with great reluctance. "There are times I could use a good man who's not on the payroll."

I nodded, and Susan linked her arm with mine as we walked away. After a few steps she poked me in the arm.

"Good man, huh?" she asked.

"She must be thinking of someone else." I smiled.

CHAPTER ONE HUNDRED NINE

"THIS IS RIDICULOUS," Angelica said, looking at her watch. "If they say they're going to be here at ten, they ought to be here at ten!"

"Sit down." Vinny patted the plastic lawn chair beside him at the foldout table. "You're makin' me nervous. The guy's gonna be here when he gets here and that's all there is to it."

I sat at the end of the table with Susan, waiting, as my friends waited, for the FedEx driver whose delivery Angelica had been anticipating for six months. Before us on the picnic table on the lawn was spread a feast not dissimilar to the one Marni had arranged what seemed a lifetime ago to mourn my lost wife. Croissants, bagels, doughnuts, yellow napkins, and yellow paper plates left over from the memorial caught the light filtering through the trees.

We were back where we had started, and yet so far from there. The people laughing, talking, drinking coffee around me in the morning light were battle-scarred. Some of them didn't sleep well anymore. Some of them had the evidence of their fight on their skin. What Cline had brought into our town had left its mark, but right now, there were more important things to think about.

Next to Vinny, Effie sat with a black coffee in front of her, tearing strips off a croissant. Now and then as she ate, twitching whiskers would emerge from her shirt pocket and she would take a flake of croissant and present it to the snuffling nose. Crazy the rat had become a kind of household mascot in the time since Effie had rescued him from the drain, and feeding him bread, peanuts, sunflower seeds, and the occasional blueberry was an activity everyone—except Angelica—enjoyed. Effie's shirt pocket sagged with the weight of the obese rodent, drawing her collar sideways, away from her scarred neck.

As I watched my people enjoying themselves, a movement in the window above us caught my eye. Neddy Ives was watching, his arms folded, his eyes moving over Angelica as she complained to Vinny about the FedEx guy. He wouldn't join us, I knew, but even a glimpse of him in the window was better than nothing. He was changed, like the rest of us.

"I know this is Angelica's day," Susan said. "But I keep thinking about Marni."

I looked at her and was surprised to see her smiling.

"She'd have been so buzzed about this," she said. "Waiting for the books to arrive. Opening the box for the first time. She always got in on other people's excitement."

Clay was near us, leaning on the table as he listened to Susan's words.

"I still think about her all the time," he said. "I know it's stupid but...I thought just this morning that after what happened, her mother would have found out that the little heart tattoo on her cheek was real."

"It was real?" I gasped.

Susan laughed. "Of course it was."

"She told me—"

"That she drew it in every day with lip liner." Clay laughed. "Yeah. She said she was going to tell you that."

"So you all knew the tattoo was real? Everybody knew except me?"

"We helped her hide it from you when it was fresh and swollen." Susan snickered. "When you arrived home, we'd warn her. She kept her right side to you for about a week. You had no idea."

The two of them giggled together. I sat back in my chair and cradled my coffee.

"My house is full of liars," I said.

My own words stayed with me as I looked around the table. Though Susan had told me a little more about her ex-husband and her need to hide from him, I still knew nothing more about what Effie Johnson, sitting feeding her pet rat, had seen or heard that meant she had come and hid in my house. I didn't know who'd tried to kill her, and every day the secret wandered the house as she did. I didn't know why the man standing in the window above us never left his room, whether it was fear or habit that kept him away from human contact. Nick had not told me any more about what he had done in the Middle East that left him so scarred and broken, but I had a feeling that his memories and hallucinations were tied to something impossibly dark, something beyond the horrors of war.

When Siobhan had assembled the crew before me, she might have known she was taking liars, runaways, and secret keepers into our home. But even that, I would never know for sure.

I drank my coffee and watched them all and felt strangely comforted by their many untruths. This inn by the sea had become a safe place for those who were lost. It was like a harbor from the storm, accepting all, no matter the loads they carried.

"Maybe it's time," Susan said. She elbowed me in the ribs, and I stood, getting the attention of everyone at the table. Clay and Nick looked over from where they had been huddled over a newspaper, reading an article about this year's Sox lineup.

I drew a breath. "I'd just like to—"

"You can't do this now!" Angelica cried. "He's not here yet!"

"Let him make his speech." Nick waved at Angelica. "Then when the guy gets here, you can make yours."

"I'd just like to congratulate you, Angelica," I said, "on the publication of your very first novel. I was glad to hear everybody made it into the last draft. Even you, Vinny, although I don't know how you ended up as a dangerously attractive neurosurgeon."

"It's the knives." The old gangster shrugged.

"I believe from the excerpt I read that the character called

Susan is a smart-talking fighter pilot." I gestured to Susan, who grinned. "Brave and clever. Sounds about right. And then there's me. The crazed arsonist. Who knows how you got there, Ange."

"You've burned a few steaks in your life, Bill," Clay mused. "You always burn the potatoes. A few pieces of toast. Some chicken kebabs—"

"Thanks, Clay, thanks for that." I raised my glass. "Anyway, what I'm saying is that we're very proud of you. Our very own author in the house. I'm sure I speak for everyone when I say that we can't wait to—"

"He's here!" Angelica yelled.

CHAPTER ONE HUNDRED TEN

THE FEDEX MAN had followed our sign at the front of the house and was turning the corner of the porch hefting a large box. Angelica ran to him like a wife welcoming a sailor home from a decade at sea. Everyone crowded around as she placed the carton on the table and set to it with a box cutter.

As my friends huddled around one of their own in her proudest moment, I looked at the faces near me. Nick had been officially diagnosed with schizophrenia and was being treated. He caught my eye from across the group, and despite the terrible secrets he carried with him, he smiled. Clay was on the other side of Angelica, chewing his nails in anticipation. When I glanced up I saw that Neddy Ives was looking down, his head almost touching the windowpane in order to get a better view.

Angelica shoved open the flaps of the box, reached into the packing peanuts, and brought out a book with a yellow-and-black cover. A moan of appreciation went up from the gathering.

"What's it called again?" Vinny leaned in to see. He'd been asking what it was called for weeks, over and over, poking fun at his girlfriend. Angelica put the book in his hands and I saw the jacket illustration of a beautiful woman, a farmer's wife, looking out across an empty field.

"'*The Lucky Ones,*'" Vinny read.

"It's an allegory," Angelica said proudly. "It's based on a story Marni told me once. Oh, I can't wait for you to read it, Vin."

The old gangster tucked the book under his arm and started wheeling himself away. "Any excuse to get some goddamn time to myself. I'm outta here. See you guys on the last page."

CHAPTER ONE HUNDRED ELEVEN

BEFORE THE PARTY could break up, I tapped Effie on the shoulder. The fat lump in her shirt pocket was wiggling, the little pink nose snuffling for more treats.

"I've got a present for you," I said.

She pointed at her chest.

"Yeah, you," I said. I gave her a package I'd wrapped in pretty silver paper. Hearing the packet rustling, Crazy poked his head all the way out of Effie's pocket. I watched as Effie unfolded the paper to reveal a thick paintbrush.

She looked at me, questioning.

"We can start tomorrow," I said. "I'll help."

Effie grinned and punched the air. Susan clapped her hands beside me, looking up at the worn and weather-beaten house.

"It's going to look beautiful, Bill." She put an arm around my waist. "It's about time."

"I have a present for you too," I told her. "Come on."

I led Susan through the house, up the stairs, and to the loft door. I turned a handle that hadn't been turned in three years, and it came off in my hand.

"Son of a..."

I put the doorknob in my pocket, shouldered the door open. Walking the dusty steps to the big, peaked-roof room was like climbing up a mountain, exhausting but also exhilarating. I stood with her in the dim light filtering through the cracks between three wooden boards nailed over the circular window, gold dust motes swirling all around us. From my coat I took another package wrapped in paper and handed it to her.

"It's like Christmas." She laughed. She unwrapped the claw hammer and smiled at me.

"Go ahead," I said.

Susan put the claws of the hammer into the first plank and yanked the handle upward; the old, dry wood squeaked as she ripped it from the frame. In a short time, she'd removed all the planks from the window. We looked out at the pine trees and the pale gray sea beyond.

"It's going to take some work," I said. "But if you want to, I think we could make it a great room."

We held each other and watched a crab boat on the horizon heading for the harbor.

"I can hear the waves," she said.

THERE'S NO TIME TO WASTE. AND IF THEY FAIL — THEY DIE.

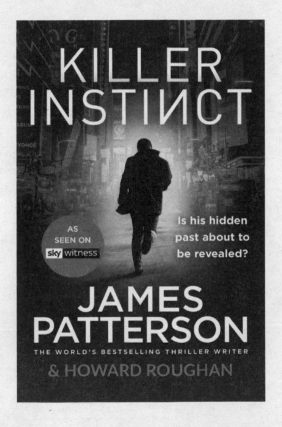

Read on for a sneak preview of *Killer Instinct*, available in paperback from May 2020

THERE'S NOTHING quite like walking into a room packed with more than a hundred students and not a single one is happy to see you...

If I didn't know any better, I'd almost take it personally.

"Good morning, class," I began, "and welcome to your final exam in Abnormal Behavioral Analysis, otherwise known as Professor Dylan Reinhart messing with your impressionable minds for a little while in an effort to see if you actually learned anything this glorious spring semester. As legend correctly has it, I never give the same test twice, which means that all of you will be spared any repeat of a previous exam, including my personal all-time favorite, having everyone in the class write and perform an original rap song about Sigmund Freud's seduction theory."

I paused for a moment to allow for the inevitable objection from the brave, albeit delusional, student who thought he or she might finally be the one to appeal to my better judgment, whatever that was.

Sure enough, a hand shot up. It belonged to a young man, probably a sophomore, wearing a rugby shirt and a look of complete consternation.

"Yes, is there a question?" I asked.

He was sitting in the third row, and best I could tell, it had been three days since he last showered. Finals week at Yale is hell on personal hygiene.

"This isn't fair, Professor Reinhart," he announced.

I waited for him to continue and plead his case diligently, but that was all he had to offer. There was no rehearsed speech on how all the other professors give their students a study guide or at least explain what they should expect on the final.

"That's it?" I asked. "That's all you've got for me? *This isn't fair?*"

"I just think we should've had a chance to prepare for this test," he said. "The only thing you told us was that we all had to bring our cell phones."

"Yes, I see. Clearly a miscarriage of justice," I said. It was a little early in the morning for the full-on Reinhart sarcasm, but sometimes these kids left me no choice. I turned to the rest of the class. "With a show of hands, how many of you agree with your esteemed colleague here? How many think that what I'm doing is unfair?"

Literally every hand went up.

I so love it when they make it easy for me…

"Wow, that's pretty impressive," I said, looking around the room. "You're all in agreement. All for one and one for all. Kumbaya!"

Mr. Rugby Shirt in the third row all but pumped his fist in

victory. "Does that mean you've changed your mind, Professor Reinhart? You're postponing the test?"

Silly rabbit.

"No, it means the test has already begun," I said. "Now everyone please take out your cell phones and place them directly in front of you. *It's time to see how united you all really are.*"

I WATCHED and waited a few seconds while everyone took out their phones. *Note to self: buy more Apple stock for Annabelle's college fund.*

Then I went to the blackboard behind me, picked up a piece of chalk, and began writing. It was my cell number. Nothing more.

"Okay," I said, turning back around to the class. "I want you all to pick up your phones and text me the grade you'd like to receive on the final exam. You can choose between an A or a B. Whichever you text me is the grade you'll get."

I wiped my hands free of any chalk, gave a tug on the notched lapel of my navy chambray suit jacket, and started walking blithely toward the exit.

"Wait!" came a chorus of voices. "WAIT! WAIT! WAAAAIT!"

I stopped. "Yes? What's the problem?"

"That's it?" they all asked. That and numerous variations on the same theme. *"That's all we have to do?"*

I smacked my forehead. "Gosh darn it, you're right. There is one other thing I forgot to mention. Actually, two other things," I said. "The first is that I'm afraid I can't give you all As. Ten of you will have to choose Bs."

Cue the chorus again. *"That's not fair!"*

"We're back to that again, huh? Fairness?"

"Why would anyone choose a B?"

"That's the other thing I forgot to mention," I said. "Perhaps this will make it easier for you all. If at least ten of you don't choose a B, then you all get Cs, each and every one of you, the entire class. I repeat, a C. All of you. No exceptions."

It was as if I'd just told a roomful of five-year-olds that there isn't a Santa Claus. No, worse. That I had *killed* Santa Claus—and his little furry friend, too, the Easter Bunny. Shock. Anger. Disbelief. *We can't believe you're doing this to us, Professor Reinhart!*

It was beautiful.

Sorry, Sigmund, I now had a new favorite final exam. The setup had gone perfectly. All I had to do was wait for the emotional dust to settle. They would all start to think. First as individuals, then together as a group. It would begin with one simple—

"Question?" I asked, pointing at Mr. Rugby Shirt in the third row. He'd raised his hand again.

"Yeah, I was wondering," he said. "Are we all allowed to talk to one another before we each text you our grade?"

I pretended to think it over for a few seconds, even scratching my chin for added effect. "I suppose I'll allow that," I said. "In return, though, I'll need to put a time limit on any deliberations. Ten minutes should be enough." After a few groans from those who wanted more time, I glanced at my watch. "Make that nine minutes and fifty seconds."

7

The groans stopped and everyone scrambled like mad to huddle up.

Later, they would learn how they were subjects of an experiment for my next book, and that the tiny cameras and microphones I had installed around the room were recording everything they said and did.

Would they be pissed? Sure. Right up until I announced that they were *all* getting an A on the final for being good sports. In fact, I could already hear the cheering.

But that was then. For now, they were a group of more than a hundred ultra-competitive students at Yale deciding collectively who would sacrifice for the greater good. How would they decide? *Could* they decide?

Would the best of human behavior prevail?

I headed for the exit again so they could all talk freely. I didn't want anything to affect the outcome, especially me. There could be no distractions, nothing to derail the experiment.

And nothing would—I was sure of it.

Silly rabbit.

No sooner had I reached the door than I heard the first *ping*. Then immediately another, followed by a few more. Everyone's phones were lighting up with the breaking news. Including mine.

Something terrible had happened. Just dreadful. The absolute worst of human behavior.

New York City, my home, had been attacked again.

I WAS redlining even before I hit the highway. One hand was maxing out on the throttle of my old '61 Triumph TR6 Trophy; the other was trying for the umpteenth time to reach Tracy. The wind was whipping past me, my cell plastered tight against my ear. To hell with my helmet.

Again the call went straight to voicemail, and again I hit Redial. *Please, please, please! Pick up, Tracy!* We should've never ditched our landline. I couldn't even try him at home.

The news alerts and tweets lighting up everyone's phones in class reported that multiple bombs had gone off in Times Square. A couple hundred were feared dead, if not more.

Like everyone else, I felt the initial shock up and down my spine. Then came an even greater jolt, straight through the heart.

Tracy had told me in the morning that he was planning to take Annabelle to the Disney Store—right in the middle of Times Square. Our adopted daughter from South Africa was only a little over a year old, and yet she was somehow totally smitten with the place. The music, the colors, the characters she didn't even know the names of yet. It all made her smile from ear to ear. She loved that Disney Store more than her binkie, bubble baths, or the monkeys at the Central Park Zoo.

At eighty miles an hour, I started to cry.

Weaving in and out of traffic, riding like a maniac, I could feel the anger in me taking over. My time in London, my years with the CIA. All of it had been dedicated to fighting a war that could never be won, only contained. Terrorism isn't merely a tactic of the enemy; it's the root of their ideology. They *believe* in destruction. They *want* death. And there are no innocent victims. Not to them.

Only to us.

A half hour into the ride, I gave up on trying to call Tracy. A half hour after that, I saw the flashing cherries of patrol cars at the entrance to the Henry Hudson Bridge. Lined up grill to bumper, the cruisers were barricading all three southbound lanes. No one was getting in.

No one was able to make a call either, I was told. At least not on their cells.

"All the carriers were forced to shut down their networks," said the second cop I approached after getting off my bike.

The first cop had all but ignored me. He was too busy directing traffic in what had become a three-point-turn festival with all the southbound cars that had been heading into the city needing to do a one-eighty. Making those turns even tighter were the piles of torn-up pavement from some recent jackhammering. *For once can there be a bridge into Manhattan that isn't under construction?*

"They're saying the terrorists used cell phones to detonate the bombs," the second cop explained. "For all we know there might be more to come."

"I need to get into the city," I said. "How do I do it?"

He looked at me as if I were deaf. Did I not just hear him? "You don't," he said. "No one gets in."

No, you don't understand, officer. I need. To get. Into the city!

I stared at him for a few seconds, hoping he might recognize me. It had been less than a year since I'd had my fifteen minutes of fame by helping to rid Manhattan of a serial killer named the Dealer. In the process, I had gained a couple of nicknames myself, including Dr. Death. For a while I was getting stopped on the street at least once a day. *Hey, aren't you that guy…?* Now it was maybe once a month.

All glory is fleeting, said General George Patton.

So much for staring at the cop. He didn't recognize me. I could've tried to refresh his memory or begun pleading my case, telling him about Tracy and Annabelle, but there was no point. He had his orders. The guy was merely doing his job. Besides, I'd already made up my mind on what I would do.

Time was wasting.

I WALKED quickly back to my bike. Running would've been too obvious. The helmet went on, and the license plate got ripped off and stuffed inside my jacket.

I flipped on the petcock, checked the kill switch, turned the key, squeezed the clutch, and started her up. One quick zig to the left, a sharp zag to the right, and I had the clear path I needed. Now I just needed the speed.

Jamming the throttle, I was redlining again within seconds.

The first cop didn't know what the hell was happening as I blew by him. The second cop, the one I had spoken to, knew exactly what I was about to do but couldn't do anything about it. He looked at me in utter disbelief before turning to the pile of torn up pavement about ten feet in front of the cruisers blocking my way.

One man's rubble is another man's ramp.

I hit the pile hard, pulling up on my handgrips even harder.

There would be no style points. It was ugly. Steve McQueen made it look so easy on the same bike in *The Great Escape*.

My back tire barely cleared the hood of the first cruiser, and I could hear my axle practically snapping as the front tire slammed the pavement. I nearly wiped out—I *should've* wiped out—but somehow I kept my balance.

There was no need to look over my shoulder as I raced onto the deserted lower deck of the bridge heading into Manhattan. Those two cops weren't going anywhere. I was already too far gone. At most, they were radioing ahead to wherever the roadblock was for the northbound traffic, but that would only be to cover their collective ass instead of catching mine.

At the first exit, I peeled off the parkway onto Dyckman Street and into the Upper West Side. Tracy, Annabelle, and I called the neighborhood home. All along, I couldn't stop thinking the unthinkable, that the two most important people in my life—the two I could never imagine living without—were suddenly gone. *Christ, this can't be happening.*

The rest of the ride was a blur as I shot between all the traffic while completely ignoring red lights. In the distance I could hear a slew of ambulances, each one louder than the next, and all of them echoing in my head. It was the soundtrack of a living nightmare.

Finally I reached the front of our apartment building, ditching my bike in the middle of the sidewalk. I sprinted into the lobby and straight for the elevator with no intention of stopping until I saw the doorman, Bobby, sitting on an upholstered bench along the wall. He was completely engrossed in his cell phone. I could tell he was watching news coverage of the bombings.

"Have you seen them?" I asked, half out of breath.

He looked up at me, confused. "Who?"

I would've been confused, too. "Tracy and Annabelle," I said. "Have you seen them this morning?"

Bobby—who everyone called Lobby Bobby, albeit not to his face—acted as if I'd just asked him to explain quantum physics. The fact that I was so panicked only made him more flustered.

"Oh. Um...no, I haven't seen them," he said. "No, wait, *I did see them*. They went out earlier this morning, before the first—"

"Have you seen them since? Did you see them return?" I was talking a million words a minute.

"I don't think so," he said. "Is everything okay?"

But by then he was talking to my back. I was halfway to the elevator. I needed to see for myself. I needed Bobby to be wrong. He was distracted. He usually was, after all. He was often talking to some other tenants or signing for a package. That's what happened.

Tracy and Annabelle had returned home. They were safe. I was going to open the door to our apartment and call out as I always did, *Where's Anna-banana?* Then I'd wait and listen for that glorious sound, the pitter-patter, her little feet shuffling along the floor around the corner of the foyer as she came running into my arms.

But there was no sound when I opened the door. No pitter-patter. The apartment was empty.

Tracy and Annabelle were gone.

"WHAT THE hell are you doing here, Needham?"

Elizabeth stared back at Evan Pritchard, wondering if perhaps she'd misheard her new boss of only two days amid all the chaos. No such luck. The guy was actually pissed off to see her.

"I'm here to help," answered Elizabeth. *What the hell do you think I'm doing here?*

"If you wanted to help me," said Pritchard, "you'd still be up in Boston, where you're supposed to be. Where I sent you."

Is this guy serious?

Elizabeth turned slowly to look at the devastation surrounding the two of them in Times Square as if maybe that might knock some sense into the guy or at least make him ease up. This was the worst attack on US soil since 9/11 and it happened in the same city—their goddamn backyard, for Christ's sake.

Times Square was no longer Times Square. It was a war zone. A coordinated series of C-4 explosions had reduced the stores and theaters to hollowed out shells of twisted metal and shattered glass. It had taken hours to tend to and clear the hundreds of wounded, which meant the dead were still everywhere, covered with bloodstained white sheets. There were too many to count, and yet that's exactly what needed to be done. That and a gazillion other things as part of the investigation. Surely it was all hands on deck for the elite New York–based field unit of the Joint Terrorism Task Force. Including its newest pair of hands, Special Agent Elizabeth Needham.

"Sir, as soon as I heard the news I just assumed that—"

"Of course you did," said Pritchard. "You thought you knew best. That's the rap on you, Needham. You always think you know best."

For a split second, Elizabeth regretted the last three and a half hours of her life, or roughly how long it took her to drive like a maniac from Boston down to Manhattan. But it took only another split second to realize that she'd do it again if given the chance, a hundred times out of a hundred.

This wasn't about her. It was about Pritchard. The guy was bitter. Big time. Six feet plus and roughly 220 pounds of resentment. Worse, he wasn't trying to hide it, not even on the heels of a massive terrorist attack. Her new boss wanted her to know that she wasn't wanted. His elite field unit was handpicked by him, always and without fail. That is, until the mayor got on the phone and told him that the FU, as they loved to call themselves, was being assigned someone new. Detective Needham was now Agent Needham. Pritchard had had no say in the matter. It was a done deal, and Elizabeth knew the guy couldn't stand it. So naturally he couldn't stand her. It was as simple— and effed up—as that.

But Elizabeth held her tongue and the dozen or so jagged-sharp comebacks that were on the tip of it. She knew what she had to do with Pritchard. Go along and get along, or at least get the hell through this miserable, horrible, tragic day. Tell the prick what he wants to hear and then figure out a way to help. Do anything. Do *something*. Search for survivors. Search for bomb fragments.

"I apologize, sir," said Elizabeth. "All I wanted to do was—"

"I get it," said Pritchard. "But look around you, Needham. Look at all the Bureau and Task Force agents who are already here. They're all trying to figure out the same damn thing: *Who did this?* And do you know what they all have in common? Not a single one of them was able to prevent it, including me. So if you really want to help, go back to Boston. Even if there's only a one percent chance your investigation leads to something, it would at least be something we might actually be able to prevent."

Elizabeth hated to admit it, but Pritchard sort of had a point. Still, why couldn't she do both? She could help here today and return to Boston tomorrow. But before she could put that thought into words, Pritchard had already turned his focus to an evidence bag filled with some charred wires that had just been handed to him. He had moved on. His newest agent, courtesy of the mayor, was now supposed to do the same.

Elizabeth walked away. She knew enough to not feel sorry for herself. How could she? She was literally stepping over the dead. As much as she tried not to, she couldn't help gazing at those bloodstained white sheets and the outlines of the bodies they covered.

Suddenly, Elizabeth stopped. One of the sheets was folded back a bit, maybe from a gust of wind. She could see a toddler's hand, a little girl. It was so small. There was a pink Hello Kitty bracelet around her wrist, and all Elizabeth could do was picture the day it was given to her and how much that little girl loved it and how happy it made her. She probably never wanted to take it off, not ever.

Elizabeth froze at the thought of this girl, her legs going numb. The only thing she could do was stare straight up into the heavens. Her years as a detective, the brutal crimes she'd seen, had tested her faith in God to the point where she truly didn't know if he existed. *What god would allow this little girl to die? What god would make all the people who loved her suffer?*

Elizabeth wanted to cry. Instead, she screamed.

In the corner of her eye, she'd seen something. Lots of them. They were in the sky and coming her way. *Everyone's* way.

The attack wasn't over.

"INCOMING!"

Elizabeth yelled at the top of her lungs, her arm rocketing into the air to point north, directly over the building at One Times Square where the ball drops on New Year's Eve.

Everyone around her turned, their necks craning to follow the line of her finger. What they saw coming toward them looked like geese in formation, only these weren't birds. They were drones. Each one was about to drop a bomb, some sort of IED. Hell, you could even see the wiring.

Shoot 'em down! Shoot them all down!

No one screamed it. No one had to.

Elizabeth reached for her gun, as did everyone else who was carrying. She unloaded the clip of her Glock 19, the sky filling with lead. *Pop! Pop-pop-pop-pop!*

BOOM!

The force of the blast knocked Elizabeth hard to the ground. The second blast—*BOOM!*—kept her there as shards of glass from the windows roughly thirty floors above rained down on her. There was no time to take cover. She rolled onto her back, changed out clips, and resumed firing. *How many are left? Three? Four?*

Whoever was controlling the drones could see what was happening. As soon as the first was hit, the others scrambled.

Elizabeth whipped her head left and right, trying to keep track of them. There was now one hovering directly over her.

Single rounds weren't cutting it. There was no way to shoot them all down before—

Shit!

The drone above her released its bomb as Elizabeth fired off the last round in her clip without connecting. She was at ground zero and a sitting duck.

The empty clicks as she continued to pull her trigger sounded like a countdown to her death. All she could do was roll underneath a FedEx truck a few feet away. It wasn't nearly enough protection. She closed her eyes.

BOOM!

Elizabeth felt the blast, the heat singeing her face and hands as the truck buckled and nearly crushed her. It hurt like hell, but it was the best pain in the world because she could feel it. She was still alive. *How the hell?*

Maybe there was a God.

ELIZABETH SLID out from beneath the truck to see what had saved her—but not before hearing it first.

The sound of the gunfire was different, though muffled through her blasted eardrums. The *pop-pop-pop* had been overtaken by the metallic *zip* of submachine guns. The cavalry had arrived in the form of the FBI SWAT team that had been canvassing the perimeter beyond Times Square. One of them had hit the bomb directly over Elizabeth as it dropped, a bull's-eye that had saved her life.

In a double-wedge formation moving up and down Broadway, the team continued to fire. Another drone was obliterated followed by one more, both before they could drop their bombs. Elizabeth's already wobbly knees buckled as she fell to the concrete again from the bombardment, her ears ringing so loudly they were stinging. She couldn't hear. She couldn't do anything.

Finally the SWAT commander yelled out, chopping his hand

through the air. The rest of his team held their fire. Everyone else with any ammo left followed suit.

All eyes remained looking up. Ten seconds became twenty, then thirty. It seemed like forever.

One by one, shoulders began to relax. Guns were holstered. The barrels of the SWAT team's Heckler & Koch UMPs were lowered.

Elizabeth felt a tap on her shoulder and turned. An EMT was talking to her, but it was nothing more than his lips moving. She still couldn't hear. Slowly, she began making out some of the words. The rest she could fill in. He was asking her if she was okay.

"Yeah, I'm fine," Elizabeth lied. She really didn't know for sure. Every part of her hurt.

He pointed to a row of medical tents set up along the nearest cross street. He was saying she needed to be looked at by a doctor.

Elizabeth nodded. It was the most her body could muster. That and hopefully putting one foot in front of the other. At least as far as those tents. She gently pulled up her pant legs, the bloodied fabric of her slacks sticking to her skin. Some of those cuts from the falling glass were well beyond Band-Aids.

She wanted to thank whoever had saved her life, but all the SWAT team members looked alike, as they always did in their combat gear, and now they all were doing the same thing—trying to clear the area. Just because a second-wave attack had been thwarted didn't mean there wouldn't be a third.

They were ushering any nonessentials down the stairs of the subway entrance at 42nd Street and Seventh Avenue. All press and any onlookers were getting the hook, even the uniformed cops who weren't part of the investigation. Elizabeth watched for a moment before spotting Evan Pritchard moving against the flow like a salmon swimming upstream. He was talking on a satellite phone, oblivious to anyone and anything. It figured.

Elizabeth shook her head and began walking toward the medical tents when she stopped on a dime. The sound was faint. A sort of revving. Like a tiny lawn mower that wouldn't start.

Her eyes darted, searching for what was making the noise. She kept looking and looking until—there, in the middle of Broadway—she spotted one of the drones that had been shot down. The bomb it was holding was still intact. *It was live.*

The rush of adrenaline pushed away the pain as Elizabeth started running. Not away from the bomb but toward it.

"Pritchard!" she yelled. He was walking straight for the damn thing and had no idea. "PRITCHARD!"

Others could hear Elizabeth. They could see her waving her arms frantically for everyone still in the street to get back. The SWAT team was now running for cover, corralling the last of the civilians down the stairs to the subway.

For Christ's sake, Pritchard!

Elizabeth ran past the drone, picking up as much speed as she could before barreling into her boss. Never mind that he was built like a brick house. She knocked him clean off his feet, wrapping her arms around him as they rolled toward the curb. He didn't know what the hell was happening, only that he was severely ticked off.

But there was no time for her to explain. Elizabeth scrambled to her feet, pulling Pritchard toward the subway entrance and literally pushing him down the stairs with her.

"What the hell are you doing, Needham?" barked Pritchard as they slammed into the concrete landing ten feet below. He was grabbing Elizabeth with both hands. He was practically shaking her. "Are you insane? You could've killed me. You could've goddamn ki—"

BOOM!

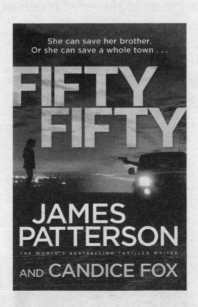

A HARRIET BLUE THRILLER

LIAR LIAR

James Patterson
& Candice Fox

Detective Harriet Blue is clear about two things. Regan Banks deserves to die. And she'll be the one to pull the trigger. But Regan – the vicious serial killer responsible for destroying her brother's life – has gone to ground.

Suddenly her phone rings. It's him. Regan. 'Catch me if you can,' he tells her. Harriet needs to find this killing machine fast, even if the cost is her own life. So she follows him down the Australian south coast with only one thing on her mind. Revenge is coming – and her name is Harriet Blue.

A HARRIET BLUE THRILLER

HUSH HUSH

James Patterson
& Candice Fox

Prison is a dangerous place for a former cop – as
Harriet Blue is learning on a daily basis. So, following
a fight for her life and a prison-wide lockdown, the last
person she wants to see is Deputy Police Commissioner
Joe Woods. The man who put her inside.

But Woods is not there to gloat. His daughter Tonya
and her two-year-old child have gone missing.
He's ready to offer Harriet a deal: find his family
to buy her freedom . . .

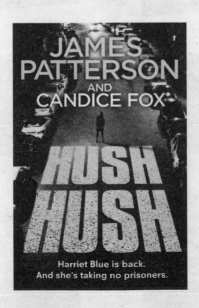

Discover the
Detective Harriet Blue series

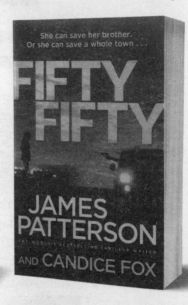

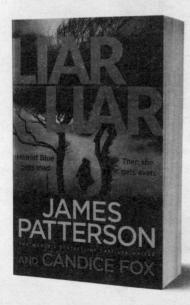

**'CLINTON'S INSIDER SECRETS AND
PATTERSON'S STORYTELLING GENIUS
MAKE THIS THE POLITICAL
THRILLER OF THE DECADE'**

LEE CHILD

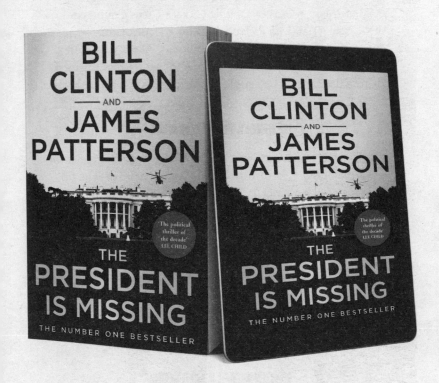

'Difficult to put down'
Daily Express

**'A quick, slick,
gripping read'**
The Times

'Satisfying and surprising'
Guardian

**'A high-octane
collaboration . . . addictive'**
Daily Telegraph

Also by James Patterson

ALEX CROSS NOVELS

Along Came a Spider • Kiss the Girls • Jack and Jill • Cat and Mouse • Pop Goes the Weasel • Roses are Red • Violets are Blue • Four Blind Mice • The Big Bad Wolf • London Bridges • Mary, Mary • Cross • Double Cross • Cross Country • Alex Cross's Trial (*with Richard DiLallo*) • I, Alex Cross • Cross Fire • Kill Alex Cross • Merry Christmas, Alex Cross • Alex Cross, Run • Cross My Heart • Hope to Die • Cross Justice • Cross the Line • The People vs. Alex Cross • Target: Alex Cross • Criss Cross

THE WOMEN'S MURDER CLUB SERIES

1st to Die • 2nd Chance (*with Andrew Gross*) • 3rd Degree (*with Andrew Gross*) • 4th of July (*with Maxine Paetro*) • The 5th Horseman (*with Maxine Paetro*) • The 6th Target (*with Maxine Paetro*) • 7th Heaven (*with Maxine Paetro*) • 8th Confession (*with Maxine Paetro*) • 9th Judgement (*with Maxine Paetro*) • 10th Anniversary (*with Maxine Paetro*) • 11th Hour (*with Maxine Paetro*) • 12th of Never (*with Maxine Paetro*) • Unlucky 13 (*with Maxine Paetro*) • 14th Deadly Sin (*with Maxine Paetro*) • 15th Affair (*with Maxine Paetro*) • 16th Seduction (*with Maxine Paetro*) • 17th Suspect (*with Maxine Paetro*) • 18th Abduction (*with Maxine Paetro*) • 19th Christmas (*with Maxine Paetro*) • 20th Victim (*with Maxine Paetro*)

DETECTIVE MICHAEL BENNETT SERIES

Step on a Crack (*with Michael Ledwidge*) • Run for Your Life (*with Michael Ledwidge*) • Worst Case (*with Michael Ledwidge*) • Tick Tock (*with Michael Ledwidge*) • I, Michael Bennett (*with Michael Ledwidge*) • Gone (*with Michael Ledwidge*) • Burn (*with Michael Ledwidge*) • Alert (*with Michael Ledwidge*) • Bullseye (*with Michael Ledwidge*) • Haunted (*with James O. Born*) • Ambush (*with James O. Born*) • Blindside (*with James O. Born*)

PRIVATE NOVELS

Private (*with Maxine Paetro*) • Private London (*with Mark Pearson*) • Private Games (*with Mark Sullivan*) • Private: No. 1 Suspect (*with Maxine Paetro*) • Private Berlin (*with Mark Sullivan*) • Private Down Under (*with Michael White*) • Private L.A. (*with Mark Sullivan*) • Private India (*with Ashwin Sanghi*) • Private Vegas (*with Maxine Paetro*) • Private Sydney (*with Kathryn Fox*) • Private Paris (*with Mark Sullivan*) • The Games (*with Mark Sullivan*) • Private Delhi (*with Ashwin Sanghi*) • Private Princess (*with Rees Jones*)

NYPD RED SERIES

NYPD Red (*with Marshall Karp*) • NYPD Red 2 (*with Marshall Karp*) • NYPD Red 3 (*with Marshall Karp*) • NYPD Red 4 (*with Marshall Karp*) • NYPD Red 5 (*with Marshall Karp*)

DETECTIVE HARRIET BLUE SERIES

Never Never (*with Candice Fox*) • Fifty Fifty (*with Candice Fox*) • Liar Liar (*with Candice Fox*) • Hush Hush (*with Candice Fox*)

INSTINCT SERIES

Instinct (*with Howard Roughan, previously published as* Murder Games) • Killer Instinct (*with Howard Roughan*)

STAND-ALONE THRILLERS

The Thomas Berryman Number • Hide and Seek • Black Market • The Midnight Club • Sail (*with Howard Roughan*) • Swimsuit (*with Maxine Paetro*) • Don't Blink (*with Howard Roughan*) • Postcard Killers (*with Liza Marklund*) • Toys (*with Neil McMahon*) • Now You See Her (*with Michael Ledwidge*) • Kill Me If You Can (*with Marshall Karp*) • Guilty Wives (*with David Ellis*) • Zoo (*with Michael Ledwidge*) • Second Honeymoon (*with Howard Roughan*) • Mistress (*with David Ellis*) • Invisible (*with David Ellis*) • Truth or Die (*with Howard Roughan*) • Murder House (*with David Ellis*) • The Black Book (*with David Ellis*) •

The Store (*with Richard DiLallo*) • Texas Ranger (*with Andrew Bourelle*) • The President is Missing (*with Bill Clinton*) • Revenge (*with Andrew Holmes*) • Juror No. 3 (*with Nancy Allen*) • The First Lady (*with Brendan DuBois*) • The Chef (*with Max DiLallo*) • Out of Sight (*with Brendan DuBois*) • Unsolved (*with David Ellis*) • Lost (*with James O.Born*)

NON-FICTION

Torn Apart (*with Hal and Cory Friedman*) • The Murder of King Tut (*with Martin Dugard*) • All-American Murder (*with Alex Abramovich and Mike Harvkey*)

MURDER IS FOREVER TRUE CRIME

Murder, Interrupted (*with Alex Abramovich and Christopher Charles*) • Home Sweet Murder (*with Andrew Bourelle and Scott Slaven*) • Murder Beyond the Grave (*with Andrew Bourelle and Christopher Charles*)

COLLECTIONS

Triple Threat (*with Max DiLallo and Andrew Bourelle*) • Kill or Be Killed (*with Maxine Paetro, Rees Jones, Shan Serafin and Emily Raymond*) • The Moores are Missing (*with Loren D. Estleman, Sam Hawken and Ed Chatterton*) • The Family Lawyer (*with Robert Rotstein, Christopher Charles and Rachel Howzell Hall*) • Murder in Paradise (*with Doug Allyn, Connor Hyde and Duane Swierczynski*) • The House Next Door (*with Susan DiLallo, Max DiLallo and Brendan DuBois*) • 13-Minute Murder (*with Shan Serafin, Christopher Farnsworth and Scott Slaven*)

For more information about James Patterson's novels, visit www.jamespatterson.co.uk